AT HIS COMMAND

HISTORICAL ROMANCE VERSION

RUTH KAUFMAN

AT HIS COMMAND
Historical Romance Version

Cover Art by The Killion Group, Inc.
Interior Formatting by Author E.M.S.

Contact: www.ruthkaufman.com

Published in the United States of America.

For everyone who encouraged me along the way.

Could she defy her king for love?

England 1453: King Henry VI sends Sir Nicholas Gray to protect the recently widowed Lady Amice Winfield from undesirable suitors. Though Nicholas intrigues her, she yearns to run Castle Rising without a man's control.

Nicholas has no interest in marriage, but can't deny he's attracted to Amice. He's surprised to finally find in Castle Rising a place he feels at home. A kiss sparks desire neither can ignore, yet serving opposing factions seeking to govern England threatens to pull them apart.

At court, the king and queen reject Amice's pleas and choose a new husband for her, a highly-ranked lord who'll provide connections and coin for the king's depleted coffers that Nicholas cannot. How can she follow the king's command when she's a scribe for his rival? How can she marry another man when she's falling in love with Nicholas?

CHAPTER 1

Norfolk, England – April 1453

Sir Nicholas Grey's scout leaned forward in his saddle, holding up two fingers to let the others know two horses approached. Nicholas heard only the slight jangling of harnesses blended with wind rattling through the trees, but relied on his scout's uncanny ability to hear what no one else could.

He and his eight men sat alert, deep enough in the forest to avoid being seen while maintaining a clear view of the road through leafless branches. Nine armed men could frighten travelers. 'Twas best to let them pass.

Each man watched, each horse sinking deeper into chilling mire as a mud-covered, black palfrey plodded over the rise in the road, its long mane whipping in the frigid winds.

"No rider," Martin, the scout, murmured.

"Look again," Nicholas replied. At first he too had thought the horse was riderless. Now he could see a woman collapsed on the animal's back. Her dark hair draped down its flank, mingling with the horse's mane. The palfrey placed each step as if trying not to jostle its burden.

Another horse, this one a brown rouncey ridden by a thin, balding man, galloped after the palfrey. A look of triumph brightened the man's face as he spotted the horse ahead of him. He bent forward, extending his hand.

Fingers like talons grasped the woman's tangled hair.

"Mine!" he cried.

※೪ ೪※

Amice Winfield jerked awake. Agony forced her head back, allowing her to see the man who gripped her hair as though he'd perish if he let go.

Harry Winfield.

She screamed. Arrows of fear pierced her as she clawed at his fingers. Her horse bolted, leaving her dangling from Harry's hand by a small clump of hair. The long strands held for a few seconds, then tore from her head.

Pain seared her scalp. She dropped into a puddle. Stunned by her fall and her stinging head, Amice could only stare at her tormentor while freezing water soaked her clothes. How she hated him. How she regretted her desperate flight from home. But what other choice did she have?

Harry gaped at the dark tresses hanging from his hand. He threw them to the ground as she struggled to rise. Panic gripped her as his hostile glare changed to a slow, confident smile.

"There's nowhere to run. I'll catch you if it's the last thing I do," he vowed. He leapt off his horse.

Amice tugged her sodden skirts, trying to haul them out of the puddle. Where was her mount? Too far away to reach without being caught, weighted down as she was. Sprays of water flew as she heaved her skirts over her arm. Heart racing, she ran for the trees. A branch snagged her. With a cry of frustration, she pulled the wet wool until it wrenched free.

Ignoring twigs tearing at her skin and icy mud that sucked away one of her shoes, she forged ahead. She gasped for air as she plunged into a tiny clearing, then came to an abrupt halt at the sight of a group of mounted men. Slimy hair slapped her face and clung to her cheek.

Panting, cold air stinging her throat, she sought a path to escape the strangers. Alarm coursed through her. She focused on the man at the head of the group. Anxiety and uncertainty warred within her though she sensed an almost tangible power emanating from him. The wind tossed his chin-length black hair as he stared down with a stern expression.

Will he help me? Am I better off with him or....? Before Amice could decide, branches snapped behind her. Harry ran into the clearing. Instinctively she moved closer to the commanding stranger.

"I am Sir Nicholas Grey," he announced, his voice deep. Confident, yet reassuring. "And you are?"

Harry's pointy nose wrinkled. She knew he wondered if he could get away with a lie. "This miscreant is my daughter. She's running away because she refuses to marry the man I've chosen for her," Harry said.

"He lies," Amice protested. "Harry Winfield was my husband's cousin. *He* wants to marry me now that my husband is dead, which all know is against—"

"This is none of your affair, Sir Nicholas. 'Tis a mere family misunderstanding," Harry said. His spindly fingers closed over her wet arm, sending a shiver of revulsion through her. "Come, sweeting, 'tis time to go home."

Silence reigned while she twisted free. Amice hoped Harry's friendly tone didn't fool Sir Nicholas. If necessary, she'd beg him to help her. All Amice wanted was to go home and live her life in peace. Without Harry. Without any husband. One had been quite enough.

Sir Nicholas studied her, clearly assessing the veracity of her tale. Something flickered in his piercing blue eyes. The intensity of his gaze unnerved her, but she couldn't look away. When Sir Nicholas broke their connection, she felt colder than before.

"I come on the king's business." He opened his cloak to reveal King Henry's badge of a chained antelope. "Which makes whatever I choose my affair."

Had Harry met his match?

"Certainly, Sir Nicholas, your business can't call for you to meddle in a father's discipline of his wayward daughter," Harry said. "You must believe me over a mere woman."

Harry's audacity no longer surprised Amice.

"He's not my father. I flee to escape him, true, but because he's trying to force me to marry him. His men control my home.

I need to reach friends at Caister Castle and get word to my cousin Cromwell," she said. "You must believe me."

Nicholas studied the pair as the petite, soggy woman spoke. She'd begun to shiver, no wonder as she had no cloak and only one shoe. With all the mud coating her gown, he couldn't guess at the quality of it. But her speech and bearing, the way she confidently met his gaze though her green eyes were filled with apprehension, indicated she was a lady. For certes she was beautiful, even splattered with grime. And her green eyes conveyed an intelligence that made him want to know more about her.

Perhaps she told the truth.

The man, on the other hand, looked as if he wanted to consume the woman whole as Nicholas had once seen a snake swallow a mouse.

"She comes with us, if she chooses," he said.

"Where do you go?" the man asked. "Perhaps we can travel together and settle this in more comfortable surroundings."

"We are for Castle Rising."

The man's mouth dropped open and the woman gasped. "Thank the Lord," she said. "You can take me home. I am Lady Amice Winfield."

Nicholas frowned. Amice Winfield was the reason he was in the middle of a forest instead of on pilgrimage. Could this bedraggled female be Lady Amice, the woman King Henry had sent him to protect?

The man didn't dispute her statement. In fact, he was sidling off toward the trees....

"Hold him," Nicholas ordered as the man started to run.

With a quick turn Martin and Thomas the Tall trapped the skinny suspect between their horses.

"Both of you are coming with us," he said.

Martin hauled the man onto his horse as Nicholas offered the drenched woman his hand. Muddy water from her garments and hair splashed him as he lifted her in front of him. His horse Merlin, in turn, shook his mane to rid himself of the icy droplets.

He'd had enough filth fighting the French. The day wasn't progressing at all as he'd planned.

She turned to peer at him, her eyes slightly darker than shoots of new grass. He couldn't look away.

"Why is the king sending you to Castle Rising?"

"I'm not willing to say, because I'm not yet convinced who *you* are," Nicholas replied. He wiped a drop of water from his nose. If he felt miserable, she must feel worse. Despite the cold, her wet clothes and danger, she'd possessed courage enough to make her case. He respected that, though he needed proof to believe. He'd learned not to easily trust women.

Her eyes widened with surprise and perhaps a hint of distress. "I've told you, I am Lady Amice. And he," she said as she pointed to her pursuer, "is Harry Winfield."

"Lady Amice would know why I was here." He signaled for the group to ride, looking at the road ahead instead of at her. Something about her struck a chord deep within. But caring wasn't part of his assignment.

"Why would I lie? I am Amice Winfield. I know of no reason for the king to send anyone to me."

"The truth will be revealed upon our arrival at Castle Rising. Not a moment sooner."

$$\text{\&} \quad \text{\&}$$

Sir Nicholas pursed his lips as if signaling the end of the conversation, but Amice refused to let him have the last word. Despite her unkempt state, though her head still stung and throbbed, she was a lady. She touched her neck, finding blood mixed with muddy water. Later she'd attend to her aches and pains. Now she'd learn what she could about this man who claimed the king had sent him to her home. Where to start?

"What is your horse's name?"

"Merlin."

"As in King Arthur's wizard? I'm fond of the tales of Arthur and his knights. I hope someday to see an illuminated manuscript. Is it true the best are not English or French but—"

"Flemish. I have one."

"You do?" She looked at him.

Sir Nicholas glared back, eyes frosty blue and cold as the wind whipping at her hair. The power he emitted was more intense up close. Yet she didn't feel afraid, but protected. "The road could be dangerous. 'Twould be best if we spoke only when necessary."

"*I* know the roads are perilous. Had there been another way to seek aid, I'd never have ridden out alone," she said. "Why don't you wear armor, if you fear danger?"

"First, I never fear. Second, we can defend ourselves. Third, the weight of armor would slow us down and tire our horses more than the weather has. Fourth, be quiet."

Amice faced front with a huff. She squeezed her numb fingers into fists. As she leaned against the hard mass of his chest to secure her position, his warmth began to seep into her.

Emotions roiled within her. Relief, foremost. Harry Winfield's sinful plot to marry her would be put to rest at last. Such a marriage was forbidden by law and religion. Anger next. She was offended that this stranger with compelling blue eyes doubted her word. Was he always so distrustful?

Exhaustion third. Her stomach growled persistently. If she shut her eyes, she feared she'd fall asleep. Her body and limbs felt stiff and cold as icicles. Except for her back, heated by Sir Nicholas. If only she could warm her hands that way. She started, shocked by the sudden turn her thoughts had taken. Yet his warmth was so soothing. Comforting.

Safe. Amice was safe at last. The horse's rocking movement lulled her. Her eyes just had to close. She fought to keep them open so she could convince Sir Nicholas to answer her questions.

What could he possibly want at Castle Rising?

❦ ❧

Nicholas felt the woman slump against him. She'd fallen asleep.

At least that would keep her silent. He gazed down, taking in her delicate, straight nose, smudged cheeks, perfectly shaped lips reddened by the cold. He couldn't deny that her beauty and spirit engaged him. And the intelligence he'd seen in her eyes made him want to know more about her. Spirit, intelligence, beauty. Three qualities he'd most appreciate in a wife. But if she was Lady Amice, he could never wed her.

His duty was to safeguard, not to take. Though an esteemed friend of the king, he brought no wealth or political connections, both of which Henry and his queen needed.

Frustration filled him. He needed no more complications. Soon, soon he'd complete his task at Castle Rising and earn what Henry had promised, time to go on a pilgrimage. He'd visit nearby Walsingham, because the king wouldn't grant sufficient leave for him to reach Rome. Still, he'd have precious days free of responsibilities and discord at court. Time to heal, and take a respite from serving his country. At two and thirty, was that too much to ask of life?

"I know you didn't want to take on this task. If you were less wondrous, the king wouldn't have insisted." Wind tossed Martin's auburn hair and reddened his long nose.

"Martin, you oft amuse me. Not today." Nicholas wrapped his fur-lined cloak around his sleeping guest, then urged Merlin forward. Even his powerful warhorse struggled in the watery muck.

Martin wiped a mud splat from his face. "'In these times of civil strife, few men can be trusted, but you've proved your worth on and off the battlefield,'" he said, repeating the king's compliments. He heaved a great sigh. "If not for your most excellent prowess, I'd be home before a toasty fire. Or seeking greater valor in battle. But no, we needs protect a damsel."

Wind snatched at Nicholas's tunic, making him wish he weren't so reliable. "Lady Amice's husband held several key estates. And she's cousin to England's former treasurer, still a powerful man and Henry's close companion. In the wrong hands, she'd make a perfect political pawn. We but watch over her till the king and her cousin find her another husband. Which I pray they do soon."

Nicholas studied the cloudy sky. They might reach their destination by noon. He flexed his icy fingers, regretting his chivalrous donation of his cloak, then turned his attention back to the oozing remnants of the road. The horses plodded as best they could, their labored breath swirling to steam in the freezing air. Each hoof slurped out of the mud.

The woman slid lower. An unbidden wave of concern washed over him. He didn't need her leaning so cozily against him, making him want to wrap his arms around her and offer comfort. Making him want to care.

"Pardon me...." Nicholas refused to call her by name until he was certain of her identity. He wanted to believe her, but had learned many women weren't worthy of his trust. He tapped her back with a gloved finger.

She opened her eyes. "Are we there?"

"Almost."

"Good." Her head dropped onto his chest. She dozed off again, almost buried in the voluminous folds of his now-damp cloak.

He sighed. His clothing had absorbed much of the supposed Amice's drippings, so that in addition to being cold he was uncomfortably damp. All he wanted was time to heal after years of never-ending skirmishes against France. Physical wounds hardened into scars. Emotional wounds festered without care. The horrific sights and sounds of bloody death planted over and over in his mind had taken root. Perhaps some time away from politics would help him pluck them out.

"Are you pleased now, my lord?" Martin asked. "This is what you get for wanting what you don't have. 'Oh, the constant pressure of serving the king, being available at a moment's notice, and never having more than an hour or two to pursue aught but the king's business,'" he intoned, lowering his voice in an attempt to imitate Nicholas.

"You twist my words. If you weren't so useful, I'd dismiss you for impertinence. I but seek a respite, which Henry granted. I think he was glad to have a request that wouldn't strain his coffers. But he needed me again after Lady Amice's husband died."

"At least you are away from the cloying court," Martin said.

True. But when would he be free?

Castle Rising lay ahead, a small square keep set in the hollow of a high mound surrounded by a brick curtain wall dotted with arrow loops. The group crossed a steep outer hill, then rode over a stone bridge and passed a tall, narrow gatehouse set into grassy mounds on either side.

The silence made the back of Nicholas's neck prickle. "Where are the guards?

He scanned the area, which offered some trees, the square crenellated keep, and a small chapel to the left with a building behind it. Another building to the side appeared to be a kitchen.

Martin snorted. "Worse and worse. You've been denied your pilgrimage to protect a tiny woman, a few buildings and a mere keep. We should've been sent to a major castle. Your plans have been postponed by an expedition not worthy of your many talents."

"We go where needed, whether or not the surroundings are ideal," he replied.

The woman lifted her head and sat up straight. She looked over her shoulder, the weariness on her face striking a chord of sympathy within him.

"The entrance is around the corner," she said.

Three sheep trotting around the corner, thick wool bouncing, drew her attention. The trio stopped directly in front of Merlin.

Amice burst into laughter, sparking joy within him. "They must've heard my voice. Hello, Isabella! Hello, Eleanor. Hello, Edward," she cooed, greeting each in turn.

She slid to the ground before Nicholas could help her, leaving a dirty stripe on Merlin's coat. The woman continued to talk to the sheep, who gathered around her eagerly.

Either she was Lady Amice or the shepherdess. Soon he would have answers. He couldn't conceal a grin at the sight of the mud-encrusted woman surrounded by three cavorting sheep.

She was even lovelier when she smiled.

Amice led them into the castle through a high, arched door on the left side of the keep. "My thanks for returning me to my home, Sir Nicholas. Now tell me who you are and why you're here."

"When you're warm and dry." He brought important news, which deserved the right time for the telling. He ignored the frown marring her smooth skin and looked up. "Impressive. Whoever built this keep recognized the defensive potential of a narrow, steep staircase."

"William de Albini began building Castle Rising in 1138...." She glared at him. "Stop trying to distract me. The minute I've changed garments, I expect answers."

They walked into a vaulted vestibule with an arcade of shuttered windows. A door to the left led into the great hall.

Several servants sat on benches, conversing as though they had nothing better to do. One, a young woman with flaming red hair that couldn't quite be contained by her simple headdress, caught sight of them and scurried over, her wide, freckled face breaking into a smile.

"My Lady Amice, thank goodness you are home! We didn't know what to do, we awaited word—" The young woman recoiled and backed away. "Oh, it's him. AAAAAH!"

Harry Winfield stood in the doorway, no longer restrained by Nicholas's men.

"Ginelle," Amice said. "All is well. We are safe. These men rescued me."

Ginelle paused mid-flight, clearly uncertain. She relaxed when Martin and Thomas the Tall each grabbed one of Winfield's arms. He struggled briefly, his futile attempt to break free ending in a seething stare at his captors.

"When Harry found you gone, he went wild," Ginelle accused, excitement flushing her fair skin. "He threw everything he could get his hands on, plates, chairs. He dragged me across the floor, shouting for me to tell him where you were and…then he ran out after you. I was so afraid."

Nicholas had his proof. The woman he'd rescued was Amice. He'd force rare words of apology from his lips. "Lady Amice, I beg forgiveness for doubting your word."

She nodded her head in gracious acceptance. "I trust it won't happen again. And that shortly you'll explain your presence here." She turned to the others. "This is Sir Nicholas Grey. His men have Harry well in hand."

A short, wrinkled man with flowing gray hair hurried into the hall. "You're safe, you're back!" He dropped to his knees. "Forgive us, Lady Amice. Harry's men watched us night and day to keep us from sending for help."

"Harry's actions hurt us all, Cyril." She turned to Nicholas. "Cyril Hodges is my steward. Ginelle is my maid."

The way Ginelle, Cyril and the others looked to her and at her told him they respected Lady Amice. He admired her confidence.

"How did you get away from Harry?" Ginelle asked. "He had you locked up so tight, we feared for your life."

Curiosity made Nicholas interrupt. "Harry imprisoned Lady Amice?"

Anger at Harry, at himself, flashed through him. He'd been so reluctant to come here he hadn't considered how far some might go to get their hands on a wealthy widow. And a lovely one, at that. Henceforth, duty would be his only concern.

Cyril said, "Harry and his men swarmed our castle and held Lady Amice under guard in her room until she'd agree to marry him. They gave her only bread and water, forbidding contact with anyone. For four days."

Amice looked as though she might faint. Her skin was pale as an angel's. Her beauty made him want to stare.

Nicholas guided her to a chair and helped her sit. He couldn't resist tucking his cloak around her. "But you could never marry your husband's cousin. Such a marriage is forbidden by the Church. You share a bond of affinity."

"All rational people know that," Amice agreed. "But Harry said some ignore the prohibition and he too would find a way around it. Mayhap get a dispensation." Her small, white hands gripped the edges of his cloak, holding it close as if to protect herself from painful memories. "Each day, I tried and tried to find a means of escape. Each evening, he'd come to me and ask if I'd marry him. By the fourth day, I was so hungry, so desperate to be free, I lied and said 'yes.'

"He believed the pretense of my acceptance and allowed me some freedom." Someone handed her a cup of steaming broth, which she accepted with a nod. She took a sip. "Harry and his men lowered their guard when I appeared to prepare eagerly for the wedding. This morn, amidst the bustle of activity on the day of our supposed marriage, I managed to ride away."

Cyril added, "After Harry went out to find you, his men tried to steal from your coffers. I locked them in your chamber and went to the village to raise a search party. I must go disband it." Wringing his hands, he turned and went back the way he had come.

"Steward, wait," Nicholas called.

The short man halted, his hair taking a moment to settle.

"Before you go, show my men Martin and Thomas the Tall where they can contain Harry."

"If I weren't so wet and hungry I'd demand this instant to know why you're here," Amice said. "You'll be shown to your chamber, and then we shall eat. I'll have your complete tale then. You've heard mine." Holding her head high, she swept out of the room, damp skirts dragging at the rushes covering the wood floor.

☙ ❧

Amice clenched her teeth as she strode to the chamber she'd use during Sir Nicholas's visit. How dare he order her people about? At least Cyril had looked to Amice for confirmation before following his order.

She'd show Sir Nicholas who was in charge. She didn't need some man, who knew nothing about her, ruling her or her home. At nine and twenty, she'd gained enough knowledge and experience to manage her household. Her husband's death had freed her of a man's rule. Of his commands and his demands.

Amice let Ginelle help her out of her ruined garments as servants brought hot water for her bath. "My lady, he is so handsome. Those eyes, the bluest I've seen. Such a fine face. And he seems strong, yet kind as well."

Amice didn't need to ask to whom Ginelle referred. She'd never met a man as attractive as Nicholas. His air of authority, the ease with which he took control and the alacrity with which he made decisions and people acted upon his orders, annoyed and made her respect him at the same time.

"Shall I attend him?" Ginelle offered, her brown eyes round with hope.

The thought of her pretty maid alone with Nicholas made her uneasy. Best keep temptation away.

"No. Please lay out my lavender gown." She'd wear one of her finest out of respect for Nicholas's standing with the king, not because she cared what he thought of her or wanted to look her best for him. And fall prey to the sin of vainglory.

She eased into the water, aching cold seeping from her tired body. Her favorite soap, scented with rose water, burned as it met the raw spot on her head. Two latherings later, she was clean. It felt good to be clean. And even better to be home.

When she was dressed, she felt almost herself again. She wore a gown of lavender wool over a cream kirtle, with flared sleeves and an elaborate border embroidered with flowers. The low neckline revealed a pleated section of the underdress. Her hair, unbound for she hated headdresses, gleamed in soft ringlets.

She touched the necklace she wore always, a square miniature of her mother rimmed by tiny amethysts and pearls hanging from an unusual chain of linked A's, her mother's initial. Adding a short, worked gold necklace set with garnets her cousin Cromwell had given her, she hoped the jewels would make her appear and feel confident and in control.

Amice descended the stairs, having offered her larger chamber on the main level to Nicholas in deference to his status. A servant busily transferred her belongings to the smaller room she'd occupied as a child. As long as she had the small painting of her parents and brother near her bed, she was home.

The head table sat on the long side of the rectangular hall across from the windows. How unsettling to see Nicholas in the lord's chair, as if he were lord of all he surveyed. Of her. But she couldn't help admiring how the way he held himself conveyed confidence. How handsome he was, as Ginelle had said.

She sensed each man watching her as she took her place beside her guest. Sir Nicholas's gaze fair burned her skin. A rush of uncertainty and nervousness kept her from meeting it. When was the last time a man had admired her appearance?

Servers carried in steaming platters, turning the men's attention from her. Stewed mutton flavored with costly pepper, haddock in creamy sauce and huge slices of crusty bread were set before her. The first meal she'd eaten in days.

Food had never tasted so good. She studied Nicholas through lowered lashes as she ate. A man as handsome as he must have women clamoring to claim him. His black hair, longer than the favored close-cropped styles, fell in shining waves against his forehead and brushed the collar of his dark blue tunic. Unlike most men, he wore no hat.

A shiver went through her as she recalled Nicholas's first look at her in the clearing, his intense gaze taking in every detail.

With him and his men added to her staff and Harry locked away, she felt safe. But thoughts of the unknown disturbed her peace as she chewed on a chunk of soft, still-warm manchet bread. What could the king possibly want with her?

Time for some answers.

CHAPTER 2

"Sir Nicholas. I thank you for saving me from Harry and returning me to Castle Rising," Amice said above the din of chatter and laughter. "I hope you won't be called upon again to take on such a dangerous task on my behalf."

"It was my duty," Nicholas responded.

"Your duty? Why have you come here?" She met his gaze, ignoring eagerness to learn more about Sir Nicholas the man.

"You truly didn't expect us? I sent a messenger ahead to alert you to our arrival."

"I didn't receive a message. Harry must have intercepted it. No wonder he was in such haste to wed." A chill raced through her at the thought of what might have happened if he had succeeded. "I didn't know you were on your way, much less the reason why. Tell me now."

His expression yielded no clue. He glanced around the room at the keen faces, each straining to hear his answer. "I'd rather discuss this privately."

Amice saw people she considered her family. Anything concerning her interested them, as their lives interested her. And as it wasn't a common occurrence for a king's man to visit, they too must be most curious as to his purpose.

Kind of Sir Nicholas to consider her feelings, but.... "I've waited long enough. I keep no secrets here."

"As you will. Best get it out without delay, then." He set down his eating knife. "King Henry and Queen Margaret have decided you should wed again. They're seeking a husband for you."

Whispers flew about the hall.

He continued, "I'm to ensure your safety until they send for you, and then escort you to court."

The king and queen wanted her to marry. And they wanted to choose her husband.

Amice's hands shook around her goblet. She hid them beneath the table and struggled for control by taking a deep breath and releasing it slowly. Then another. Maybe now she'd be able to keep from bursting into tears.

Sir Nicholas was an intruder. This man didn't deserve to know how his news affected her. He'd rescued her out of obligation. She didn't owe him her secrets.

Why did her relatives have to be so important? Many widows had the power to choose their next husbands. Perhaps Henry would present her with several candidates, allowing her the final choice. Why, she'd be willing to pay for such a privilege.

She had to take matters into her own hands before it was too late.

"If there's nothing else you need, I shall retire," Amice said.

"Have you nothing to say? I'd hoped the news would please you." His eyes, the shade of yarn her mother used to call the sky at twilight, revealed none of his thoughts. "Lady Amice, are you well?"

Mother. If she and Father had lived, would Amice be so alone, in this unfortunate position?

What was it to Sir Nicholas who she wed? "Have you ever been married?"

He shook his head. "No."

"Then you can't know what it is to live with a spouse you didn't choose. One husband picked for me was quite enough. But we're all at the king's command, aren't we?" Tears threatened. She swallowed them back despite a suddenly dry throat and stood. She wouldn't cry in front of him, let him think her weak. He'd rescued her once already today. She couldn't bear another hint of concern or compassion. "Perhaps in the morning you'd care to survey the area."

"I would. I'm sure your steward can show us what we need to see. We need not trouble you," Nicholas replied.

Clearly he thought her a delicate flower of a lady, or one lacking intelligence. She couldn't keep rancor from her voice. "I know these lands better than anyone, even Cyril."

"Very well. We'll leave after we break the fast."

He had given, now she must. "Very well. Good night."

As Amice climbed the stairs, dizziness assailed her. She swayed slightly, putting her hand to her head. Summoning strength, she made her way up the stairs by clinging to the stone wall, hoping no one had seen her waver. She was rarely ill. Days without food and long exposure to the cold combined with the impact of Nicholas's news must have taken their toll.

She made it inside her door, then collapsed.

☙ ❧

Someone screamed. Nicholas, on his way to his chamber, retraced his steps. Taking the stairs at a run, he collided with Ginelle as he burst into the hallway.

"More evil is at hand," the maid wailed. "My lady is ill. What if Harry poisoned her food? I can't open her door. I think she's wedged against it."

Pushing slowly and carefully, he opened the door, then picked up Amice and carried her to the canopied bed. Setting her gently on the soft mattress, he rested her head against the pillows. She was still as death, her skin pale.

He sucked in a breath. If anything happened to her, he'd fail his king. Fail himself. Surely that was why concern and worry warred within him, tiny spears and daggers lancing his gut.

He felt Amice's forehead, recoiling as his hand met burning heat. "She has a fever."

"What are we to do? She usually takes care of the sick." Ginelle wrung her hands.

Nicholas had a rudimentary knowledge of tending battle wounds, but was at a loss about curing fevers. What had his mother done when people took ill? "Is there someone who knows what to do? If so, I'll fetch him. You change her clothes and cover her with quilts."

Ginelle, seeming calmer now that there was a plan, vague though it was, said, "We've no physician. Sometimes Maia, the cook, she's got herbs for things."

"Well, then, we'll have to make do." Nicholas had seen physicians at work and reasoned Amice might be better off without one. His sister, Margaret, almost died after a physician bled her in an effort to realign her humors. Her recovery had taken months.

By the time Nicholas returned with Maia, Amice was tucked beneath several quilts. She rolled to the side, exposing a red spot on her cheekbone.

The three looked at each other in horror, eyes wide.

"Red spots. She's got plague!" Ginelle burst into tears. "We're doomed. We'll all catch it and die horrible deaths."

Who could forget the outbreak in 1434 that had killed rich and poor alike? Almost everyone knew someone who had succumbed.

Maia approached the bed, leaning back as if she didn't want to get too close. "Thank the Lord, I don't think it's that," she said. "She must've scraped her face when she fell. I'll mix a drink she must take every hour. Won't work if she doesn't. Maybe some cucumber with honey and oil too, that's good for fever. Or some fennel...no, that would only be if she stays ill." She turned to look at Nicholas. "Milord, there is nothing you can do here. We'll wake you if need be."

He wasn't used to being told there wasn't anything he could do. Still, he had no choice but to trust the cook. His insides twisted as he looked down at Amice's unconscious form. The desire to protect her, help her, filled him. And not just because he had been ordered to, or because completion of his duty depended on her safety. Somehow, it was more than that. As if she was a valued friend. Someone important to him.

A peculiar way to feel, knowing her for such a short time. He hadn't had strong protective feelings for anyone since his mother died. How could he care for someone he'd known less than a day? Perhaps it was only that he felt the need to protect her after what she'd endured at Harry's hand. Yes, that must be it.

Nicholas went to his room, *her* room, but couldn't sleep

though the huge bed and soft linens proffered comfort. Too much had happened this day, several it seemed, all rolled into one.

He was in a castle he'd never heard of until two weeks ago, protecting a woman to whom all sorts of unusual things happened. And a beautiful, intelligent woman, too. He turned on his side, inhaling the same rose scent Amice had worn at dinner. The sweetness tantalized him. He pushed the sheets away, ignoring the cold night air.

He remembered how Amice had yelled in outrage at Harry. He laughed. She was a bit outspoken, but to the right man that would be a blessing. If only he were the right man for her.

Where had that thought come from?

❧ ❧

Amice's eyes adjusted to the darkness. She was in her old bed with the green velvet curtains drawn. Her head throbbed as if she'd spent too long in a crowded hall and queasiness gamboled in her stomach. She tried to sit up but fell back against the pillows, alarmed by her feebleness.

She remembered falling to the floor. 'Twas a fever, nothing more. With deep breaths, she forced herself to relax her tense shoulders. She'd not die young like her parents and brother. She'd never understand why God chose to kill so many in plagues and wars. Why He'd chosen to take her family. The only way she could think of them without the ache of loss making her weep was to believe they were in a better place.

I will not leave this earth without attaining my goals. I will have and love a family of my own and give them the home and childhood I was denied. No one could hear her vow, but she felt better for having made it.

Ginelle poked her head through the curtains. "Thanks be to God. I thought I heard you moving about. Are you feeling better?"

Amice nodded. "A bit."

Ginelle opened the curtains and handed Amice a wooden tray with bread and a bowl of broth. "Everyone will be happy to hear you've recovered. Maybe life can settle down again."

"At least I won't be forced to marry Edwin's cousin, the slimy toad," Amice said, pushing herself into a sitting position. Though at any time, she could be forced to leave her home.

"But soon you will marry, and someone of the king's choosing. This one is sure to be handsome and kind." Ginelle set the tray on Amice's lap. "Mayhap like Sir Nicholas."

What would it be like to wed a man like him, close to her age? As Ginelle had said, handsome and kind. The way he'd wrapped his cloak around her made her smile. The way he'd taken control of Harry made her feel safe.

"I'm happy enough on my own. I don't want to marry unless I can choose my own husband. Would I could find a man to love...that would be ideal." She sighed. "It's my own fault. The sin of pride. I should've accepted cousin Cromwell's assistance after my parents died. Because I refused his coin, my suitors were few."

"Beauty isn't always enough to snare a man, more's the pity. You can't blame yourself for doing what you thought was right," Ginelle said.

Amice picked at the bread in her hand. "I suppose not. Most men want a bride who can add to their coffers and holdings. A truth I ignored."

"All marriages aren't as dreadful as yours." Ginelle picked up the spoon and handed it to Amice.

"Even in an arranged marriage, there should be things a husband and wife can share. Simple things, like riding together, enjoying a meal." Amice scooped up some broth and let the liquid trickle back into the wooden bowl.

"Every woman hopes for a good match. You'll find one this time around, I'm sure. I'll be back for the tray."

Amice closed her eyes and rested against the pillows. Thoughts of the past had stolen her appetite.

Her marriage to Edwin had been as lifeless as a plant without water. As a girl she and her friends had dreamed of good marriages, of happy homes. What she'd gotten instead was an old man uninterested in anything but his money and lands.

Ginelle and other girls in the village often giggled and swooned over men, but Amice was convinced they made up stories for fun. Edwin had never praised her beauty. His kisses didn't make her melt. They made her want to rinse out her mouth. Amice likened lovemaking to farming. Plow the field, sow the seeds and hope something grows.

How she'd wanted to have stories like theirs. But the other women knew Edwin, knew his lank gray hair and spindly frame wouldn't earn deep sighs, knew his mean-spirited ways wouldn't evoke sagas of love.

And it was her fault. She'd been so worried about not depending on her cousin she hadn't thought ahead. If only she'd known how many factors made up a marriage, how many ways a bad one could cause misery.

A new husband would be found, likely without her even having a say. A wealthy widow with highly ranked male relatives such as her cousin, Lord Ralph Cromwell, oft lost her say in choosing a second husband. But managing Castle Rising for Cromwell, she had authority. People listened to her and acted upon her decisions. She felt accomplished and fulfilled watching the keep and village flourish in her care.

Could she attain her dreams now? What were the chances of happiness with this unknown groom? Best to find a way to avoid marriage altogether.

All of this worrying and remembering had worsened the pounding in her head. She closed her eyes again, wishing she could pray for guidance.

But she was on her own.

❧ ❧

Nicholas pulled aside a heavy, embroidered curtain surrounding his bed. The sun told him it was nigh upon midday. How could he have slept so long? Why had no one wakened him to tell him of Amice's condition? He dressed in haste and hurried to her chamber without breaking his fast.

Amice was sitting up in bed, still pale, but clearly better. As comely as the day before. Relief joined the sense of protectiveness that encompassed him in her presence.

She motioned him into the room. "Thank you for fetching Maia."

"What was in her potion? It worked quickly." He moved

closer to the bed. Her dark curls tumbled over the pillows. Were they as soft as they looked? *Stop that. Do not think about her beyond her safety. Beyond duty.*

"'Tis a secret, naturally. Eggs, barley, I don't know all of the ingredients." She shook her head, sending curls bouncing. He clasped his hands behind his back. "That ride we discussed…we can wait until you're well. There are plenty of tasks close to the keep."

Nicholas took a few steps toward the door then turned. To reassure himself that she was better. Not to glimpse her beauty once more.

"Why did King Henry send *you*?" she asked.

He shrugged and took a few steps closer. "He doesn't always give reasons. I suppose because he knows me so well. We're the same age. When we were eight, his tutor, the Earl of Warwick, recruited me to be his companion at swords."

"Why haven't you married? I'd like to think when he makes matches he doesn't only move people as if they were chess pieces, but also rewards good service." Nicholas saw hurt mixed with curiosity. She lowered her lashes, as if she'd revealed more than she'd intended.

How to describe the vagaries of life with the king? Some thrived, others gasped for air like fish on a hook. Helping her adjust wasn't part of his task. Nor was telling her why he hadn't wed. Yet he wanted to.

"Of course he rewards some of his fidelis with titles, lands, and marriages. He offered me a bride a few years after he married Margaret. I chose to serve him in the war with France rather than abandon a new bride."

"That I understand." She sighed. "I wish he'd offer, not command me. I don't like being told what to do."

"Neither do I." They shared a smile. "I'll return to see how you fare later."

Their gazes locked. Had her annoyance at his arrival faded? Now she seemed intrigued by him. Just as he wanted to learn more about her. Not only because she was one of the loveliest women he'd ever seen, but because her people respected her rule.

To follow that path would surely lead to peril. He was her protector. Nothing more.

No matter what he wanted.

⋇⋇ ⋇⋇

By mid-afternoon, Amice was sure all traces of her illness were gone, but Maia insisted she remain in bed.

"I'll not have you taking sick again. Rest," she ordered.

She decided to agree with the cook. "I will, but please bring my desk. That way I can accomplish something."

Maia nodded agreement to the compromise and fetched the small wooden writing desk. "Why you like to spend so much time with a pen in your hand I don't know, but if it'll keep you still today, fine with me."

Maia departed with a smile, leaving Amice free to write. First she'd compose a letter to King Henry, offering to pay a fine in return for the privilege of not having to wed again or at least permission to choose amongst several candidates. Then she would delve into her manuscript.

In addition to her dream of having a family, Amice had a secret goal of writing books. That dream sprouted years ago, when her cousin Cromwell first told her about Christine de Pizan, a Frenchwoman who'd written many books and had even been the biographer of King Charles V. He'd seen Queen Margaret herself reading one of de Pizan's works, *The Book of the City of Ladies,* about the role of women in society. If only she, Amice, could write such a book that might enlighten and inform others. Even the opportunity to read such a book would surely be one of the greatest events in her life.

The desire to write had become part of her the way a branch was part of a tree. She'd tried to share her unusual enthusiasm. Cromwell's nieces, Joan and Maud, couldn't understand why Amice would want to waste her time on a useless pursuit. Nor could Edwin.

She'd ignored the naysayers and persisted. Somehow the act of writing made her feel less alone. In whatever time she could spare, she worked on a book about how to manage a castle. Since few of the residents at Castle Rising could read, she hadn't hidden her work, only what she was trying to accomplish.

What would Sir Nicholas think? The thought flew into her

mind, unbidden. No matter, for he'd never see a word of it. He'd never get to know her that well. For some reason, her chest tightened, as if her heart were shrinking.

Amice finished and sent off her letter. Would the king help her?

❦ ❦

Nicholas visited Amice before he went to sleep. Some color had returned to her pretty face. A weight lifted from his shoulders, akin to removing his armor. Unbidden came the thought of how nice it would be to see her every day, whether in the midst of chores or in repose.

Something about her called to him. Well, he'd just have to stop listening.

She was writing on a small lap desk. Ink smudged her delicate fingers. Smiling a welcome, she indicated a stool. "Thank you for visiting again."

"I'm glad to see you—are well." He brought the stool close to her bed and sat, catching a hint of her rose scent. The longing to breathe deeply tugged at him. Not because she was particularly enticing, but because any woman would smell far better than his men after a hard day's work. "My men and yours are getting to know each other. We've been testing their skills in the bailey. That Douglas is very quick with his sword."

Her smile faded into a frown. "I hope he doesn't have to use it on my account. I wish…everything would be different if my parents hadn't taken my older brother, Edward, to London." Her voice cracked. She swallowed. He thought he saw the glint of tears in her eyes, and had a sudden longing to comfort her. "None of them came back. The plague swept through London and took my entire family along with it.

"I can't forget. Never to see my beautiful mother again, never to hear her sing in lilting French, be lifted high in Father's strong arms, or walk proudly with Edward and listen to his stories when he visited from the castle where he fostered to be a knight."

He took her hand. She started at his touch, but he hoped the strength in his fingers, the warmth of his skin would soothe her. Make her feel less alone.

"I'm sorry for your loss." He pulled his hand free and bid her good night.

Amice was intelligent. Lovely. Her laugh made him want to…. But soon she'd be promised to the king's choice, whether she chose to wed or no.

Best that he focus on their differences. Find reasons to draw them apart, not together.

❧ ☙

Amice's hand was cold now, and her heart as hollow as the tree she'd learned to read beneath. A stinging rain of memories washed over her as she'd told her story. What had made her share her secret with Nicholas? Made him touch her, and her feel such warmth and peace in return?

At that moment, she wished she'd never met him, hadn't glimpsed how satisfying being with a kind, caring, comely man near her age could be.

Ah, how she hated change.

Her family's possessions had meant little because she was alone. Though she loved the folk of Rising, the kindliest friend would never care for her as much as her mother.

Soon after, the king's council gave control of Castle Rising to her cousin, Lord Ralph Cromwell, then treasurer of England. He sent his nieces, Joan and Maud Stanhope, to live with her. That helped, for the sisters accepted Amice as one of them. But a void remained deep inside. She couldn't find it in herself to forgive, as Christians were supposed to do. She'd failed.

Years later she learned the significance of being in her cousin's care. Though not penniless, she had no great properties to offer as her dowry, nor were her funds significant enough to entice prospective grooms. When Amice realized Cromwell would have to dower her if she was to marry anyone of import, pride grew in her like an ugly weed. She refused his generous offer of a dowry. He made auspicious matches for Joan and Maud. And she'd had to accept Edwin.

She'd adjusted to all of those changes on her own. She'd tried to pray, but found no solace.

Nor would she find any now.

The unknown frightened her. She'd have to leave the only home she knew, go to court, and marry a stranger. And she had to face Nicholas again, though she was as averse to that meeting as she was to washing a huge pile of laundry. He brought out feelings in her, concern, curiosity, awareness of him as a man, that she didn't dare profit from. He was not for her.

She shouldn't strengthen their fragile friendship.

She had to make the most of her remaining days unwed. Including maintaining her routine and keeping contact with Sir Nicholas to a minimum. No good could come from getting to know and like him more than she already did. From wanting him to touch her again.

Tears dripped down her face and her head pounded anew. So much seemed out of her control. In addition to writing to the king, there had to be something else she could do to prevent her life from changing so drastically. But what?

She vowed to find a solution.

CHAPTER 3

Nicholas was already drawn to Amice in a way he'd never experienced. Had never wanted to experience. He was supposed to guard her from men who might want her or her resources, not want her for himself.

The king couldn't send for them soon enough. He didn't want to spend another day, much less a fortnight or a month, wanting what he couldn't have.

Martin knocked, then entered, a cup in his hand. "I know that look. That's exactly how you looked whenever a certain duchess was near."

Martin was the one person who could read him, and a very annoying talent it was.

"I made sure my interest never amounted to anything. I'll put a stop to this, too."

Even if Amice were attainable, the last thing he needed was a woman to complicate his life. He wanted to simplify his existence. Be at peace. In his experience, women were far more likely to contribute to chaos. After only a short while near Amice, his thoughts were as difficult to sort out as the competitors in a melee.

"Let me guess who so inspires you. The cook? No, far too plump. The fair Ginelle? No, you don't like redheads, nor those with a penchant for the dramatic. Why then, it must be...the beauteous Amice?" He placed a hand over his heart. "Ah, the lady of the land. You can, of course, count on my discretion in this matter."

"May not a knight admire a fair lady?" Nicholas vowed to be

less transparent. If Amice saw what Martin had, he'd be discomfited.

Martin snorted. "You're not a troubadour, to sing of longing and praise from afar. Does she know? How does she feel about you?"

"Martin. We are not writing another *Roman de la Rose*. She intrigues me." That was all.

"What a conundrum, since she'll be pledged to another."

On his way to the evening meal, Nicholas thought about what Amice had said about not wanting to marry again. Had she been so unhappy that she had no expectation of happiness? She offered him insight into a woman's mind, something he'd never been interested in before.

Still, he was intrigued and wanted to know more. Even though she'd soon wed another man.

Around them, residents of Castle Rising ate and laughed, taking pleasure in the reward of a good meal at the end of a good day's work. No frowns or sidelong glances like those at court.

Nicholas began to understand Amice's pride in calling Castle Rising home, from the indoor kitchen and combination buttery and pantry that made life easier for the servants and allowed food to always be served hot, to the garderobes with ventilation slits, separated from the hall by an L-shaped passage, ensuring that no unwanted aromas permeated.

He no longer felt like a mere visitor, but was starting to feel at home. Here. With her. He'd need a stronger guard around his heart.

"My thanks," he said to the server who delivered stuffed capon. He took a bite. The spiced fowl surpassed his expectations.

"You're a king's man," Amice said from the opposite end of the table. "You must know here in East Anglia many support Richard, Duke of York. I've heard he and Henry are often at odds, and because of York's close blood connection to the throne—closer than the king's himself—Queen Margaret sees him and his family as a threat to any children she might have," Amice said.

"I'll always support the king, but what is true is true. King Henry trusts those around him and is easily influenced by others.

Much of the work done by his father has been undone. Many of the lands Henry V gained in France have been lost back to the French."

Amice ran her fingers around the rim of her silver-trimmed cup. He couldn't help but notice her slender wrists and delicate, oval nails. And wish he could hold her hand again. "How can you ensure Henry trusts the best men? York's views seem sound. He's had many successes as Henry's aide."

Nicholas was at once impressed that Amice had such strong opinions and dismayed to uncover a sizeable area where their beliefs differed. "How did you come to be so interested in political maneuverings? Most women at court think nothing is more important than who will marry whom or what color their next gown should be. Yes, York and others have urged reform. Each faction wants its favorites in command. I can only offer advice when the king asks it of me."

"So we are at odds, sir. You must follow Henry, and my upbringing lends me to favor the Duke of York."

He looked down at his half-eaten capon with dismay. Amice's cook served foods as tasty as those he'd enjoyed at court, but their discussion had diminished his appetite. "Debating such issues in the privacy of one's home is one thing, discussing them publicly is another, and a war over them is another thing still. Yes, I will support Henry if it comes to that. As it already has, and might again."

"Even if you believe York would be a better leader, and could quell the factions? Guide England to more prosperous times?" Amice questioned.

He shifted slightly to see her better, amazed by her perception. "What I believe is of no import. Henry is our anointed king and I am his man. I was raised with him. He may be more pious than most kings, but he's the rightful ruler. My duty lies with him."

Amice pushed her trencher away, perhaps as glad as he the meal and the discussion had come to an end. That their views on such an important issue as the governance of England were so disparate bothered him as it must her. Even so, he simply enjoyed her company, this peaceful interlude before the king remembered to find her a husband.

Perhaps that was what made these days all the sweeter. The fact that they could end at any moment.

⁂

Her blond, gray-eyed page Robert marched into the hall as she and Nicholas were breaking the fast. Despite their differences, having him at her table made her home feel even more welcoming. A dangerous way to feel.

"Someone approaches." He puffed out his tiny chest.

Amice nearly choked on a bite of bread, but managed to swallow. Not so soon. She wasn't ready to leave. Against her better judgment, she wanted more time with Nicholas.

"He has a lute on his back. He must be a minstrel or troubadour. Maybe even a jongleur," Robert added with a little dance. "I want to learn to juggle."

Relief rushed from her in a whoosh. She didn't like being happy one moment, so startled the next she'd assumed the worst. "I'm sure we'd all enjoy some music after supper. It's been a long while since a performer has come to us."

"Has it?" Nicholas stood. "I'll speak with him before the gates are opened."

"You think he's an avaricious suitor disguised as a minstrel?"

"I won't know until I meet him. Wait here."

She stood and faced him. "This is my home. You're not my husband, I'm not under your rod. You can't tell me what to do." Jumbled emotions made her sound petulant.

Would every issue result in a battle of wills, as if they were rams butting heads? Being at odds with him made her shoulders tense and her stomach churn. But so did giving in. Who was she without authority? A mere lump of clay, serving no purpose but to be pushed and pulled or left alone at the whim of others.

"I'm here to ensure that no harm comes to you. I'm doing that." With his wide stance, shoulders back and head high, Nicholas looked every inch a knight. Impressive and comforting at the same time.

"And that means you can order me about like a servant?"

"The king trusts me, but you don't?" he asked.

"Of course I trust you."

"Then let me do my job."

Life was so much simpler, less confusing, before he arrived. So much she wanted now she couldn't have: Nicholas to care for her as a woman and to stay at Castle Rising.

"Perhaps we could make decisions together," she suggested.

"I've never discussed defensive strategies with women. Not their purview." He sat back down. She joined him. "Why not? If the visitor has a nefarious purpose, he might also have cohorts hiding in the trees, planning an ambush. I'll talk to him from the walls."

"Thank you. I've little expertise in defensive strategies as you say, but I'd like to learn. I'd like to know what's being done on my behalf at my home and contribute where I'm able. Maybe some women are content to let men tug their puppet strings. I'm not one of them."

"Very well. You may— Would you care to accompany me to the wall? But I need you to agree to remain behind a merlon in case he or any companions wield bows and arrows." He stood again and held out his arm as if he were escorting her to a dance.

"Yes." With a smile of satisfaction, she also rose and lightly rested her arm on his, wishing the warmth of his skin permeated his wool tunic. She sensed his power, his strength. And she had to admit, she was proud to be walking with him. If only for a moment, she could pretend she was his lady.

Nicholas duly approved the minstrel's admittance. Amice welcomed seeing Nicholas display his leadership skills.

After supper, all were sated on Maia's fish pie with figs and raisins and ready to hear the minstrel, Geoffrey of Arundel. Long brown hair dangled beneath his hat. His particolored tunic was worn at the sleeves.

"What news do you bring?" Nicholas asked.

"I came from London, where all still talk of the recent Parliament and new taxes. But with your indulgence, I'd rather amuse than inform. Would you prefer a song or a *chanson de geste*?"

Amice loved the long poems centered on myths and legends. "Do you know any about King Arthur?"

"Of course." In a mellifluous voice, Geoffrey launched into

the tale of Gawain, Arthur's nephew and friend to Sir Lancelot whose honor was tested. Then he sang a song. The gentle lute strumming and the verses of love lost brought tears to some of the women's eyes.

Amice lifted her chin, trying not to blink and keep her own tears from falling. She wished she could take Nicholas's hand, to share the moment more fully.

As the "huzzahs" and applause faded, Amice smiled. "Geoffrey, that was wonderful. It's been too long since I've heard the like. My thanks for sharing your talents."

Seated next to Nicholas, her people enjoying the respite, Amice could not have been happier. She'd commit the evening's events to paper and always carry the memory with her. With her uncertain future, she feared she might need pleasant memories.

❧ ☙

After the minstrel was given lodging for the night, twinges of what could only be jealousy pricked Nicholas. Merely because Amice had admired another man. A handsome, talented one at that, with a voice to make ladies melt. He'd seen the like at court, and been subject to the swooning that went on for days hence.

He sat alone at the table staring into his empty mug. Amice entered the hall, humming the minstrel's plaintive tune. The fact that it had stuck with her irked him.

"I wish he could sing for us again," she said, a wistful tone in her voice. "The way he made me experience the lovers' sorrow, not just through the beautiful notes and well-written verses, but how he sang...." She heaved a sigh worthy of any woman at court. "The pacing, his use of artful pauses. I'll have to think on how I might apply some of his techniques to my writing. I should have asked him for another song, a happier one. I'd have loved to see how he conveyed joy and pleasure."

Her gazing upon him was bad enough. He didn't want to hear Amice sing Geoffrey's praises. But why should what she thought bother him? She couldn't marry a minstrel, and he'd be departing in the morn. Their paths might never cross again.

Yet the adoring look on her face even now rankled. He wanted Amice to admire him, as she'd seemed to when they stood on the parapet. To wax poetic about him as she took his arm. He shook his head. More the fool he, for it could do naught but to salve his pride.

She couldn't marry him, either.

Not that he wanted her to.

❧ ❧

A week later, on the first of May, Amice awoke at dawn and ran to the window, opening the shutters as if she were a young girl eager to go outside and play. The sun peeked over the horizon; the sky was awash in pinks and golds, promising a beautiful May Day.

She threw on an old gown of brown linen and hurried to join those who foraged in the hunting fields of Rising Chase to gather the may, branches and flowers they'd fashion into wreaths and garlands. Morning dew on May Day was said to bring luck.

As she selected leaves to weave into her hair, Amice wondered what Nicholas would think. Would one such as he, used to finery and feasts, look down upon their holiday? Would he be bored by the games, find the dances foolish? Everyone, except perhaps Father Heydon of St. Lawrence Church in Rising, appreciated the importance of the ceremonies dating back to pagan times. The earth needed to be encouraged to yield to spring.

She smiled. Whatever his views, she looked forward to Nicholas's presence at this special celebration.

Though she hadn't yet come up with another way to avoid marriage except her letters, though good or bad news from court could come at any time, she wanted to live every moment at Castle Rising to the fullest. Each moment in Nicholas's company made her want another. Despite their differences, no man had made her laugh, none had made her feel so at ease. Contented.

And sometimes, the way he looked at her made her think he saw her as more than a friend. As a woman. Those times made her wish for more…more time, more togetherness, more closeness.

If only…. No. She couldn't think of what she wanted. But she took extra care with her appearance nonetheless.

❧❧ ❧❧

Nicholas watched Cyril supervise the maypole decorations in the bailey, shouting commands as morning breezes blew his hair upward.

At court, servants made ready. Nobles participated only in the dancing and eating. The ladies might weave a garland or two, more for sport rather than achievement or to share tasks. Here, everyone worked wholeheartedly, from Amice and Cyril to the stable boy, Harold. Even Amice's page Robert had a task, for he busily scurried toward the outside kitchen.

Nicholas wanted to join in the fun, but felt uncomfortable asking how he could help. He sat on a tree stump, the sun warm on his face though the air was cool, alone in the midst of activity. Would he always feel the outsider? Because he frowned on the intrigues of court life, he hadn't minded holding himself aloof there. Here, camaraderie called to him. Would they welcome him if he could bring himself to ask Cyril for an assignment? Watching wasn't enough. But it was better than not being there at all.

At length the tall birch pole stood ready. Dozens of colorful ribbons, streamers and garlands dangled, awaiting the dancers who took their positions.

Nicholas's heart cried out, "Please ask me to join you." Sinful pride prevented him from asking aloud.

Amice wore a flowing green gown embroidered in blue. White hawthorne flowers and leaves peeked out of her dark curls. Amice's smile, her pleasant yet decisive demeanor when people asked advice, made him like her all the more. A wonderful lady of the manor.

She laughed, moving gracefully into place, her back to him. But perhaps she heard his silent cry, for she turned and started toward him. He smiled inside as she continued her approach and held out her hand.

"Come," she said. "Everyone must dance."

The others shouted and waved for him to join their circle.

He was welcome. Tears filled his eyes, a bittersweet ache tightened his throat. When was the last time he had cried? He forced himself not to blink, knowing he'd melt into the very ground with embarrassment if anyone glimpsed how much this meant to him.

Amice's hand nestled in his as she led him to the circle.

Yearning sliced through him at the feel of her smooth skin, joined by a sense of belonging. He didn't want to let her go. More the fool he.

"Go," Amice whispered, releasing his hand. "We saved the place of honor, next to Ginelle, the queen of the May, for you."

Touched by her thoughtfulness, Nicholas took his place. He would've preferred to stay by Amice, for guidance in the dance and to have another excuse to hold her hand, but this position provided him a better view.

As the musicians struck a lively tune, the dancers began their clockwise steps. Even Nicholas knew they had to go clockwise to follow the pattern of the sun. When the others added stomping with their right feet, he joined in as best he could.

He didn't want to miss a step, but watching Amice's glowing face and slender form while keeping track of Ginelle's feet proved a challenge.

❦ ❧

Amice smiled as Nicholas grasped the simple pattern, noting his graceful movements. He seemed to be having a good time, and hadn't even tried to refuse when she asked him to join them. Joy filled her as the dancers moved as one.

Their gazes met across the circle. The rest of the world disappeared. She no longer heard the music or laughter of those around her. Could he know her smile was only for him? Did he watch her with equal fascination, or did she just happen to be in his line of sight? The day took on a new meaning because he was there to share it.

After other dances came the games, including races and contests in jumping distances, archery, and ball throwing. Nicholas won the archery competition, and accepted his victory ribbon from Queen Ginelle with as much grace as he might have shown Queen Margaret had she bestowed him with a title.

❦ ❧

They feasted upon bread colored green with parsley, green peppermint rice and fruited beef. Seated next to Amice, Nicholas felt happier than he had in years.

Amazing how quickly things could change for the better. One minute he bemoaned being the outcast, the next he happily cavorted in the midst of the festivities. Had he ever been as at ease? Felt so at home? In his travels, he'd seen others prize their homes, but he hadn't truly appreciated the significance until this visit to Castle Rising. Until he met Amice and basked in her glow.

How would he find contentment without such a home for himself? Without her?

❧❦

The next day, on her way to the inside kitchen, Amice found Maggie the laundress and Agnes the weaver jostling for position in an open doorway.

"Ah, Sir Nicholas," Maggie sighed. "What a body on that one, eh?"

Unwillingly, Amice understood.

Nicholas worked his horse in the bailey as other men engaged in mock battles. Sounds of clanging swords and pounding hooves filled the air. He rode shirtless.

"I've never seen the like," Agnes said. "But really now, if he was your man, would you want others all agog, wantin' him, too? There's not a woman in this place who doesn't hope he'll glance her way. And more." She patted her brown hair into place.

"Everyone? Even Lady Amice?"

Amice, who'd been about to encourage them to return to work, stopped short. The two were so focused on the men they hadn't noticed her approach. She couldn't resist the temptation to listen.

"Why not? After that awful husband, you can be sure she's wantin' a good man," Agnes said. "That Master Edwin, always pokin' at whoever was passin' by. And so old and cranky too."

Amice gasped in shock. How could this have been going on

and she'd known nothing of it? Add one more black mark to the tally against Edwin.

"Can any be trusted? How do we know they all aren't after the next female that catches their eye?" Maggie asked. "Or whatever other part responds," she added with a giggle.

Amice had heard enough. She walked by cheerfully calling, "Hello, Maggie. Agnes."

With a quick curtsy, Maggie picked up her basket of linens and walked off. Agnes also bobbed before returning to her loom.

As she continued her journey upstairs, Amice couldn't stop herself from watching the men. From the safety of the shadowed window, her eyes sought Nicholas as a flower seeks the sun.

His long black hair tossed about as he turned Merlin in tight circles. Not overly bulky like those of the blacksmith, Nicholas's muscles accentuated his broad chest and added to his powerful aura. His arms flexed as he changed his grip on the reins. The rhythmic movements emphasized his masculinity.

A deep, powerful yearning filled her. She looked forward to their every meeting with a thirst strong as a hot August day after hours of gardening. That need could be satisfied with a cool drink from the well.

How could her need for Nicholas be met, when he'd come to take her to her new husband? She didn't even know if he felt the same. He, who could have most any woman to wife.

Maggie and Agnes were right.

All of the characteristics she'd hoped for in a husband had found their way to Nicholas. He was intelligent, hard working, considerate, an interesting companion. And the most attractive man she had ever met, with a compelling gaze, a nose with just enough shape to give it character, a square jaw. And his smile moved her, made her want to make him smile.

Perhaps she only yearned for what she couldn't have.

Amice stepped deeper into the shadows. She'd allow herself one last look before willing herself to get on with her day, to help the cook determine what supplies to order.

Nicholas looked around as if he sensed her presence. He frowned. Had he sought but not found her?

She backed away. His head snapped in her direction. Was he that aware of her? He picked up a sword and joined the mock fray but kept looking toward her window. His obvious lack of attention to his opponent earned him a thwack on the shoulder.

Smiling, he parried the blow and continued his battle. She smiled, too.

⁂

As Amice tied her overgown over her kirtle of pale blue the next morning, she heard a knock. Who could it be at such an early hour, and who would come to her chamber? Word from the king? Had Harry escaped again? A sense of foreboding filled her as she opened the door.

"My shirt has a tear." Nicholas walked into her room as though it was a perfectly normal thing to do. He looked quite offended as he pointed to the back of his shoulder at the sleeve's seam, as though the shirt had torn itself on purpose.

A gasp of relief preceded her peal of laughter. "Let me see it." Amice approached, feeling heat emanating from him. She jumped as the feel of him sent a shiver through her finger to the rest of her, and looked at her finger in surprise.

"What is it?"

Amice's hand flew to her side. "Just a small tear. I can mend it."

Nicholas pulled the shirt over his head and turned to hand it to her. They were alone in her bedroom and he was shirtless. They stood, staring at each other, the shirt still in his outstretched hand. The sound of her breathing seemed loud in the quiet room.

His hair, a few shades darker than hers, shone as the rising sun streamed through the window. She couldn't ignore the lure of his blue eyes. His scent, now familiar and welcome, floated into her senses. A simple need brought him to her. Suddenly mundane sewing turned into something special.

It seemed natural for them to be standing so close.

Amice had seen him shirtless from afar, and thought that was wonderful. But it was nothing compared to him up close. She saw the contours of each muscle, the black hair on his chest, the breadth of his shoulders. His chest rose and fell with each breath, making her want to lay her head against it to know the warmth of his skin, hear the beat of his heart.

She couldn't meet his gaze any longer, so she looked down. A mistake, for she wound up gaping at his lower half. His legs were encased in tight cotton hose and worn thigh-high leather boots. Without a shirt or tunic, his powerful thighs were on display. As was the outline of his manhood. Her cheeks flushed.

What would he do if she touched him? Could she be so bold? She moved her hand toward him, anticipating the feel of his skin against hers.

"Amice, I've wanted to tell you something." She froze as he looked at his feet. Swallowed. What was making such a confident, well-spoken man hesitate? "I—"

Robert raced into the room at full speed and ran straight into Nicholas.

"Oof!" Nicholas caught his balance before toppling onto her.

"Oh, here you are," Robert said. "I didn't hear you awaken. I went to the stables and Merlin was still there, I went to the hall, the bailey...."

Amice bit back a smile. Robert worried his hero would leave and do something exciting without him. Confusion wrinkled his brow, perhaps because the two of them had been alone in her chamber. But he was too well-mannered to ask questions.

Amice glanced at Nicholas. The mood was broken. What might have happened had Robert not interrupted them? What might either of them have said or done? She yearned to know.

"I tore my shirt and brought it to Lady Amice to repair." Nicholas ruffled the lad's hair.

Amice fetched her sewing basket from her coffer. After preparing a length of thread and a needle, she took the shirt from Nicholas and set to work. She tried to focus on the torn fabric, resisting the temptation to look at him instead.

Ginelle poked her head into the room, her red hair tucked demurely into a simple headdress.

"Oh!" she exclaimed, her eyes opening wide as she took in the scene before her. "Oh," she repeated, noticing Robert behind Nicholas. "Maia wanted to know how much white bread you wanted her to make today."

"I'll speak to her in a few minutes."

Ginelle nodded and left.

Amice turned to Robert. "Don't you have lessons with Father Heydon this morning?"

The guilty look on his face answered the question. He dutifully started toward the door. "What are you doing today, Sir Nicholas?"

"If Father Heydon tells me you worked hard on your studies, you may come hunting with me this afternoon."

Robert's face brightened and he ran off.

They were alone again. What had he been about to say? She wanted to tell him how she felt, because she might not have another opportunity. But what purpose would it serve? If she knew he felt the same, each glance, each word would be bittersweet. Maybe the knowing would bring them closer together. But again, to what purpose…to be wrenched apart when she was handed to another?

Amice broke the thread. That's all that held them. A mere thread of interest. No point trying to strengthen it. "Here."

He examined her handiwork, running a finger over the tiny stitches. She imagined that finger on her arm.

He opened his mouth as if to speak, but turned and left.

It was for the best.

Keeping secret her interest in Nicholas went against her nature. Perhaps because she couldn't discuss the issue, it took on excessive importance. Like the last bolt of silk at a fair. After purchasing several she wanted, somehow the last bolt she didn't buy and now couldn't afford seemed all the more desirable. Of course, she could exchange one bolt for another.

She still couldn't see a way to change her situation. And any day, she could run out of time.

That evening, Amice tried to concentrate on Cyril's tallies and supply orders as she sat in her solar, but her thoughts kept straying like wayward sheep. When would news arrive? Who would the king…? No. Focus on salted meat. Rye and wheat flour. Peas and beans. Then if—when—she had to go to court, Castle Rising would fare well in her absence. She didn't want to worry about her home in addition to her future.

She set down her quill and idly rubbed her tight neck. Closing her eyes, she savored a rare moment of privacy. Of quiet. The quiet before the storm.

Her mind wandered. She saw Nicholas seated at her table. Talking, laughing, his smile illuminating his strong features, setting his blue eyes asparkle. She hadn't wanted him there, not at first, because he was an intruder. Now she wished he'd leave because she admired and was attracted to him. If she had to wed, a man such as he might not be a hindrance, but an asset.

She didn't want merely a man such as he. She wanted him.

Amice sat up straight. What if she could wed Nicholas? Her people already liked him. She already liked him. More than she should. The way he made her feel....

It wasn't too soon to consider this plan. She didn't know how much time she had. And many matches were made without the bride and groom knowing each other well, or at all.

He might not hold a high enough rank, the king might have other plans for him, but it was worth a try. She'd write the king again and amend her request. Shoving the tally book aside, she reached for a piece of parchment, hope filling her heart for the first time since Nicholas revealed his news.

Eagerly, she dipped her quill.

A foul-smelling hand grabbed her mouth, pulling her tight against a bony chest. Nails dug into her cheeks. She couldn't scream, couldn't wriggle free.

"I will have you to wife, Sir Nicholas and his men or no."

Harry.

Her heart battering her ribs, she jabbed the quill into his hand. Ink splattered her eyes. She blinked against the sting.

"Aaaah!" He stumbled back.

She jumped to her feet and headed for the door.

He grabbed her skirts, pulling her off balance. She crashed to the floor. Pain burst through her hip as she fought for breath.

"Help! Hel—!"

Harry scrambled atop her, pressing her down. She couldn't draw in air.

His uninjured hand slapped over her mouth. "I will have you. You belong—"

Suddenly his weight was yanked from her. She sucked in a huge breath.

Nicholas, fury in his gaze. He punched Harry in the jaw.

Harry dropped, making the wood boards shake beneath her. Two of Nicholas's men dragged him out.

Amice sighed with relief as Nicholas reached for her and helped her to her feet. His hands were warm and reassuring in hers, which were ice-cold. She didn't want to let go. She wanted him to wrap his arms around her, keep her safe and—

"Are you all right? You're shaking."

Her hip ached and she'd bruise, but she was otherwise unharmed. Her body, at least. Fear nipped at her heart. She nodded, not yet able to find her voice.

"I don't know how he freed himself, but I'll ensure that he's locked up tight this time. I'll send for the sheriff." Nicholas helped her to a chair by the fire. He drew the matching chair close and sat beside her, a comforting arm around her waist.

She breathed in his scent, her soap mixed with his essence. Warmth, not just from the fire, filled her. She resisted the urge to move her chair closer still.

He wiped ink from her cheek. The gentle tracing made her feel cared for. Protected. She wanted him to do it again.

"How can I thank you?" Amice asked. "I shudder to think what would've happened if the king hadn't sent you. It didn't occur to me to hire guards after Edwin died. If I'd known Harry was lying in wait, a snake ready to pounce...." Another shiver racked her. "His determination frightens me."

"You're safe now. He won't harm you again."

He wrapped his arm tighter around her waist. She so wanted to rest her head on his shoulder. To rely on his strength and trust that somehow all would be well.

"I admit that I wasn't pleased with this assignment," Nicholas said. "I thought I could better serve the king at court, protecting him from his enemies. But now that I've met you, spent some time with you...lived in a home rather than moving from castle to castle or with no roof over my head while at war.... I want you to know that I've enjoyed being here more than I expected."

"I've enjoyed having you here," she admitted.

His eyes were dark as the ink. Intense. After a long moment, she broke the connection.

She'd make sure to send that second letter to the king. Today.

CHAPTER 4

Then Maud decided to visit Castle Rising. At first Amice was overjoyed to see her cousin, also recently widowed. Maud was tall and fair, with the palest skin, facts Amice had known but not paid much attention to until she saw her laughing with Nicholas over a cup of wine. Did he prefer women closer to his height? Did he prefer flaxen hair?

The way Maud latched onto Nicholas as a drowning man clutches a passing branch made Amice's chest burn. But she had no right to wish Nicholas smiled at her, not her cousin. No matter how much she'd enjoyed their conversations and having him here, Nicholas was in no way hers. Nor could he be unless the king acquiesced to her wishes. She hadn't even been brave enough to tell him how she felt.

He could be Maud's. The thought rankled, persisting like a nagging cough. If Cromwell decided he was a suitable choice for Maud's second husband, she didn't know how she would bear it.

Every morsel of Maia's normally flavorful meals tasted the same. No activity, not even writing, held her attention for long. Because her thoughts kept turning to a certain dark-haired man and his annoyingly beauteous and pleasant companion.

Each moment he spent with Maud was one less he could spend with her. His hours at Castle Rising were running short.

The next afternoon, Amice was engrossed in dying wool. She sought a special deep blue that met her exacting specifications, a combination of the right amount of woad with orchil to add a

hint of purple. She'd have denied it if anyone suggested she tried
to match Nicholas's eyes.

Dyed wool and people were very much alike. Expose people
to new influences, and they changed, just as wool changed with
the application of dye. But if there were too many colors in the
mixture or the fabric was soaked too many times, you could wind
up with a shade you didn't intend or like.

Amice felt like over-dyed wool. Her usually pleasant humor
turned to moodiness and rancor. Ever since Nicholas arrived, she'd
been plagued with want for what couldn't be. That desire, which
had begun sweetly, as a touch of blue might remind one of the
palest sky, had darkened into irritability. Nicholas was the excess
dye that turned her from her favorite purple into a grim black.

She moved around the large vat atop its fire, stirring the wet
cloth with a tall wooden pole. Hot and sweaty, two conditions
which did nothing to improve her mood, she raised a spotted
blue hand to push a damply recalcitrant curl off her forehead.

Nicholas and Maud returned from a ride, faces flushed from
their exertions. Maud walked toward the keep, waving and
laughing her farewell. Nicholas handed the reins to Harold.

Possessiveness seethed in Amice, steamy as the water in her
vat. She stomped toward him. Much like a fish, her mouth opened
and closed. Everything she thought of to say seemed childish.

"You aren't here to dally with my cousin. You go riding when
things need to be done. Shall I inform the king you've been lax in
your duties?" She wanted to be calm, to show she had no interest
in him. But she couldn't prevent the stream of complaints from
leaving her lips, knowing all the while she sounded the shrew.

"What things?" He stepped closer.

Each was momentarily silenced as the heat radiating from
their bodies met with a clash. Being susceptible to him fueled her
anger.

Shaking her dripping pole, she continued, "I've barely been
able to get a word with you since Maud arrived. There are
important things to discuss, and you've been too busy with her."
Her cheeks colored from more than the flames' heat. She'd not
only sounded childish, she'd basically confessed her jealousy.

❧ ❦

"What things?" Nicholas repeated. He stepped closer, grabbing Amice's pole so she couldn't accidentally whack him in the head in her fury.

What angered her so? Bits of hair curled on her reddened cheeks, begging him to push them away. Her green eyes sparked with gold as she glared at him. Even Amice's fury enticed him.

Exactly why Nicholas had welcomed Maud's arrival. He could talk to Maud without wanting to hold her hand or hold her, without stirrings of desire. Without being sad when their time together ended. Yet he'd missed Amice. His friend. His...what?

One of his hands closed over hers. The simple contact elicited a rush of longing, almost making him relinquish his grip. Why did he react to her so strongly?

"Going riding with Maud, as though you had nothing better...."

Without thinking, he stopped her reproach with his mouth. He'd wanted to do that for so long. The sweet taste of her heightened his excitement.

This, at last, was what he'd waited for, swirling vibrations of yearning, as he kissed her in the bailey.

In the bailey! Instantly, his passion cooled. They were in plain view. Fortunately, no one seemed to be paying attention.

"How dare you kiss me?" she hissed. "If you try that again, this will stop you." She brandished her pole as she hurried back to her vat.

Nicholas concealed a grin as he watched Amice poke viciously at the wet wool. His impulse to smile vanished. Henry and Margaret trusted him to safeguard Amice until they agreed on a groom. Compromising her in any way was unforgivable. Yet Amice had but to enter a room and all activities but being with her lost their luster. Being inches away from her lovely face, her slender body, made him lose control. Unforgivable.

He'd conquer his desire with the same determination he'd used to fight those who trespassed on English soil. His weapon against invaders was his sword. Against the lure of Amice, he'd have to rely on self-discipline and denial.

❧ ❧

"The wool is too dark now. I'll have to start over," Amice called as Nicholas walked away.

Her flushed cheeks stood testament to interrupted desire, but Amice hoped he thought her heightened color was due to the heat.

With his warm lips moving upon hers, longing for more had filled Amice so that she'd barely been able to stand. She'd wanted to melt into him, let him whisk her to her room. Surprise at her strong reaction, at being kissed in public, led her to snap at him rather than indulge further.

Better he believed she had no interest in him. Leading him to think otherwise could only result in disaster.

※ ※

Hours later, Robert ran into the hall, shouting, "My lady, my lady, the watchman says a messenger approaches. 'Tis believed he wears the king's livery!"

Though her heart skipped a beat and dread flooded her, Amice fought to keep her face calm for the benefit of those watching. She took another stitch of her embroidery as if nothing were amiss. "Thank you, Robert."

"He's expected anon." The boy puffed out his chest and stood proudly at attention a short distance from Amice.

Other servants hurried into the hall.

Despite her suddenly dry mouth, she said, "Maia, prepare food for our visitor. I'm sure he'll be hungry and parched."

She tightened her hold on the cloth to keep herself from wringing her hands or throwing them into the air. Tears came to her eyes, but pride forced them back. She wouldn't cry in front of her people or Nicholas. Of all, she didn't want him to think her defeated.

Hope flared. What if the messenger brought a response to the letter she'd sent the king, not a summons to court?

Servants paused where they stood, arms filled with clean linens or dirty ones, brooms halted mid-sweep. Eerie silence permeated the hall until the messenger was announced.

"I bear a message from His Grace Henry VI for the Lady

Amice Winfield and Sir Nicholas Grey," the thin, balding man proclaimed loudly for all to hear.

Nicholas and Amice stepped forward as one. "I am Sir Nicholas and this is Lady Winfield. The message is for both of us?"

"Aye, my lord." He handed Nicholas a parchment sealed with thick red wax.

The crack of the seal breaking seemed loud as a matchlock gunshot in the silence. When they had finished reading, Nicholas lowered the letter and looked at Amice.

He turned to the messenger. "Tell my liege we are on our way, and look forward to greeting him anon."

The servants began whispering. Their lady was going to court. Activity resumed with renewed energy.

Amice took the missive, hoping she'd misread it. "The King to all in Greeting: The attendance of Amice, Lady Winfield, is requested at Westminster. We shall introduce Lady Winfield to her new betrothed in our presence...our man Sir Nicholas Grey is recalled to the service of his king.... Depart with all speedy and convenient haste.... Witness the King at Windsor, 26 May."

King Henry either hadn't received her letters or had chosen to ignore them. Why should he grant her request when he wanted her to wed? She'd lulled herself into believing life at Castle Rising would stay as it was, with Nicholas an important part of it.

Suddenly she regretted her efforts to resist her feelings for him. Parting would be painful in any case. Why hadn't she allowed herself to embrace the joy, the comfort, of caring for a man, even for a short time? She'd squashed girlish dreams she should have reveled in. For they might be all she'd ever have.

Amice sighed. The king wanted to meet her. Misery over the main reason for her journey overwhelmed any excitement she might've felt at being so honored.

"We ride at dawn. Leave your men behind. Take only two servants. Quarters can be crowded," Nicholas said. "You'll need to arrange for provisions."

The flurry of commands startled her. Nicholas clearly thought only of preparations needed for travel. The warm, agreeable man she'd come to know had fled, leaving the efficient commander in his place. Had their time together meant so little that he could move on so easily?

Amice went about the tasks at hand, numb as if she'd stood all day on the parapets in mid-winter. Ginelle proffered various garments to pack, but Amice barely noticed what went into the satchels. Yes, that was the way. Feel nothing and nothing will matter.

Will away your desires and you won't be sad when they don't come to pass.

She couldn't sleep. As the hour of departure approached, she burst into tears, crying all the harder that she had to cry at all. She loved Castle Rising. Her home, the place where she remembered her parents and the happiness they had shared. She felt safe here. She knew where everything was and knew everyone she saw. At court, only two servants would comfort her, with occasional visits from her cousin Cromwell. She'd be an outsider.

While a short trip to see some of the world would be opportune, she didn't want to live anywhere else. Her new husband would probably take her to his home, unlike Edwin, who hadn't cared where they lived. She'd been happy running her home as she saw fit.

She'd been far happier with Nicholas in her life. She'd miss his companionship and his contributions to running the estate. Though she'd only admit it to herself, she'd miss just looking at him. Wishing he might kiss her again, even if he didn't, was better than not being with him at all. Simply watching him work and relax in her home gave her a sense of satisfaction, of internal peace. Of family. If only he could have been the one chosen for her.

On the other hand, he was a knight. What wife wanted to fear for her husband's safe return, or live alone for months while he was on campaign? A perfect situation if a wife didn't like her husband. But if she had to wed again, Amice wanted to more than like her husband, she wanted to love him.

What were the chances of that?

Harry ground his teeth as he crossed his narrow cell for the three hundred and thirty-fifth time. What else was there to do but walk, count and plan?

Anger burned within, keeping him warm despite the chill. The cell was clean enough, but such quiet and solitude could rot a man's mind.

"Everything is Amice's fault." How could he hate her and want her to wife at the same time?

While Edwin was off getting married, Harry had persuaded Edwin to leave him in charge of the estates for the first time. He'd worked diligently, eager to impress his cousin with his accomplishments.

His plans changed the instant Amice rode into the courtyard. The most beautiful woman he had ever seen. Her hair, of darkest brown, was mostly hidden under a golden headdress, but Harry imagined it flowing down her back. Her skin, so smooth and pale, her fine features and sweetest of smiles called to him.

The problems of being a mere cousin had converged. Edwin, the heir, had the estates, the responsibility, everything. Of course Edwin received a wonderful bride while he had none.

"While I, ever so much handsomer, was supposed to feel lucky even to have a place to live," Harry told the door, which did not reply.

"I had to get rid of Edwin. It was my turn to have it all." Three hundred and forty-two. "Hunting can be a very dangerous pastime. I'd return from the hunt alone, the grieving cousin. No witnesses to suspect me.

"I was finally the eldest Winfield. But Edwin bequeathed everything to Amice. Wasn't it enough she had her dower lands? She had to have what should've been my inherited birthright as well? Not one manor or field for me. Not one tree."

He'd come so close to persuading Amice to marry him. Until that king's man Sir Nicholas arrived. He'd managed to free himself, only to taste imprisonment again.

Harry punched the wall, then gasped at the pain. Cradling his throbbing knuckles, he completed the three hundred and fiftieth pass.

There had to be another way to have Amice. And a way to make Sir Nicholas pay for foiling his plans and putting him through the humiliation of prison.

But what could he do with only unyielding walls and a silent door at hand?

He had to get out. Again.

※⃛ ⃛※

Nicholas reclined on his comfortable bed for the last time. He'd enjoyed Castle Rising much more than he'd expected to. Time away from court was what he'd wanted, not the seclusion he'd once anticipated. He realized he wanted to belong, to be part of a household. He'd thought himself happy fighting Henry's battles, that his satisfaction came from helping the king achieve his goals, from striving for the good of England.

Compared to the pleasure and sense of completion he derived from training the men and spending time with Amice, the splendor and intrigue of court seemed tarnished as an unused candlestick. The rush of battle no longer intrigued. The reprieve he'd sought from endless banquets, political debates, gossip and shallowness of many courtiers wouldn't suffice. If anyone had told him two months ago he'd feel this way, he'd have laughed.

Martin interrupted his reverie. "So, back to the life we love, eh? I'm sure Belinda will be happy to see you."

Nicholas sighed. Since his arrival at Castle Rising he'd not thought of her.

"Too bad no sensible man will take her to wife," Martin said. "Poor Belinda, three husbands but no children."

"Mayhap she'll find another wealthy widower who needs a wife to raise his children."

"Or you could marry her, like she wants," Martin teased.

"You know I have no interest in marriage." *Unless I can wed Amice.*

He sat up straight so fast his head spun. What had made him think that?

Wed Amice. Until now, he'd not shared the compelling need most men had to sire heirs. With Amice as his bride, the prospect sounded appealing.

But that could never be.

Martin laughed. "I think you fear falling in love. You see

caring so deeply as a weakness to which a powerful knight should not succumb."

"Would it were that simple." His earliest memories of visits home were of his parents' vicious quarrels. And they'd married because they believed they were in love, not because their families arranged it. Somehow, over the years, their feelings had disintegrated into bitter unhappiness. Whether the sameness of daily life or the demise of emotions caused the decay, all who lived in their household were exposed to their misery.

Nicholas could still feel the anguish as he huddled behind a door, doing his best not to cry as they shouted, wishing he could escape their suffering. And his own.

"Misery seems inevitable when a man and a woman are stuck together for their entire lives. How could any man possibly be with one woman for so many years and not find her annoying?"

As his friends wed, he'd grown more convinced marriage was a horrible lot. He'd not found a woman he could tolerate even with time apart while he was at war. How could he be expected to find a life mate? Belinda had seemed the perfect solution.

Until Amice. Who he couldn't have.

"Belinda won't relinquish you without a fight, but she'll land on her feet like the cat that she is." Martin smirked. "I've seen the moon-sick way you stare at the Lady Amice. Though she is small, her hips look wide enough to—"

"OUT."

Martin wasn't afraid to step out of bounds if he thought doing so was in Nicholas's best interest. Which made him both valuable and annoying. He'd spilled a few grains of truth, Nicholas acknowledged.

After spending so much time with Amice, he could no longer endure Belinda. She'd been a means to avoid being completely alone. He realized now that he'd still been lonely, that even his appreciation of Belinda's sexual maneuvers paled in comparison to the contentment his friendship with Amice brought. And if they could've delved beyond kisses, he knew their intimacy would surpass anything Belinda could offer. Sex had been just that with Belinda. Not making love.

He'd come to truly care for Amice. How could he stop?

Though the hour was early, he sent a servant to finish his

packing and walked into the hall. Amice was already in her customary chair by the hearth, clad in a fox fur trimmed cloak. Her red and puffy eyes proved she'd been crying.

"Amice?" he said softly. "What troubles you?"

She jumped. Nicholas's heart wrenched as the last stubborn tear trickled down her cheek. He sat beside her, but she wouldn't meet his gaze.

"I wish I could lie and say, 'Nothing.' My mother often warned me that my inability to tell even the whitest of lies would get me into trouble someday. Any lie would haunt my conscience. The truth will come out anyway, so why lie, get caught, and not be trusted?" She rose and walked to the hearth.

"What is it, Amice?" Something truly bothered her. Something he sensed had to do with him.

"I don't want to go," she blurted. "I don't want to leave my home and I don't want to marry a stranger."

He walked to her. "Will you miss me?"

He had to know if he was part of the reason she was so distressed. Whether he would or could act on her answer, he wasn't sure, but he had to know how she felt.

Amice looked bewildered. Either he'd read her deepest thoughts, or he'd been wrong to think their time together meant anything to her beyond mere companionship. Which? He clenched his teeth to keep from asking again.

"There was something you were going to say the day you brought your torn shirt for repair. What was it?" she parried.

"Never mind. I shouldn't have brought it up." Nicholas regretted his question. What he'd wanted to share went far deeper than being missed. Telling her now would only make her feel worse about leaving Castle Rising.

She took a deep breath and let it out slowly as if doing so could help her decide what to say next. "Of course I'll miss our time together, Nicholas, very much," she said as smoothly as any courtier.

Nicholas waited for more, suddenly feeling as if his future hung on her answer. This was the first time since the kiss that they'd talked of their feelings. He steeled himself to remain still, not betray his anxiety by shifting his weight from one foot to the other or tapping his fingers on his sword sheath.

She continued, "I've never had a friend like you."

That was all? Nicholas burned to know the truth. If she felt as he did, could there be some way for them to be together despite the obstacles in their path?

Someone had to make the first move.

Nicholas would take up the gauntlet and prove Martin wrong. He wasn't afraid to care. He could be strong enough to let Amice know how he felt.

The decision somehow freed him. Nonetheless, he struggled with his choice of words. So confident on the field of battle, when talking to women at court, he was unsure of himself now. *Because I care about Amice.* Nicholas was reluctant to admit that his feelings for her continued to strain his self-control.

Perhaps there'd be a better time for this conversation, when he'd had an opportunity to analyze his true feelings. Angry at himself for wavering, he bit back his hastily decided upon confession.

"I'll miss you too." Admitting that was easy, but by no means complete.

Martin would gloat, were he here.

"Won't I see you at court?" she asked.

"We'll often be in the same room attending the king and queen, but whether we'll be able to speak privately, I can't say. You will, naturally, be expected to spend time with—"

A spear of jealousy stabbed his gut. He didn't want her to get married, either. The thought of another man having the right to talk to her, walk with her, hold her pretty little hands, wed and eventually take her to his bed infuriated Nicholas. The idea of another man touching what he had not, out of his sense of honor, allowed himself to touch beyond a single kiss filled him with unaccustomed envy.

What could he do? The king had chosen. Why would Henry change his mind? He already had the benefit of Nicholas's services, so no great political alliance would be made. But as a reward to an honored friend and knight? A slim possibility.

He hadn't known how important Amice would become to him, despite their differences. Nicholas had never felt such possessiveness for a person before. The very thing Belinda had demanded of him, he'd freely given to a woman he'd known only a short while.

Maybe he was imagining his feelings. A perfect example of what he'd oft heard minstrels sing of, wanting from afar but not being able to obtain. The longing, the sighing, the wishing for what could never be he'd once thought foolish and feigned were all too real.

At that moment, however, he wasn't far from the object of his interest. She gazed curiously at him, dark curls shining in the firelight. Her eyes, made brighter green by crying, so close to his. Yes, he confirmed, one eye was greener than the other.

He gently put his hands on her face, her skin against his fingers soft as the tufts of her fur collar. He lowered his head, his mouth inches from hers.

How many times had he daydreamed such a moment? Her cheeks were flushed, her mouth slightly open. His arms supported her as she leaned back, looking up at him as if trying to read his thoughts.

He lowered his mouth to hers and was pleasantly surprised when she instantly wrapped her arms around his neck. Her warmth enveloped him and desire claimed him. He drew her closer, his hands gently cupping her neck, feeling her smooth skin.

For once reality surpassed dreams. Imagining the need flowing through him wasn't as wonderful as living it.

"More," she breathed.

He was happy to comply, sliding his arms around her to pull her against him. It was never like this with Belinda, never. Ashamed his thoughts would turn to another woman at all while kissing Amice, he released her. He wanted to tell Amice about Belinda, so there'd be no secrets, but didn't want to spoil the moment.

He couldn't describe the swirling in his stomach, though he recognized quite well the stirring in another part of his anatomy.

"Nicholas," she began, but he stopped her with a finger on her lips.

"Later. Others are coming into the hall. We must get under way," he said.

Was that sorrow or relief in her gaze? Releasing Amice

despite the desire that pulsed through every fiber of his being, Nicholas stormed outside. He hoped the summer winds would return him to his senses. What might he have promised her if he remained in the spell of her nearness? He wanted her so much he'd almost violated his honor.

When had being with her, sharing his days by her side, become what he truly wanted? How could he have such thoughts, which could bring dishonor on them both if carried out?

What he wanted couldn't matter. Nothing could come before duty to his king and his country, not even his feelings for Amice.

He wouldn't allow himself to touch her as a husband touched a wife ever again.

CHAPTER 5

ondon is only a day away, a day away, the clip-clop of the horses' hooves sang scornfully. Amice's stomach churned. Dust and misery choked her.

She didn't notice the weather or the countryside they rode through. Not since her parents and brother died had she felt so despondent, so purposeless. All she could seem to do was think about Nicholas abandoning her in the hall the morning of their departure. He'd kissed her, and she'd wanted more. Her heart had rejoiced in his attentions. She'd felt changed for life.

Her tongue still hurt, she'd bitten it so hard to keep from calling him back. The futility of acting upon any feelings they might have for each other in light of Henry's impending announcement had prevented her from saying the words she longed to say. But she couldn't deny how his kiss made her feel. The tingling sensation remained, deep inside, making her yearn for more. She could still feel the warmth of his hand on her face, smell his clean scent, sense the security of his arms holding her.

Again she wracked her brain for any means for them to be together. No option she could think of would serve any purpose but to briefly delay the inevitable. Still she wanted…was it sinful? She wanted to make love with Nicholas, to feel his hard body against hers. She imagined waking in the cozy warmth of his arms, watching him sleep as early morning light crept in, carefully brushing stray locks of hair from his eyes. How could she have such thoughts, which would bring dishonor on them both if carried out?

Nicholas moved his horse close to hers. "You have your duty, as I have mine."

He'd read her thoughts. Their gazes met, but Amice made no reply. They'd barely exchanged two words since leaving Castle Rising. What more could they say?

Nicholas signaled the party to stop. Amice was glad for the respite; she'd never ridden for such an extended period. She waddled into the trees lining the road, eager to stretch her aching legs and back. To be alone, if only for a moment.

Sitting on a wide, slightly damp oak tree stump, she inhaled woodsy air. A bird flitted from branch to branch as he sang a cheerful tune. How lucky the bird was, to be free to fly wherever he wanted, whenever the impulse struck. Why did women have to be told where to go and when?

The uncertainty of the life awaiting her in London made her head pound. She closed her eyes, concentrating on the peaceful forest sounds, from several different birdcalls to the slight, sibilant rustle of breezes whisking through the trees. Was that a brook in the distance? Peaceful, relaxing sounds to ease her soul.

Then came heavy footsteps, crushing twigs and leaves in their path.

Nicholas, his blue eyes dark, glared down at her. "Did you think I wouldn't find you? That I wouldn't notice you and your horse were gone? Where did you think to hide?" he demanded.

She stood. "I wasn't running away. As you said, where would I go? I but sought a few minutes to myself. I tied my horse with the others."

"She's not there now," he said. "We've been searching for you."

A flush stained Amice's cheeks. "I'm sorry for the trouble. I just needed—"

"Next time, let me know," he ordered abruptly, offering her his hand to help her over the bracken.

The caring Nicholas was gone, the stern commander in his place. But his hand was strong and warm, sending a tingle up her arm.

How would she stop caring about him? Wanting to be with him?

❧❦

Nicholas couldn't speak another word until his breathing slowed. He, the calm one, had nearly panicked when Ginelle informed him Amice was missing. Unfortunately, it wasn't only the disruption of his duty to escort her safely to court that ailed him, but the cold fear of Amice alone and in danger. Without him to protect her, like she'd be as soon as they reached the king. He'd be there, but no longer charged with her care. How long would he miss his role? Miss her?

As they rode, Nicholas thought of all they'd left behind. Though he'd spent mere months at Castle Rising, he saw it as home. Never had he felt so comfortable, so much a part of life. Where else had he belonged? Not the manor house outside London, where his mother lived. Not at court, which rarely stayed long at any single holding, partly because the king wanted to be among his people and partly because feeding so many courtiers sapped surrounding flocks and fields.

Thus continued his roaming lifestyle until he was ordered to Castle Rising. There he'd found the home he'd not known he wanted until he experienced it. Of course, he admitted reluctantly, Amice was a large part of that. She helped make Castle Rising thrive, for him and for the other residents. Just when they were settling into a challenging yet pleasant routine, it was taken away.

Nothing good lasted. His father died when Nicholas was eleven. Then plague took his brother at the castle where he fostered. Nicholas had loved them both. His overbearing mother was no consolation. He'd hated leaving his younger sister Margaret with his mother, but he knew he couldn't remain at Greystone or take her with him. He'd avoided seeking an intelligent, interesting woman for whom he might come to care, only to wed her and endure the slow, painful deterioration of their relationship. Or her death.

Until now. Amice had slipped into the cage containing his heart forged of memories of constant quarreling and loss. Seemingly without any effort, as though it was meant to be. Yet here they were, arriving at court, where he'd have no part in her life. Instead, he'd see her wed another. More proof that caring for someone yielded more pain than pleasure.

Amice interrupted his thoughts. "What is life like with the king? I'd know something of what's in store. I should have asked sooner. I admit, I didn't want to. It would've made the inevitable more real."

How to explain the crowds, the conniving, the strictures? "To start with, hundreds of people serve him. I'd say about two hundred fifty have designated functions. There are clerks, valets and grooms, who are considered below stairs. Above stairs are chaplains, jewel house officers, the keeper of the wardrobe, esquires of the household and such. They work in shifts," he explained. "Margaret has her own staff. There are always numerous visitors and petitioners in attendance. There isn't room for everyone, so many buy or lease homes near the king's various castles."

Amice stayed silent for once, as if trying to imagine her place amidst the mass of people he described.

He knew she'd hate the bustling court where she'd oft be told what to do. And it was unlikely she'd feel welcomed or at home, the way he had at Castle Rising.

He had no way to soften the blow.

❧ ❧

Westminster Palace stood on the north bank of the River Thames, a cluster of buildings more imposing and grander than Amice had imagined. As they neared the arched entrance, a young page wearing the king's livery approached and demanded their names. When they presented the king's letter, the boy snapped his fingers. Nicholas's men and their horses were escorted away.

"The king expects you to join him for the evening meal," the page announced as he led Amice, Nicholas, Ginelle and Robert through the many corridors.

Numerous people hurried and scurried every which way as if on missions to complete the most important of tasks. At last they stopped, in front of a door that to Amice looked no different from many of the others. She had no idea how to make her way back to the entrance or how she would find anything.

"Your rooms are here, my lady," the page said, bowing slightly. "I shall call for you in three hours."

With each step away from all she knew and loved, she found it harder to breathe in the musty air. There was too much to absorb at once, the vast palace, so many new people, her upcoming meeting with the king. The revealing of her groom's identity. Add to that how she already missed being at Castle Rising. With Nicholas. She felt as if several stone had been added to her weight.

Without further ado, the page turned and walked on. Nicholas didn't follow. The boy turned and impatiently tapped his dark red leather-booted foot on the stone floor.

Nicholas said, "I know the way. That will be all."

"I was told to bring you straightaway to the king and I will," the boy retorted defiantly.

"You're new here."

The boy nodded. "Yes, I'm Lucan, of Gloucester."

"Then I'll forgive your behavior. You don't know me?"

The boy's widening eyes revealed the first stirrings of fear.

"You'll soon learn. I caution you to mind your station before you open your mouth and get into trouble," Nicholas advised.

Lucan had the grace to turn red. "I await your convenience, my lord."

Robert, peeking out from behind Amice, giggled at Lucan's discomfort, and received a scathing glare in return. Nicholas guided Amice a few steps away from the others.

"I must go to the king," he began. "If you need anything, send Robert to me and I will come. Don't send a note. It could end up in the wrong hands. Remember that the simplest, most innocent message can be misconstrued. Gossip flourishes here, and most are quick to judge. I wish you well." He drew in a breath, as if he wished to say more.

Amice hoped for words of kindness, to hear that he'd miss her. But he left with Lucan and disappeared around a corner.

Her heart sank. Tears of frustration threatened. Nicholas was gone. Who knew when or if they'd regain the closeness they'd shared? His presence had been her only comfort, but now she was alone in a place so foreign to her it could just as well be another country as the king's castle. No longer did she have the responsibility or authority she so appreciated. Instead, she was at the mercy of another, and expected to meekly do as ordered. A prisoner, albeit in an appealing, large cell.

At least Nicholas had said he'd come to her if needed. She didn't want to need him in that way.

She looked at Ginelle and Robert, who seemed as uncomfortable as she. *Well, at least these two are left to me.*

As Ginelle unpacked, Amice inspected her new chambers. A tiny sitting room led to a chamber with a bed wider and larger than her own, hung with cream wool curtains heavily embroidered with colorful leaves and flowers. Several tall windows overlooked a manicured courtyard, beyond which she could see a knot garden and a forest. She looked forward to walking the grounds, one thing to take pleasure in, at least. The windows' red glass borders lent the room a rosy glow in the afternoon sun. A tiny maid's room completed the quarters.

Where was Robert to sleep? She'd worry about that later. She needed to wash away the dust of the road, refresh after her journey and prepare for her dinner with the king.

"Ginelle, please find someone to fetch water for a bath." She opened a chest and took out a comb.

"But my lady, whom shall I ask?" Ginelle too seemed at a loss.

Amice snapped the comb in two. "If I knew, I'd have told you."

"I wish we were at home!"

"I'm sorry, Ginelle." Amice knew she'd need more control over her emotions. She took a deep breath, then let it out. "I wish we were home, too."

Ginelle, wringing her hands, stepped cautiously into the corridor.

A page leaned on the wall across from their door.

"My lady wishes a bath," Ginelle began nervously.

"It shall be brought shortly." The page hurried away.

"Why couldn't Nicholas—someone—have told us how things are done here," Amice muttered while arranging gowns on the bed. "What am I to wear? Ginelle, see if you can find someone else to ask what one wears to meals."

Nicholas hadn't included attire in his rendition of court life.

She should've asked, either on the road or at home while there was time to have new gowns sewn, if needed. She'd been too busy worrying. Too busy resisting the idea of going to court in the first place. Too busy taking pleasure in Nicholas's company.

Ginelle left Amice to ponder her gowns.

"I asked another page, who sent for a maid," she reported.

A few moments later, a knock sounded. Ginelle opened the door.

"My lady, I am Adele. I was told you're interested in the fashions of the day. Here, fine ladies such as yourself prefer bright, cheery colors," the young, fresh-faced maid said. "If I may, I'll help you select a gown."

Amice nodded her acceptance and gratefully accepted the bright blue silk overdress and low-cut kirtle the woman handed her. "Thank you."

The maid curtseyed and departed.

Wearing the blue silk and her favorite amethysts, Amice was pacing furiously in the sitting room, heels clicking on the wood floors, when Lucan returned to escort her to dinner. They wove through corridor after corridor, her nerves tightening like balled yarn as the sound of many people talking in unison grew louder and louder. What was everyone doing?

She'd envisioned an intimate dinner with the king and queen. Obviously there were many more guests than she'd expected.

At last they reached a wide doorway. Amice took in the scene before her, surprise and confusion knotting her stomach. Everyone stood, heads bowed, in the midst of a rather extended grace.

The page began making his way through the great hall, so vast it dwarfed Castle Rising's. Long tables ran the length of the room, with a raised table across the back. To the right, a fireplace as tall as she barely contained a huge blaze, though it was warm outside and in. Finely woven tapestries of knights in battle covered several walls.

The praying continued as Amice peered at the high table, trying to determine which man was King Henry, who she knew to be in his early thirties. A hint of excitement prickled. She was going to meet the king and queen of England.

In front of the tallest chair stood a man dressed almost

completely in black. Instead of tunics worn by most of the noblemen, Henry wore a long gown with a rolled hood, much like those common men wore in the towns they'd passed on the way to London. The bright gold cross dangling from his Lancastrian chain of "SS" links called attention to the solemnity of his clothing. His small crown had a border of tiny crosses instead of jewels.

To his right stood a beautiful woman with large eyes and a rounded face in a rich, dark blue velvet gown, whom she assumed to be Queen Margaret. Her hair, reputed to be blond, was hidden beneath her headdress with an oval padded roll on top. To Henry's left was the only empty seat she could see. Next to that she was relieved to see Nicholas.

Immediately her tight shoulders relaxed. Her breath came easier. She'd never seen him so richly dressed, in black velvet with silver thread at the collar. A sense of contentment washed through her, cleansing as a spring rain. She forced her gaze from Nicholas to seek out the page. How had he disappeared so quickly? There he was, almost at the high table.

The crowd sat, leaving her one of the few still standing except for servers carrying heaped platters hither and yon. Sensing many eyes upon her, she drew herself up regally and continued on, weaving gracefully around the tables. She knew she looked her best. The din quieted as Amice curtseyed to the king and queen. The sibilance of whispers rose above her pounding heart as the king raised her to her feet.

"Welcome," Henry said, his voice nasal and thin. He looked down his nose at her with what seemed to be great disdain. He opened his mouth as if to say something else but turned to address the other guests instead. "We welcome Lady Amice Winfield."

The whispers flourished with renewed vigor.

"Come, sup with Us so we can get acquainted," Henry said, indicating the vacant chair. With that, he turned to his food, as if already uninterested in the new arrival.

Amice's stomach was too squeezed to think of eating. She couldn't stand the suspense another minute. Who was she to wed? When? As she drew breath to speak, Nicholas turned to her with a bright, clearly forced smile. So his court persona was yet another facet of him. Would she ever again see the Nicholas she had come to know, care for and already missed?

"Whatever we discuss, keep smiling...as though we spoke of the venison or some such thing," he said.

"Where is he?" Amice demanded with an equally forced smile.

"He's expected very soon." Nicholas took a bite of roasted eel in red wine.

"Who did the king choose?" She picked up her small, chased silver eating knife, but the aroma of the sauce made her queasy.

"I don't know," he answered. "I tried to find out, but Henry wouldn't reveal his name."

The servitor brought more wine.

"When is someone going to tell me something?" she asked angrily. "This waiting, the not knowing, is worse than what will be. You can't make plans without facts." Recovering with a stiff smile, she changed the subject. "I'm glad to see you, a familiar, friendly face. But why are we seated here? And where is my cousin Cromwell?"

Nicholas leaned close, whispering, "No matter what, smile."

Her eyes widened, but she did as he bid. Many had stopped eating and appeared to be avidly studying the events at the high table. Amice hoped their expressions were bland enough to mask the true nature of their conversation.

"The question is, 'When is your wedding?'" he said.

He looked so handsome, with candlelight brightening his eyes. She needed his comfort, but how? He couldn't even take her hand or even say too much lest a neighbor overhear.

"When?" Her voice came out a whisper.

"In three weeks. The king and queen plan to attend."

Her knife fell to the table and slid to the floor with a clatter. Henry turned to her with a raised eyebrow.

Amice knew she blushed as a server retrieved the utensil. Never had she felt so awkward, so unsure. In three weeks she'd wed a man she'd never met, whose name she didn't yet know. How she wished to return to her satisfying life at Castle Rising. With Nicholas.

Henry said, "We're certain you will be pleased with our choice."

Amice clutched her jeweled goblet, her knuckles turning white as the stones dug into her palms.

He continued smoothly, "We see no need to waste time in this matter. The wedding will be in three weeks."

She couldn't resist a quick glance at Nicholas, but couldn't read his expression. The man on his other side was leaning so far toward them that his hair dangled over Nicholas's plate. Thankfully the king had spoken softly.

Amice had no choice but to risk Henry's wrath. This might be her only opportunity to protest the marriage. Her only audience with the king and queen. She'd never forgive herself if she meekly accepted her fate, though ordered by the king. She had to try to change it, though her arsenal of options was limited.

"Your Grace, I am most honored that you think highly enough of me to select a husband for me and have made the effort to do so," she began. "However, I would rather not wed."

Henry turned in his tall chair to peer more closely at her. He seemed curious, not angry. "What say you?"

"I'm content to remain at Castle Rising, to continue managing it and the lands Edwin bequeathed me. I'll gladly pay a fine for this privilege. Or perhaps I could make a generous contribution to Eton College, the school for poor scholars you established? I've heard how important education is to you, that you want students to learn both virtue and the sciences. Whatever amount you think appropriate...." She was babbling. Her courage faded faster than a winter sun at twilight.

Henry looked sympathetic, even as he shook his head. "What the individual wants is not important, but what is good for England and our Lord. I didn't ask to be king, as you didn't ask to be wed. But I am anointed by right and must do as I see fit. That is my duty. Your duty is to marry, to strengthen an alliance. God almighty, the Lord of all, is compassionate and merciful." Henry shifted in his chair, as if he found the discussion distasteful. He turned to Queen Margaret, who'd been trying to overhear the exchange. A frown marred her brow.

Learning that Henry didn't want to be king surprised Amice. Yet given the myriad problems he faced, such as France wanting its sovereignty, the arguing among his own advisors Nicholas had told her about, and Richard, Duke of York's claim that he was the rightful king, combined with the pressure of weighty decisions, Amice couldn't blame him. She strained to get another glimpse of the queen, whom she knew to be near her own age, and at last with child for the first time after seven years of marriage.

Henry had been the wrong one to approach. Maybe Margaret would help her.

The seemingly endless meal was almost over. Amice nibbled on a piece of bread, not as soft or flavorful as Castle Rising's, making her miss home and Maia all the more. She surveyed the other guests. Most wore black, brown, or another subdued color. Why was she one of the only people garbed in a bright shade?

As they rose to leave, Queen Margaret motioned to her. "Lady Winfield, it's most obvious you haven't been informed of my husband's preference for somber dress." Her accent revealed her French heritage.

Amice grew hot with embarrassment, but held her head high despite chagrin that the first words the queen spoke to her weren't of welcome but disdain.

"Henry dislikes colorful garments, and as you can see, most accede to his wishes. Once at a Christmas play, women were brought to dance before the king. Though it was the fashion, so much of their flesh was exposed that the king left the room. In future, please keep in mind that the king is quite modest and offended by such displays as you make with your gown."

The whispers hadn't been mere musings about the new arrival. They'd all been laughing at her. The maid who'd advised her on her choice of gown had known this would happen.

A painful way to learn a lesson. She'd be more careful whom she trusted in the future.

"As to your marital situation, do not anticipate assistance from me. We need you to make this marriage," Margaret informed her. "Your wishes have no import."

Worse and worse. Neither Margaret nor Henry cared to reconsider their choice of husband. This unpleasant beginning to her court visit didn't bode well for things to come.

But Amice refused to be a pawn manipulated by king and queen. Somehow she'd find a way to make her own moves.

❧❦ ❦❧

Near the other end of the hall, Belinda Carlisle observed the high table as best she could between bustling servers and pages blocking her view. When she saw Nicholas, her slow smile was quickly replaced by a frown. She couldn't bear to watch his cheerful banter with the beautiful new arrival. Who was she to be so highly seated?

Envy sliced sharper than a sword. He hadn't even let her know he'd returned to court.

After Belinda's third husband set her aside, she'd sought out Nicholas, an exceedingly handsome favorite of the king, who gave her access to lords and ladies she wanted to know. Many a woman wished to claim him. The prospect of capturing a prize in the face of competition encouraged her to try harder.

She'd thought Nicholas easy prey; he was a man. But Nicholas spent time with her on his terms, not hers. Nor had he professed to have any feelings for her. Still, she enjoyed the pride she felt attending court functions on his arm, the envious looks from other women, questions about his prowess to which she offered only enough information to keep them asking more. The lack of a suitable replacement kept her from complaining too often.

She was only twenty-five, so perhaps there was still time to ensnare him completely. Perhaps she hadn't tried hard enough, been bold enough.

Her smile returned as an idea came to her. How she adored having a plan.

❧❦ ❦❧

Nicholas sighed as he entered his quarters. His head ached from the noisy hall and the strain of making polite conversation. Sitting next to Amice, ever aware of their impending separation, unnerved him. She'd looked so lovely despite concern and uncertainty about her situation. He'd wanted to ease her fears and bring a genuine smile to her face. To be alone with her and make her his.

He paced in the narrow antechamber. *I don't want her to marry someone else.* He'd found the one woman who might change his distaste for marriage. He'd come to care for her, respect her. Desire her.

Why can't I speak the truth to Henry? Why can't I ask for her?

He answered his own questions. "Because Henry needs her marriage to benefit England, not his friend."

The strength of his feelings for Amice weighed on him, but he didn't know how to rid himself of them. Wanting what couldn't be.

A noise from the next room broke his train of thought. Silently he unsheathed his dagger and stepped toward the door, wishing he were wearing his sword, now propped next to the bed. He looked into the bedroom, lit by a fire.

Someone was in his bed.

As he drew near, he heard a stifled giggle. Belinda's blond head appeared from under the covers.

Nicholas jammed his dagger back into its sheath. "Belinda. What are you doing here? Do you think to cause some kind of scandal to force me to wed you?"

Her smile didn't waver. "I wanted to welcome you home. You've been away so long," she answered, as she slowly drew back the covers, revealing her nakedness.

Not even a stirring of interest.

Her audacity in coming uninvited to his rooms irked him. And he hoped she hadn't overheard his musings. If anyone had seen her, he'd have to find a way to extricate himself from that quagmire. And if word got to Amice....

"I was going to tell you this tomorrow, but since you're here...." He had to be blunt. No vague phrases that could be misinterpreted. "Whatever we had is over. I never made you any promises. I'm sorry if you believed something would come of it."

She jumped out of bed, seemingly unconscious of the cold floor or her nakedness. Her smile changed to a snarl. "Is there someone else? That new woman? What can she offer that I can't?"

"I don't owe you an explanation."

"I know you want someone you can't have," Belinda said. "Why bother with whoever she is when you can be with me?"

Belinda *had* heard him. At least he hadn't mentioned

Amice's name. She didn't have enough information to use against him.

Slowly, she walked forward, offering herself, pressing herself against him. Her scent seemed sickeningly strong. "Don't make me your enemy, Nicholas. You'll be much better off with me as your friend." She ran a hand over his shoulder and down his arm.

Ignoring her veiled threat, somewhat surprised that her lush body no longer enticed him, he said, "Belinda. There's nothing between us, nor has there been. Just leave."

He walked around her, picked her clothes up from where they were piled neatly on a chest in the corner and handed them to her.

A knock sounded at the outer door. "Get dressed," he ordered. "And be quiet."

Nicholas opened the door to find Robert. "My lord," he began.

"What's amiss? Has something happened?" He regretted his harsh tone, not wanting to frighten the boy.

"N-nothing, my lord. It's just that…here."

Nicholas took the proffered note with some dismay, remembering his earlier request that Amice not risk undue gossip should a note fall into the wrong hands. But he smiled as he read it. Amice was worried that her precious servant would be corrupted by staying in the page's quarters. How quickly she learned the ways of court.

And how clever she was. By entrusting Robert to his care, she'd be able to send as many messages as she wanted without arousing curiosity.

"You may stay with me, for now. I'll send for a pallet."

Robert's face lit up. "I'm much too old to stay with Ginelle and Lady Amice, or other boys. I want to learn to be a knight, just like you."

Belinda chose that moment to saunter in. "Hello, young sir. Goodnight, Nicholas. I adored visiting with you. And look forward to our next meeting."

She kissed him on the lips and trailed her hand down his body before Nicholas could stop her. She walked out, hips swaying seductively.

Robert's mouth dropped open. The boy focused on a crack in the stone floor.

Nicholas resisted the urge to wipe his face on his sleeve. He leaned his forehead against the arched wooden door as he locked it, which he'd always do from now on.

He knew he didn't have to explain anything to Robert, but wanted to. What did a boy of his age know of such things? Would he tell Amice what he'd seen? She wasn't calculating enough to have sent Robert as a spy.

"Robert, I didn't invite that woman here. She let herself in after the meal, and waited for me. I was sending her away when you arrived."

Had he restored Robert's trust?

Robert smiled. "I'm already learning from you. A good lesson, my lord. Send all uninvited women away posthaste."

Nicholas sighed with relief. One cannonball dodged. Who knew how many more would be fired at him?

CHAPTER 6

Amice felt as though she were hauling a heavy cart up a steep hill. She couldn't let go, but holding on strained her endurance more each day as she waited for word of her groom. She'd asked for details, but none were given. To leave her less time to protest? Each day she learned more of the routine of court, listened to countless conversations about people she'd met and some she hadn't, walked in the gardens and flew hawks with the women. There was naught else for her to do but attend Margaret. No accounts to manage, no stores to order, no one seeking her guidance, no decisions to make beyond what to wear. She had asked for, but not been granted, a private audience with Margaret in a last, desperate hope to persuade the queen to her cause.

As predicted, though they were often in the same room, Amice and Nicholas hadn't had the opportunity to speak privately. She knew he trained, hunted and was often closeted with the king and his advisors, but she wanted to talk to him. Be near him. Know his thoughts.

She wanted to scream.

Despite spending hours with the pen dangling from her fingers, hoping for inspiration, even writing was no longer a source of accomplishment or pleasure. Perhaps she'd left her muse at Castle Rising.

Though surrounded by throngs of people, loneliness pinched like a gown tied too tightly. Her thoughts often strayed to Nicholas, who'd seemed to settle in with ease. Had their time at

Castle Rising meant anything to him, or was it a mere diversion until he could return to court, where he truly belonged and preferred to be?

Late that night, a boisterous storm kept her awake. Each clap of thunder made her jump and condensed her quarters into a tiny, suffocating box. She had to escape the constraining walls, even for a few moments. She doubted that women often wandered the halls alone at night, but she didn't care.

As lightning flashed and thunder cracked, she wrapped a cloak around her. She made her way to the great hall, completely deserted at this hour. No servants made their beds on pallets, as they did in many castles. The spacious solitude calmed her, contrasting with the storm. Her peaceful side and rebellious nature warred with each other. She smiled at the comparison, the first smile she hadn't had to force since her arrival.

Pulling a bench away from the wall, she sat, listening to rain splash against the windows and thunder roll across the sky. The roiling weather echoed the turmoil of her emotions.

Soft footsteps disturbed her thoughts. *Can I never be alone?* As she turned, a burst of lightning revealed a man. She gasped, thinking she'd seen Nicholas gazing out the far window.

How her imagination could play tricks on her.

The hall glowed with another series of lightning flashes as rain beat ever harder.

Nicholas *was* there, his face illuminated by brief brightness. He mustn't have seen her in the shadows. His long, dark hair was loose, his expression hard. White light reflected harshly on the planes of his face, making him appear a wild warrior. What troubled him so?

As if he could feel her gaze on him, he looked up slowly, staring through the darkness. She felt his stare as though it was a tangible thing.

Her heart lightened. A few moments with him, stolen though they were, would make her feel better.

"Who's there?" Nicholas's voice sounded hollow to him in the empty hall, and was almost drowned out by a thunderclap.

Another flash revealed Amice. He hid his surprise, wondering if his thoughts had conjured her. He sat beside her on the bench as the thunder rolled.

"Well met, at this hour. What brings you out, and alone?"

"The storm, of course. I couldn't sleep." She drew her cloak tighter about her.

Her nearness tugged at him, drawing him nearer on the bench. He'd missed her company, missed her smile. Quelling a strong urge to take her in his arms, to feel her against him, he chose a safer course. "How do you find court?"

"It seems worlds away from Castle Rising. I have little to do, and miss my responsibilities. I haven't even seen my cousin Cromwell, who's off on some task for the king. Each day seems endless with waiting. The suspense…. I fear each page hurrying by is the one carrying the message that the chosen man has arrived. I wish I'd never come. I wish I could go home. There, are you satisfied?"

The bitterness in her voice shocked him. He'd thought her resigned to her fate, an honorable marriage to please both king and queen. Believing in her acceptance was the only thing that had made the past two weeks tolerable.

He started to speak, but his words were lost in a crash of thunder. Waiting until the noise quieted to a low rumble, he tried again. "The weather must be adding to your misery. When the sun shines, you'll feel better."

She shook her head, sending her curls flying, brushing his shirtsleeve. "No. I won't." After a long moment, she said, "Thank you. Are you happy to be back with the king?"

"'Tis my duty."

"That's not an answer." Her eyes shone an eerie golden green, like a cat's, in the short bursts of light. She sat quietly, perusing his face as lightning flickered, as if memorizing every inch.

He recalled their departure from Castle Rising, the stirring kiss they'd shared. His loins tightened. Of its own volition, his head moved toward hers, to build on that moment and make it new. She didn't move, but accepted his mouth on hers as if she'd been waiting for it. Waves of warmth crashed with the thunder, driving the dampness of the night from him.

Only their lips touched, then their tongues. They explored each other's mouths with deep, thirsting kisses.

❧ ☙

Amice savored the taste of him, the pressure of his lips on hers. Sliding closer, until their chests met, they kissed in the flare of the storm. Delicious warmth centered on her chest, where he pressed against her.

How long she'd waited for this.

Her cloak slipped off her shoulders as he slid his arms around her. His muscles bunched as he pulled her closer. Only the thin gown separated them now. His tongue sought hers as his hands caressed her back. Warmth, desire, everywhere. She wanted more.

Having him so near was torture. A teasing, wonderful glimpse of what could never be.

"This will get us nowhere. I am not for you." It took all of her willpower to push free of his embrace. She ran from the hall and back to her chamber, where tears burst forth with all the force of the storm.

She'd experienced the freedom of the hall only to return to her cage. Just as she had barely begun to enjoy Nicholas, only to be returned to the prospect of an unknown groom.

❧ ☙

The only thing that brought Amice pleasure was the queen's library. She'd never seen such a vast collection of books, available to anyone able to read.

Reverently she opened each volume to reveal treasures concealed by the decorated bindings. There were elaborately illuminated romances, various histories. As expected, she found a worn copy of *Roman de la Rose,* the long poem of courtly love written nearly two hundred years ago.

Two volumes that surprised her were written by Margaret's father, René, king of Anjou. Then she came across a book that brought tears of delight to her eyes. Queen Margaret had a copy of *La Livre de la Cité des Dames, The Book of the City of Ladies,* the very book she'd been yearning to read for years. She read the cherished tome as slowly as possible, in small sections, to savor every word.

Oh, to be able to write like Christine de Pizan. Most women didn't talk of things Christine wrote about, leading Amice to believe she alone in had unusual ideas. But here they were, preserved on the pages. Women should be educated, could contribute beyond wifely duties. Christine wrote to avenge wrongs done to women throughout history.

The rustle of skirts interrupted her concentration. She almost dropped the precious book when she realized Queen Margaret stood before her.

Amice jumped to her feet, clutching *The Book of the City of Ladies* to her chest. She curtseyed. "Your Grace."

"Are you fond of that book?" Margaret inquired in a tone requiring no answer. "My grandparents were among Christine de Pizan's patrons. They gave it to me."

Amice was pleased to find a subject she could discuss with her queen, one not as delicate or painful as her upcoming marriage. "Yes, Your Grace, I've longed to read this. She writes so cleverly and wisely."

"I am particularly fond of her discussion of the queens and princesses of France." She perused the shelves, her velvet-clad back to Amice. "I couldn't sleep, and thought to find a book myself."

"The volumes your father wrote are quite impressive," Amice added. She desperately wanted the queen to accept her. Perhaps like her, even.

Margaret turned and smiled, the first time Amice had seen her do so. "Chivalry is his passion. He helped illustrate the tournament book." Holding a volume of statutes under her arm, she studied Amice with a thoughtful expression. "Do you write as well as read?"

"Yes, Your Grace," Amice answered. "And I keep the tallies at Castle Rising." Letting go of the reins and leaving her steward in charge had been a challenge.

"When this marriage issue is resolved, come to me. I can always use another scribe."

Amice dropped into a deep curtsy. She hadn't expected such an honor, especially after she'd alienated the queen by trying to avoid her arranged marriage. She wished her parents were still alive, to be proud of her and share her accomplishments.

After Margaret left, thoughts of the beautiful queen prevented Amice from reading. Amice knew Queen Margaret was highly intelligent and poised for power. But none of the terrible things Amice had heard about her seemed to be true, such as that she favored France over her new home, England.

How did Margaret handle the pressure of being queen, when Amice was nearing her breaking point over the choice of a husband? Did the queen, who could command hundreds, have what she really wanted?

Amice doubted she herself ever would.

❦ ❦

Seated with the king and a small group of advisors, Nicholas frowned as he watched Belinda and Amice talking on the other side of the Painted Chamber, a hall replete with biblical paintings covering the walls and ceiling. A group of men blocked his view, making him shift in his chair.

Being alone with Amice last night still haunted him. He'd remained in the hall, eyes closed, breathing slowly to still the pounding of his heart. To calm surging desire. If she hadn't had the strength to leave, what would they have done? There, in the hall, where anyone could enter? Again having her in his arms made him forget his duties, his honor. He remained weak where she was concerned, despite many prayers for strength and more on her behalf every morning and every evening.

The king had pledged her to another. Thank goodness temptation would soon be removed.

He tried to convince himself he meant it.

She and Belinda slowly walked out of the room, heads bent close. He barely resisted the urge to jump to his feet.

What was Belinda up to? What if Amice confided in her? He signaled for Robert, seated on a fat velvet pillow, plucking ineffectively at a lute. Nicholas thought of sending for vellum to write a note, then thought better of it.

"Never mind, Robert, I'll go. Come for me if the king needs me."

He knew Robert returned to what he called his instrument of torture with great reluctance. Nicholas had assured him a true knight was well-versed in many areas, including music. So play he would.

Nicholas found the two women—one who wanted him, one he wanted—seated on a stone bench beneath a vine-encrusted trellis. Belinda wore blue brocade, while Amice wore a deep green gown that accentuated her eyes. He vowed to commit each moment with her to memory, in case it would be his last. The row of pearls trimming her neckline reflected late afternoon sun. A cream undergown peeked above the neckline. A mesh headdress with a short transparent veil that floated in the gentle breeze hid her hair.

He shook his head to make himself ignore the effect her beauty had on him, to clear fond memories of their days at Castle Rising and concentrate on what they were saying. And gleaned that he'd arrived in time.

"Lady Winfield, if I may interrupt, I've just come from the king and must speak with you."

He sensed Belinda bristling with curiosity as Amice paled.

"Of course," she said. "Belinda, I'll see you anon."

Pathetic that he was glad for any excuse to speak to her. He trained for the rigors of battle and had survived. How would he gird himself against the lure of Amice?

They crossed a vibrant patch of purple and blue irises toward a secluded clump of hawthorn bushes. At that moment, Nicholas's message took priority over his concern for propriety. He had to worry about Amice more than who might spy them walking off alone and what gossip might erupt.

"I must tell you before you hear the news from someone else. As unwelcome as it may be," he said.

Amice looked out over the rolling hills. She lifted her chin, obviously bracing herself. "Tell me, then. Who is he?"

"Who is who?" Nicholas asked, perplexed.

"You said you came from the king. I assumed he'd finally announced who I am to marry."

Her loveliness at that moment, with late afternoon sun casting a rosy glow on her face, eyes as green as the leaves behind her and glinting defiantly, the breeze filling the air with her sweet rose scent, overwhelmed him. He didn't want to tell her about Belinda. He wanted to tell her how much he cared. That he wanted her more than he'd wanted any other woman. The words hovered on the tip of his tongue.

This could be their last moment alone, ever.

"No, no, not yet," he began. "I did come from the king, but that was merely an excuse to get you away from her."

"Lady Belinda? She seems quite friendly."

He wanted to take her hand, both to reassure her and just to touch her, but didn't. "Seems is the key word. Belinda wants to wed with me and has for years. She was, well, we used to…."

❧ ☙

Amice gasped, stifling the spears of jealousy stabbing her.

She'd thought she'd made progress in her quest to stop caring about Nicholas, at this moment striking as a knight depicted in one of the queen's novels. Clearly not. Forgetting him would be far easier if she didn't see him hither and yon, sparking her memories and dreams. Making her long to create more.

"She was your mistress?" she whispered.

"Yes. But there is nothing between us now. Nothing at all."

"Why are you telling me? Your amours or lack thereof can be of no import," Amice hedged, unbidden images of Nicholas and Belinda together, laughing, talking, bodies entwined, filling her mind.

"I trust very few people, and she isn't one of them. I wanted to alert you to the truth in case she's befriending you for the wrong reasons."

Her stomach churned afresh. How could she tell who was sincere and who wasn't? "Thank you for the warning. I assure you I'll be careful." She relaxed her shoulders, which she hadn't realized she'd tensed. "Nicholas, what is the purpose of life?"

"For me, to serve God, king and country."

"And for me?"

Amice noted his answer to this question did not come as quickly.

"To serve God and king also, and to serve the country by producing heirs for your lands. Each of us must do what he or she can."

"'Must do.' You believe what you said the night of the storm. To choose our own way is wrong. Forbidden. The king has not only the power but the right to choose for me. For us."

"Marriages are often arranged thusly among the nobility," he agreed. "'Tis rare for either the bride or groom to have a say."

Amice cringed. Nicholas seemed so matter of fact, impersonal. Their interlude of closeness had ended. There was no point telling him she'd been drawn to him almost from the first moment she'd seen him. That she wanted to return with him to Castle Rising and continue the life they'd barely begun. Bringing her feelings out in the open, baring her heart to him, could only lead to greater despair when she wed another.

He plucked a purple flower and handed it to her with a smile. Warmth flooded her. The simple gesture, the petals soft as silk against her fingers, meant more than it should, because it was the first thing he had given her.

She was promised to another. What she felt for Nicholas was of no consequence to her duty. What did a few conversations, a few brief embraces truly mean? Amice lifted her chin, her face set, hardening her gaze, hoping her eyes were as green as marble.

He couldn't know how difficult these days at court had been, the irksome dejection that had drained her spirit at seeing him talk to others but not her. To occasionally be part of the same group or at the same table, knowing though they were feet apart, the gulf between them was miles wide. She had to get away before her will dissolved into her feelings and she threw herself at him, begged him to find a way to marry her. Her need for this man would be her downfall if she let it.

She gathered her skirts to leave.

Nicholas grabbed her elbow. "Amice, wait. You don't understand...."

In spite of her resolve to be strong, tears filled her eyes, for in his voice she heard despair as deep as hers. Amice sensed his frustration with what must be as she felt his desire for her flowing from his body. She couldn't stop herself from reaching out to him, taking the opportunity to feel his arms around her once more. One last kiss to remember always.

Nicholas enveloped her in his strong embrace, his hard-muscled arms holding her close. He ran his hand through her hair. In that moment, everything felt better. Felt right.

Her heart soared high as the birds she'd seen in the forest on their way to court. Amice wanted to laugh, to sing out her happiness.

He bent closer, closer, until she felt his breath. Their mouths melded with ease, as if they were meant to touch. The searching heat of his kiss stunned her, overwhelming bittersweet knowledge that this was all they would ever share. Warmth flooded her from fingers to toes. She wanted to savor every second. If only this moment could last forever.

But he ended the kiss and released her. Amice wanted to laugh, to sing out her happiness. As she wished for another, she saw passion in his eyes. Beyond that, was there love?

CHAPTER 7

Fotheringay, Northamptonshire – June 1453

Belinda arrived in Richard Plantagenet's receiving chamber to find the third Duke of York pacing furiously. The train from his fur-trimmed robe snapped as he turned. The Earl of Salisbury, the duke's brother-in-law who had arranged this meeting, also named Richard, waited patiently in an elaborately carved armchair, thick fingers folded over his substantial paunch.

"What has it all come to? What is it for? Must we continue to tear apart our own country?" York asked no one in particular.

She slid back the hood of her oversized black cloak. The duke gasped as her blond beauty was revealed. She acknowledged his admiration with a nod. As long as men responded in this way, she wasn't yet old. She might find another husband.

"It was difficult for me to get away. And a woman traveling alone is such a rare sight," she said. "I was stopped several times. I told them my husband abandoned me on the road and I sought shelter with my sister."

"So you are good at creating tales, Lady Carlisle." York settled in a chair opposite her and crossed his legs, the hem of his fur-trimmed robe pooling on the carpet. "Salisbury said you wished to tell me your story yourself. Please tell me why I am to entrust you, a woman, and one who can lie with ease, with my cause."

Belinda bestowed one of her special, slow smiles upon him. "Your Grace, while attending the queen, I hear many things. But I'm certain you're wondering why I'd betray King Henry to help you. My second husband, the only one I truly cared for, was killed during the Jack Cade uprising. I can't forgive those currently in power for allowing rebellion."

York would be the next king. She'd heard conversations at court, knew how lords feared and respected him, heard tell of his vast riches and power. Instead of drowning with Henry's sinking ship, she hoped to join a captain on the rise. Then, when the Yorkists overtook the Lancasters, she'd be assured of a place in the new court.

Perhaps even a better one than she had now.

Belinda could produce tears on demand. She let her eyes fill, then struggled to keep the tears from falling, for if they did they might stain her silk gown.

The duke ran his fingers through his straight, cropped blond hair. "Are you an heiress? Do you have soldiers and knights at your disposal?"

"No. But I'm highly placed with the queen and can be discreet. I can pass on information about the king's strategies. I can foment rumor." The slight frown and shake of his head told her York wasn't convinced. What else could she do? "I can seek out others to aid your cause."

"What do you expect to gain? How do I know you can be trusted?" the duke demanded. He began to pace. "What reward do you expect for your services?"

Belinda kept her eyes on her hands. Why hadn't she thought to wear a rosary? A pious façade might help sway him. "I ask nothing, my lord, but to know I am avenged."

"I've been betrayed too many times to believe everything I hear," York said. "But I will allow you one chance."

He was looking at her mouth. She slowly moistened her lips with her tongue. "It's a bit warm, might I have something to drink?"

"Of course, please forgive me. There is hippocras." There were no servants present, so York himself walked to the pitcher on a side table.

Belinda studied him as he poured. Not quite as large as

Nicholas. His hair was shorter, straighter…but he was quite attractive, and reputed to be the wealthiest man in all of England. Unfortunately, he was also married. But spouses came and went and not all men were faithful.

As he handed her the cup of heavily engraved silver, she made sure her fingers grazed his, very lightly. He started at the touch.

Belinda had come to offer information. But she could offer much more. Slowly, she took a sip, looking at him over the rim. She had to prove her intelligence and quality. No other man she knew was worth the effort. Except Nicholas, of course.

She took another sip. "This isn't from Bordeaux."

"A discerning palate. It is Mediterranean," Richard said. "Even with the supposed truce with France, I'll not drink from their cup."

"Thank you, Your Grace, for the wine. Now, what would you wish of me?" She smiled modestly, as if unaware of the innuendo.

"Either you tell the truth or you are a very good liar. A pair of eyes as beautiful and insightful as yours ensconced in Henry's court would be of value." He drank, then set his cup on the small table. "Report any knowledge you think I might find of interest. Don't bring or send documents. And if you should be discovered, of course we never had this conversation.

"The laws of primogeniture dictate that I am the rightful heir to the throne, as a descendant of an older son of Edward III than Henry. I will be king. Though I have no desire to resort to secrecy and spies, unfortunately such methods have proved the only means to obtain valuable information. And, as you said, foment rumor to cause uncertainty."

"I understand, Your Grace. I'm honored to assist you however I can. And if you need more to come to your aid, I know of several who'd be willing." She had no idea at the moment who those people would be, but it sounded like a powerful thing to offer. "There are many who believe, as we do, in your cause."

"We are in agreement, Salisbury. Thank you, Lady Carlisle, for your offer. I look forward to hearing something of use from you soon." He turned toward the window, dismissing her.

Belinda was fairly confident that she could persuade York to add her to his retinue after proving her usefulness through devotion to his political and perhaps personal desires. But to get him to accept Nicholas too, whom he knew to be devoted to Henry, would be much more difficult. Maybe that was the way, to persuade York that having one of Henry's most respected men on his side would be to his benefit.

Belinda smiled like a satisfied cat. She'd found the way to get Nicholas away from Amice. Once he was free, he would turn to her.

And they would marry.

Amice was picking listlessly at an uneven stitch at the tip of a falcon's wing when the page summoned her. Heart in her throat, mouth dry, she tossed the troublesome tapestry onto a velvet-cushioned bench and followed the boy.

The time is at hand.

Her temples throbbed as they traversed the corridors. She looked for Nicholas, in the futile hope he'd whisk her away or at the very least offer support. But he was nowhere to be seen, nor was he in the long, narrow Painted Chamber where Henry and Margaret awaited on their thrones.

After a respectful curtsy, she took a deep breath. The weeks of delay and fear of the unknown made the suspense all the worse. She hid her trembling fingers in the folds of her dark blue gown.

Willing nervousness away, she glanced at the many amazing biblical paintings. Those depicted with such piety seemed to mock her. She felt cold and empty inside, as if she'd been abandoned at the bottom of a dry well. Empty and alone.

She concentrated on the others in the room. A few miscellaneous advisors, and someone partially hidden in the shadows of heavy curtains.

Henry spoke, drawing her attention from the shadowed man. "Lady Winfield, your betrothed is at hand. I present Lord William Talbot."

The man stepped out of the shadows and bowed. Amice studied him unabashedly, as he studied her. She saw a tall, thin man, somewhat older, with thick brown hair interspersed with gray, dressed in a diamond-patterned knee-length velvet doublet belted at his waist. He smiled slightly as he bowed. Altogether an attractive man. *But he's not Nicholas.*

What could she do? The king himself bade her to wed. How could she put her selfish desires against the wants of her king? She should be honored she had value enough to be given to the son of the great commander who for decades served England so selflessly.

There was no way to refuse.

The king continued, "Your marriage will reward the efforts of one of my most stalwart commanders, his father, John Talbot, Earl of Shrewsbury. Unfortunately, he must soon leave to join his father and brother to continue our campaign in France. The wedding needs wait until Lord Shrewsbury returns."

She hoped her relief didn't show on her face though it rushed from head to toe. Had her reprieve been granted? If they didn't have to wed until Shrewsbury's return...with the sad state of the war, who knew how long that would be. Or what events might intervene. She held back a grateful sigh.

Amice awaited dismissal from the royal pair. Henry wore his customary black, his round-toed shoes disdaining fashion. His only jewelry was his necklace of "SS" links and a ruby cross. The somber costume made Margaret seem all the brighter, with her heart-shaped gold wire headdress and heavy necklace of square gold links studded with jewels.

"We shall have the betrothal tomorrow," Margaret said.

Air whooshed out of Amice. Her heart sank.

Whispers fluttered through the room.

Amice froze, stiff as if she'd been standing outside in December. She was doomed. A betrothal was almost as binding as a marriage. Tomorrow she would belong to this man she'd just met, but hadn't even spoken to.

How awkward to stand staring at one's all-too-soon-to-be betrothed in the presence of a crowd including the king and queen.

Her tongue seemed stuck, so she was grateful when Lord William broke the silence. "My liege, how can I thank you for the gift of such a beauteous bride? With your permission, we take your leave to walk in the gardens, that we might become acquainted before I depart for France."

His voice was pleasant enough, but not as rich or deep as Nicholas's. She shook her head. How would she stop comparing the two?

The king nodded his approval. Amice barely heard the hushed congratulations as they walked from the chamber, side by side. They continued through the halls in silence, as if by unspoken agreement waiting to talk until they were alone. Outside, she barely appreciated the sunshine and pleasant breeze. He led her to a small carved bench nestled beneath a large oak tree.

What did one say to one's just-met, soon-to-be groom, days before his departure for war? She knew nothing about him but his name and his father's reputation. She could offer no words of caring or love.

A jeweled brooch winked from the brim of his hat. "I wanted to marry before I leave, in case...." He stopped. "I wanted you to be my wife, in case I fail to return. But the queen wouldn't have such a rushed event. If I had the time, I would talk of your beauty, praise your hair, for isn't that what women want to hear?

"Instead, I must bid you farewell to make ready for war. I didn't know I'd be sent away so soon, or I'd have come to court earlier. But problems on my estates needed resolving."

He smiled and took her hands. His were cool, his fingers short and thick, not long like.... "Have you no favor for your departing knight? No sweet kisses for your lord?" he asked with such tender gentleness that she smiled too.

She liked the way the corners of his eyes crinkled, noticed the rich brown of his eyes. But she preferred blue.

"Had I known, I'd have worn some pretty ribbons or gloves, but all I can give you now is this." She pulled the necklace she always wore over her head. The slender chain sparkled. "It was my mother's. This is a portrait of her. The border is pearls and amethysts. My favorite stone," she added.

Her fingers itched to snatch the necklace back. She grabbed her skirts instead. What had she done? She'd offered her most precious possession to this man she barely knew. The man soon to be her betrothed. Had she loved him, the gift would have been her only means of sending part of herself. Parting with her only connection to her mother now seemed foolish.

She could tell by the way William carefully accepted the gift, the way his fingers lingered over the back of the pendant, that he knew its value.

He looked at Amice. "Your face will follow me to battle. I look forward to being your husband. But I cannot accept your most generous favor. Perhaps a scarf or veil? I can send my squire to fetch one, if you like," William said.

His kind offer touched her. The time to take the necklace back had passed. "No, I want you to have this. It would please me to know it can bring comfort to someone else." She pressed it into his palm. "Please. The necklace has brought me peace in difficult times."

He nodded, understanding. "I'll wear it always." The chain just fit over his head, amethysts catching the light. "There. Until I return. For you and for the sons we shall have."

Tears gathered. Henry had found her a good man. Was he with her now only to be taken away by this endless war? She could be a friend to him, at least. She raised her face, and he offered a gentle kiss. A kiss of peace. Not a kiss of love or desire.

"I must go, but will see you on the morrow. While I'm away, I'll write when I can and tell you of France and of my dreams."

"I will write as well." She couldn't promise to tell of her dreams. At the moment she wasn't sure what they were, but she knew they didn't involve him. And that made her feel guilty.

They stood and returned to the castle as silently as they had left it.

The next morning, Ginelle hovered like a delighted butterfly, oohing and aahing as she helped Amice dress. Amice's heart and soul ached as she prepared for a ceremony she wished to share with Nicholas, not a near stranger.

The plighting of her troth, exchanging words of future consent such as "I will take you to be my husband" and signing contracts with a priest's approval meant nothing, yet bound her like mortar to brick. The king's and queen's presence, an honor granted to few, felt more like jailors ensuring that their prisoner obeyed.

Amice wished she'd been brave enough to ask Nicholas if he'd agree to a clandestine marriage, in which they'd simply exchange their consent to wed each other. No priest was needed, no witnesses either, for the commitment to be valid. But she didn't want a marriage the Church believed was a sin. If she had to be married, she wanted a real marriage, and with the right husband.

Her heart was heavy as a millstone. Here she stood in all her finery, signing binding papers with William and all she could think of was Nicholas. He stood at attention near the back of the church, staring straight ahead.

During the next few days, Amice felt obligated to spend as much time with William as he could spare. They walked in the gardens and sat together at meals, appearing to the court as if they were getting along rather well. If she'd never met Nicholas, she might have found some contentment with this man. Unfortunately, she knew she'd constantly compare the two. Nicholas would always prevail.

She often sensed his gaze on her but willed herself not to glance away from William, even for a second. Though she hungered to have any connection with Nicholas, she had to appear the devoted betrothed both for William and herself. He was a soldier on the eve of battle. No matter what she felt, she'd do her best to make his last moments with her pleasant ones.

She tried to care for William. But there was nothing in her heart for her betrothed beyond friendship. Nothing close to deep caring or love. Maybe they didn't have enough time. Maybe it wasn't possible to force feelings. He was an interesting companion, a pleasant person, but that was all. She didn't yearn to be with him, didn't crave his closeness, or think of him constantly. The touch of his hand didn't make her insides melt or spark the faintest hint of desire.

Amice refused to admit there'd never be more with William, refused to acknowledge Nicholas's presence filling her heart. She'd simply await William's return and try harder to love him. Try harder to forget Nicholas. It was her duty.

If she failed, her life would be miserable.

❧ ❧

A week later, in his chamber, Nicholas couldn't sleep. He

couldn't contain his frustration. He'd known Amice was the only woman for him since their kiss in the garden. Maybe before, but hadn't wanted to accept it.

He'd not want another. Ever.

Such words didn't come easily to him, even in his thoughts. So how could he say them aloud? He wanted to tell her that seeing her everywhere but not being able to spend time alone with her made him long for the closeness they'd shared at Castle Rising. He wanted her to know, yet he didn't. Indecisiveness made him uncomfortable.

To Nicholas, Amice seemed happy...unless she was putting on an act to please Henry and Margaret. She gazed into William's eyes, too often, he thought, and laughed too frequently. Had his friendship with Amice meant more to him than to her? No matter, now. She and William were betrothed. He was nothing but an erstwhile admirer who lacked the courage to express his feelings. As it should be, he had to admit.

The betrothal had nigh ripped his heart out. He hadn't wanted to watch them together but couldn't seem to stop himself, even going out of his way to find them and see what they were doing. He couldn't bear the sight of their heads bent close. Worse was seeing William hold her hand. And the two of them together at meals made his stomach turn.

At least the almoner would be pleased, having more tasty scraps of capon with its sauce of blanched almonds and ginger or pieces of meat pie to offer the poor.

Amice was lost to him.

❦ ❧

The morning William was to leave, several ladies cornered Amice after an early mass. Two Elizabeths, Lady Grey and Lady Roos, were the first to descend upon her. Their incessant chatter gave Amice a headache at the best of times, but today their words fell hard as a sledge hammer on a swage.

Lady Roos pulled at the chin strap supporting her tall headdress. "Tell us about your wedding gown, Amice. Will it be trimmed in fur or beads? How long will—"

"—your veil be?" Lady Grey continued without pause. "Have you chosen velvet for the gown, or brocade?"

The ladies seemed genuinely interested. Even in her tense mood, Amice didn't want to snap that she hadn't even begun to consider what she'd wear to a wedding she didn't want or know when would occur. So she smiled her now customary false smile. She'd fit in while at court, no matter what.

"Lady Roos, perhaps you'll help me choose by telling me what you wore at your wedding?"

Obviously flattered, Lady Roos launched into a tediously detailed explanation of her attire from bodice to hem, interspersed with lengthy observations from Lady Grey. This allowed Amice to nod politely at appropriate intervals while turning her thoughts elsewhere. She lost track somewhere between the description of the rings Lady Roos wore on her first and second fingers.

They followed her outside, still talking, as she went to bid Lord William farewell. The morning air was stagnant, the sky cloudless. She'd never seen so many people gathered in one place. All about her squires and commanders shouted orders as they took their places in the procession. Horses whinnied. The din made her head pound harder yet. If only she'd had time to seek out some wood betony or boil some heather.

Thankfully William had told her where his men would gather. As she handed him one of her scarves as a favor to decorate his armor, another knight caught her eye, one with broader shoulders and longer, darker hair. Just a few feet away sat Nicholas, atop a brown horse instead of Merlin. Her hand faltered. The blue and red scarf floated to the ground, delicate silver embroidery glistening in the sun.

She bent to retrieve it, sudden dizziness fogging her head. She braced herself against William's horse, seeking reassurance in the familiar animal scent, the firm flank. Nicholas, going to France? Why hadn't it occurred to her he'd be going, also? Why didn't he tell her?

William reached for the scarf as she handed it up, looking down at her with a proud smile.

She was officially betrothed now. Nicholas wouldn't encourage her to be unfaithful or try to tempt her. Had he told her he was leaving, what would she have done? Did he know she'd have wanted to spend time with him instead of William? To be in his arms, arms forbidden a woman betrothed?

Now, Nicholas wouldn't even look her way. They were to part without even a shared glance. If he fell in battle, or if she went to live on William's estate, this might be the last time she saw him. How could he leave without creating a final memory?

Hearts didn't break, they were torn into pieces, like a condemned man being drawn, hanged and quartered.

"Farewell, my Amice," William said.

"Farewell, Ni…William. God go with you." Even as she spoke, Nicholas was on her mind. What sort of woman was she, to crave another with her betrothed beside her?

She waved as William mounted, then rode off with the others.

Nicholas guided his horse out of line and turned back.

He's looking at me! He couldn't leave without bidding me farewell.

Joy filled Amice, even at this moment of parting. How she wished she could offer him a favor. But her smile was only for him, and she knew he knew. She raised her hand to wave again, not to William but to Nicholas. If she'd known he was leaving…but she couldn't send him off with her kisses.

Amice cringed. There *was* someone who could bid Nicholas a public farewell. Belinda ran unashamedly after the departing knights, grabbed Nicholas's arm and offered him a glove in an effort to mark him as hers in front of everyone. He accepted her favor, but didn't kiss her, even as she tugged at his arm, Amice noted with satisfaction.

She let out her breath as the last of Henry's men faded from sight. The waiting would begin. Again.

She hadn't realized how much she'd counted on Nicholas just being there. Though their day-to-day contact was minimal, and the only real conversation they shared was in her daydreams, mere morsels were better than his absence, the nothingness of the present.

Far better than the fear that harm might befall him or William in battle.

CHAPTER 8

Harry awaited his daily repast of brown bread and cheese. It had taken two weeks to get his stern-faced guard to speak through the small, barred opening in the door. Another to learn his name, as bland as the man's appearance—John. Day after day he'd tried to convince John how time had shown him the error of his ways. To no avail.

There was another approach Harry itched to try. He'd only get one chance. Lying awake night after night, the squealing of rats setting his nerves on edge, he'd considered every possible outcome. The chance of failure was high.

Would today be the day he'd find the courage? It had to be, for he could take no more silence or endless hours of pacing that had worn out his leather boots.

John rapped on the door, the signal for Harry to stand against the far wall, hands behind his back. Humiliation burned his empty belly.

The key creaked in the lock. As soon as John began to open the door, Harry lunged. He flung the door wide and punched John in the gut as hard as he could.

"Oof." The guard bent over, dropping the bowl of food.

Harry ran.

❧ ☙

With so many men gone, the life of a queen's lady became more tedious.

Unmotivated, Amice wrote only occasionally. Reading took concentration and focus she couldn't muster. She spent most of her time waiting with the queen for word of the war. Her means of pleasure was long walks around the castle grounds. She'd discovered a gentle hill covered with soft grass and colorful meadow flowers that reminded her of Castle Rising. If she closed her eyes halfway, she could almost believe she was back at home.

One afternoon she sat near a rhododendron bush, trying to write. Her companion was a greyhound puppy, Galahad, a descendant of Nicholas's first dog, Lancelot. Nicholas had placed the pup in Robert's care. Robert had been thrilled by the responsibility, but had agreed that Amice could borrow him, just for the afternoon. Knowing the pup belonged to Nicholas made her feel closer to him, no matter how many miles away he was.

Staring morosely at the blank page, she inked her pen again.

A soft voice from the other side of the bush made her pause. Belinda. She peered through the leaves to see Belinda reading softly from a letter.

"Spread the rumor that Henry is ill. If we don't receive word of this rumor in two weeks' time, we'll know you have failed. If you're caught, you are on your own."

Amice's mouth dropped open. The lovely Belinda, a spy? For whom, and for what purpose and reward? Amice sat motionless, afraid of discovery. She didn't dare breathe until she was certain Belinda had moved on.

Galahad, sensing an intruder on their solitude, began to bark. Amice closed his tiny jaws between her hands. Too late. Belinda's head appeared over the flowering bush. Amice released Galahad and knocked over her ink, which spilled into the grass and on her skirts.

"What are you doing here?" Belinda's light blue eyes flashed with anger.

Amice was annoyed to have her special spot invaded, and annoyed to have overheard Belinda. She didn't want Belinda beholden to her, or to have the responsibility of deciding whether or not to keep her secret. More importantly, she still couldn't get beyond the fact the blonde beauty wanted to marry Nicholas.

Instead of behaving as though she'd heard nothing, Amice said, "So you add spying to your list of questionable activities."

Belinda's fair skin turned bright red. "You are a spy yourself, hiding behind bushes, not making a sound."

"I was here first." She blotted some of the ink with her handkerchief. "You might as well tell me the whole story."

Belinda rounded the bush, clutching her skirts. "I owe you nothing," she hissed.

"Would you prefer I tell Margaret what I've heard?"

"You have no proof. She wouldn't believe you," Belinda retorted.

"She has no reason to doubt me. And as the letter you hold implies, the power of rumor must be great."

Belinda opened her perfect mouth as if to speak, then shut it. "If I tell you, what will you do?"

"I don't know. But I'll go to Margaret straightaway if you don't." Perhaps she was starting to fit in at court after all.

Belinda paused, as if weighing her options. Glancing right and left, she joined Amice on her blanket. She tucked her skirts closer to her legs, avoiding the ink stains.

"All right. I'm helping the Duke of York."

Amice couldn't hide her surprise. How did one such as Belinda convince a noble such as the duke that she could be trusted? "And how did that come about?"

"I don't need to tell you every detail."

Amice liked the feeling of power being in the right place at the right time yielded. "I asked for, and will receive, the whole story, or off I go." She rose to her knees, a trail of ink dripping down the side of her gown.

"Oh, very well. One day I happened upon his brother-in-law, the Earl of Salisbury. We had a conversation about the duke's situation and the rightness of his cause. What could I do but offer my services?"

Amice frowned, doubtful Belinda would even consider a discussion about any matter more serious than the design of a new headdress or who might be dallying with whom, but she remained silent. She wrapped and unwrapped a curl around her finger.

"I don't believe you."

Belinda pouted prettily.

Amice could see that trick working on men, but it didn't

move her. She set her jaw and crossed her arms. "I have nowhere else to be, nothing important to do today."

Or any day, for that matter.

"All right. I've heard rumors of York's increasing strength. Should he gain control of the throne, I want to join his court. Are you satisfied?"

Amice nodded. "That I believe. What is the duke having you do?"

"You heard me read the letter." Belinda tucked an errant strand of blond hair under the wire mesh of her headdress.

"I did. But how will you spread such news so it's not traced back to you?"

"I haven't gotten that far," Belinda admitted. "Stop that!"

Galahad was worrying the hem of her gown between his teeth. Belinda pulled the offending hound to the side and pushed him toward Amice. "Here, control your animal," she bit out, as if glad of an excuse to change the subject.

"He's not mine. He belongs to Nicholas."

Belinda pursed her lips, then frowned. "What is that to me? Now you must keep your part of the bargain and remain silent."

Amice smiled again. "I never promised not to tell." Belinda opened her mouth to retort but Amice held up her hand. "What if I said I wanted to join you?"

"Why?"

Galahad turned in circles, oblivious to the ink and to his companions' intense conversation. After completing his series of inked paw prints, he rested his head in Amice's lap. He put his nose between his tiny paws and closed his eyes.

Amice petted the sleepy pup as she prepared her answer. What should she say...she wanted to feel important, wanted to be needed? That she missed her home and Nicholas so much she'd do almost anything to add excitement and responsibility to her life? Telling Belinda her reasons would shift the power balance between them, but she'd come this far....

She looked at Belinda, whose eyes narrowed with suspicion.

"I've always believed in York's cause, but didn't see a way to offer aid until now. It would also increase his trust in you if you were able to bring him more loyal assistants."

"I'll consider informing His Grace of your interest. What can you offer him?"

Amice knew better than to say, "Whatever you can," guessing Belinda's involvement might at some point include more than she, Amice, was willing to give. "I can write, quickly and with a clear hand. Perhaps he needs documents copied."

"That idea I like," Belinda said. "I'll think on it and report back to you."

Why did Belinda walk away with such a satisfied smile?

CHAPTER 9

France, Near Castillon – July 1453

nstead of missing Amice as he traveled through France, Nicholas forced himself to concentrate on the matters at hand. Such as how to succeed at their task: relieving the beleaguered English forces under siege at Castillon.

The journey of John Talbot, Earl of Shrewsbury's six-thousand-man army had progressed smoothly. It was rumored their opponent, Jean Bureau, led anywhere from seven to ten thousand Frenchmen. Were Nicholas in charge, he wouldn't attack without proof and a clear understanding of their opponents' weaknesses.

Nicholas wanted to learn about the man Amice was to marry. He was predisposed to dislike William and found nothing to change his impression. The man's tedious descriptions of previous successes didn't help.

As the time to fight drew near, tension increased. Nicholas could feel it in the humid air, see it in the tightness of the men's faces. Early in the morning, Talbot took five hundred men at arms and eight hundred mounted archers, including Nicholas and Lord William, to lead the attack.

"I hear Bureau has more cannon and bombards than anyone in all of Europe," one of the men offered.

"I hear he's got the balls to go with them!" another added, rewarded by the raucous laughter of nervous knights.

Nicholas ignored the banter. He had a bad feeling, and feared his prayers for victory would go unheeded. The English weren't equipped to fight an artillery battle. But they had their orders.

Focusing on the road, he rolled his shoulders to ease his aching muscles. Annoying rivulets of sweat trickled down his back. Though it was barely daybreak, the air was hot, thick and damp. Dense forest hindered any breezes that might have broken through the heat.

Ahead was a small priory, which a scout reported was filled with French soldiers. Taking the priory was no challenge. The taste of victory increased the knights' confidence along with their lust for French blood.

One of the injured French cried, "You cannot win. We have cannon, so very many! You English dogs will perish. We built a wall of guns...." The man died.

Had he spoken true? Sir Thomas Evringham, their standard bearer, was sent to investigate. Talbot, clearly invigorated by their early success, encouraged the men to drink wine while they waited for the rest of the men to catch up. But it seemed to Nicholas as if the man's words had dampened some soldiers' spirits.

A dust-covered messenger interrupted their respite.

"The French are retreating," he gasped. When all stared at him in surprise, he repeated, "The French are retreating! They're leaving!"

Sir John beckoned the man over. "Who are you? Are you sure of this?"

"I escaped from Castillon. Many horses were fleeing the French camp...."

Talbot turned toward his men. "We ride," he shouted.

Nicholas didn't recognize the messenger. He prayed their commander was right to trust him.

Distant cannon thunder heralded their approach, surging into ear-numbing explosions as they rode closer. Nicholas and the rest halted abruptly as Castillon came into view. He'd never seen as much artillery in one place. The dying man had told the truth. Mounted on a wall of earth were more culverins than he could count. Plus heavy bombards and newer, lighter cannon that loaded from the back, not the muzzle.

So many shots fired that the noise never abated. The roar was deafening. A huge cloud of dust grew in the distance...the retreating French?

Should the English retreat? Were they mad to attack?

As they splashed across the Lidoire River, wet clothes and armor slowing their progress, a shout rose above the din. "How are we supposed to beat them?"

Then another, "We're coming from behind. With a sneak approach they'll not get those guns on us!"

Talbot yelled, "Where in hell is that messenger? Did he see those horses or did he lie? The French are still here!"

He ordered them to dismount and fight on foot, following the tradition of only using horses to carry soldiers to the battlefield. Talbot alone would remain mounted. At his age, fighting on foot clad in armor wasn't feasible, and he could better command his troops from on high. He gave the signal to move forward.

Nicholas tensed, then shouted along with the others, "Talbot! St. George!"

The archers made the sign of the cross on the earth and kissed it before taking up their positions. English longbows picked off a few of the French. But hearts plummeted when Sir Thomas Evringham was the first to fall. A bad omen. Someone grabbed the standard before it was trampled, and the battle was joined.

The lighter guns shifted position with surprising speed and fired into their ranks. As if that wasn't enough, from the south across the Lidoire came hundreds of fresh French soldiers. The battle turned into a complete rout. Those the guns didn't kill, the Frenchmen did.

"No retreat!" Talbot cried, in an effort to recall men running toward the Dordogne River. Too late. Too many were fleeing.

Pungent smoke filled the air, thick clouds swooshing by as Nicholas fought to breathe and see. Everything seemed to be moving slower than normal.

The smell of death.

Cannon shot slammed into Talbot. His horse collapsed, trapping him underneath. As Nicholas fought his way to his fallen commander, a French soldier hacked at Talbot with an ax. An arrow pierced Talbot's son in the neck.

Blood splattered Nicholas. Suddenly his left leg stung.

Struggling to stand but failing, he sank to the trampled ground. With growing horror, he examined his thigh. A piece of cannon shot must've gone through his leg. Blood seeped from both sides.

A hand appeared through the haze. Lord William. Nicholas struggled to rise, biting back a scream of pain as William hauled him to his feet.

"I can't tell how bad it is," Nicholas shouted. "Leave me. I don't think I can walk…. I'll crawl, stay close to the ground. Get away now!"

William looked to the safety of retreat, toward the fray, then at Nicholas. Even through his pain, Nicholas knew the war raged in the man's conscience. Would William have tried to help him if he knew what he'd been to Amice? What he wished he could be? As always, his thoughts were of her.

"For God's sake. Go, man, go!" Nicholas encouraged, dropping to his hands and knees.

"No. We go together."

William put his arm around Nicholas, helping to support his weight. They ducked instinctively as a whining ball burst behind them. After a few seconds, they rose and pressed on.

Pain seared him with each step. He couldn't keep up.

"Let me go!" Nicholas yelled, his words lost in another cannon blast. "Save yourself!"

They'd only managed to cover a few feet when William shoved Nicholas down, sending shafts of fire radiating through his leg as he landed with a grunt. The earth behind them exploded, showering them with stinging bits of rock and soil. He caught his breath.

"That was close." He strained to look at William, who lay partially on top of him. "Hurry, we've got to get out of here!"

He pushed William's arm, but there was no response. "My God, William, move!"

With a mighty shove that hurt his injured leg, he raised himself on his arms. William slid off of him. Nicholas inhaled dust and smoke. Coughing and spitting, he tried to remove the grit from his mouth as William tried to rise. His helmet was gone, his head covered in shiny blood.

William's mouth moved. He beckoned Nicholas closer.

Resting his weight on his good leg, Nicholas bent toward the wounded man.

"I'm the one who isn't going anywhere," William said. "You go. Tell everyone how it was and why some of us had to die. Don't let this go unremembered..." His voice trailed off. "For God, for England and for Henry." He coughed, blood spilling from his mouth. Nicholas could barely hear William's hushed tones over the fading sounds of fighting. "I was to be married...."

William was dead.

Nicholas dropped his head. Was he to blame? Anguish battered him, thicker than the smoke, hotter than the pain in his leg. He'd fought before, seen men die. Nothing equaled the horrors of this day. The absurdity of archers and knights trying to battle hundreds of guns, the waste of life, disgusted him.

Another blast hit nearby. He curled into a ball. As he unwound, something caught his eye. A sparkle amidst swirls of smoke. William wore a chain around his neck, almost hidden by sweaty dirt. He'd take it for Amice. As he tugged the chain free, he recognized the portrait of Amice's mother. His heart wrenched. Had she come to care for William so much in such a short time she'd parted with her favorite necklace?

His hands shook as he pulled the chain over his bare head, his helmet lost long ago. He could only think now of getting to safety.

Of staying alive.

☙ ❧

The remnants of Henry's forces huddled beneath a stand of trees in a vain effort to avoid a downpour. Nicholas rested against a tree. Cool rain ran down his neck and arms, leaving watery streaks in the soot, but couldn't soothe the fire in his leg.

There was no physician. He'd have to ask someone to help bind the wound, knew he should try to clean it, but for the moment another pain tormented him.

William had died saving his life. Though Nicholas encouraged William to escape, to abandon him, the fact remained that Amice's betrothed died trying to help him. How could he return to face her, when, because of him, her betrothed would not?

Why did so many good Englishmen have to die? Why had he been spared? "Nicholas. We can't stay here, the French may pursue us. Can you travel?" asked a soldier with dried blood on his face and armor.

"My leg, I need to bind it. Then I'll be able to ride."

One man positioned himself at Nicholas's head to hold his shoulders against the pain, another at his feet to keep him steady. A third pulled a relatively clean piece of cloth tight around the wound.

With that, more agony than Nicholas thought possible coursed through him, and he felt no more.

He awoke in a barn, lying on his back in a pile of fresh-smelling straw. Moonlight shone through broken slats in the roof. A bottle of wine and some hard bread lay beside him. His leg throbbed and his rambling thoughts continued their torturous paths.

He'd survived the battle, but his troubles were nowhere near over.

❧ ☙

A week after the soldiers departed, Amice answered a knock at her door. Sitting and waiting for news with the queen so aggravated her she'd asked for an evening alone. Had she already been recalled to service?

Belinda swept in, closing the door. "The duke has agreed," she said without preamble. "You shall copy documents. I'll serve as courier. Here's your first assignment." She set several rolled parchments on Amice's table. "He wants three copies, which I'm to pick up tomorrow."

Amice unrolled several blank sheets of parchment and a long, unsigned letter. She'd have to work through the night to make three copies. "By tomorrow?"

"Time is of the essence." Belinda tapped her foot. "I thought you wanted to help. Will you do it or not?"

Guilt whisked through Amice. Working for York while living in Henry's castle? But York was the rightful king and would be a better leader. Time would pass faster. And her life would have purpose again.

"I'll do it."

"Good. If York is satisfied, I'll bring more work. And payment."

When Belinda had gone, Amice opened her ink, picked up her pen and set to work.

Clarendon – August 1453

The king and select members of his household retreated to the forest manor of Clarendon, ostensibly for him and Margaret, with her advancing pregnancy, to escape the heat and propensity for disease in London in the summer. Amice was glad for the sojourn to the royal hunting lodge near Salisbury and change of scenery.

She wasn't as glad that York continued to send documents for her to copy. Yes, she wanted to help his cause. Yes, she was glad to have something of import to do. But working in secrecy against the king and queen, having to trust Belinda, combined with her worries for Nicholas and William made for restless nights. If she were caught, she'd likely be tossed in the Tower, or worse, burned at the stake.

"They come, they come!" An out-of-breath guard raced into the hall.

Finally. A messenger from France. The few reports so far hadn't been good. As Amice and the courtiers hurried outside, she knew something had gone very wrong.

The women's veils fluttered in the hot drafts, their finery contrasting with the mud-covered, dejected men on horseback or being carried on litters. No one spoke. No cheers, no words of welcome, just desperate silence as they waited to hear the tale.

Amice's breath came in spurts. Most of the soldiers probably had returned to their homes. But where would those close to the king go? She bobbed from side to side searching for the face she'd dreamed of each night and thought of each day. Where was he? Where was Nicholas?

She checked herself. Where was William?

A soldier broke away from the small cadre of troops, dismounted and knelt in front of the king and queen. His armor was dented and covered with smeared, brown stains Amice didn't want to identify. He took off his helmet, revealing brown hair plastered with sweat.

"My liege…." His voice broke. "I know not how to tell you. We have lost. We have lost all. They had hundreds of cannon, there was so much blood. Four thousand Englishmen perished. My lord Talbot and his sons among them."

Amice gasped along with the rest. Some burst into tears.

Four thousand archers, soldiers and commanders dead. William, dead. Sorrow filled Amice at the death of a prominent man, a good man, at England's losses. But all she could think was, "What of Nicholas? Who will they find for me now?" Was she selfish to be more concerned about her future than mourning one already dead? A man she'd barely known.

"And how many of our enemies died?" the king asked.

The officer bowed his head.

"How many Frenchmen? Answer me!"

"Around one hundred, Your Grace."

More gasps.

Amice snapped to alertness. Where was Nicholas? She put her hand to her mouth, fearing the worst. Struggling to remain calm, she fought the urge to cry out his name and race toward the survivors. As long moments passed, Amice worked herself into a frenzy of fear.

Her will crumbled when she saw Nicholas's tousled, matted head appear as he raised himself to his elbows on a litter among a handful lined up on the grass. Oblivious to what anyone would think, she ran to him and dropped to her knees, tears falling onto the trampled ground. He must've been sorely wounded to allow himself to be carried home. Love, fear, uncertainty and more rushed through her, buffeting her like gusts of wind. What could she say?

Nicholas stared straight ahead, his eyes vacant. He looked right through her.

How badly was he injured?

"Nicholas? Nicholas?" No response. Fears renewed, barely able to draw breath, she scrambled to find assistance.

The king's physician, William Hatclyf, hurried by. His doublet was badly stained. Who knew with how many men's blood?

"We need help, please!" she cried. "Sir Nicholas is ill!"

"My lady, many need my aid. A few are bleeding, almost to death. I'll send someone for him as soon as I can." He glanced at Nicholas's sweat-covered face. "Hmmm. An infection of some kind, most like." He took a step closer and sniffed. "Possibly a putrified wound."

Amice couldn't smell anything but damp air and sweat. She tamped down a scream. Panic wouldn't help him, or her. "Is there anything I can do in the meantime?"

"See if you can get him to drink something. And pray, my lady. Pray for us all."

Pray? That was the doctor's advice? Amice had to try. But the words wouldn't come. Because she was so frightened, her head too full of dire thoughts to make room for hope?

She entwined her fingers and bent her head. "Dear God, please heal Nicholas. Make him well, so he can return to your service. And may William Talbot find peace by joining you in Heaven. Thank you."

She'd said the words, but didn't feel any better.

That evening a summer rain pounded the lodge, not cooling the air but increasing the dampness. Amice wiped her neck with a scarf. She'd waited outside until Nicholas was carried away. They'd refused to let her accompany him, but she vowed to send Robert to see how he fared. She'd give Robert something to take with him, so if Nicholas awoke he'd know she was thinking of him. He might not recognize her glove or scarf…it would have to be a note.

She flew to her desk, scribbling as fast as her pen would go on a scrap of parchment she'd used to practice a decorative border of ivy and flowers. She summoned her young page.

"Robert, you must find Nicholas and give him this. If he isn't awake, tuck it in his clothing so he'll find it. Then hurry back and describe all that you see."

"But it is late, my lady. Shouldn't you be abed?"

Amice was touched by his concern. "No matter how long it takes, tell me how he fares."

❧ ☙

Nicholas was still in Castillon. Cannon fired blast after blast, but he heard no noise. William yelled, bits of rock and earth flew past, but all was silent.

Sweat streamed down his back. The fires of hell surrounded him, searing his flesh. Why was the fighting still under way?

"Nicholas."

His name came whispered on the breeze, loud against eerie silence that should've been clamor. He squinted into the glare. Amice stood before him, wearing a flowing gown shimmering like gold in the blistering sun.

He panicked. What was she doing on the battlefield? How did she get here? If he couldn't save her, she'd be shot and killed. He couldn't lose her....

Amice floated over the bloodstained ground, lips curved in a serene smile. He ran to her, shouting for her to get down. No sound came from his mouth no matter how hard he tried to speak. She was mere feet away. Nicholas reached for her but grabbed air, not flesh. She melted into him, filling him with coolness and peace, then passed through and continued on her way.

Had he really seen her?

The force of the din's sudden return almost knocked him to the ground. All was as it had been. He knew he relived the battle but couldn't stop. He was there and he wasn't; he watched the events as a spectator, not a participant. But still the suffering, the grief, the fire, pierced deep into his very bones.

How could he free himself from this torment?

CHAPTER 10

The wait for Robert's return seemed endless. How could time pass so slowly? Finally Amice gave in to frustration and paced the chamber. She was ready to search for Nicholas herself, despite the late hour. Whoever cared for him would know she was supposed to be in mourning for her betrothed, and would be appalled that she sought entry to the bedside of another man so soon. Ah, the strictures of court.

Tension gripped so tightly that when Robert finally arrived she wanted to shake the information out of him. Tears ran down his sweet little face, the sight melting her anger fast as butter in Maia's hot pan. She knelt, gently holding his shoulders.

"Robert, what happened?"

"Oh, my lady, he is so very ill. He didn't wake up when I called to him, he's gripped by a terrible fever. Those physicians were sawing at someone, they didn't see me. There was so much blood, men were moaning and screaming. Please don't make me go back there!" He fell to his knees. "I want to be strong, but sometimes it's hard to be a man."

Heart full of sympathy for Nicholas and Robert, she enveloped her page in a hug. She would not cry.

❧ ☙

There was no other way around it. She'd have to go to

Nicholas herself. Who else was there to help him? Perhaps in the middle of the night her errand might go unnoticed.

Amice covered her head with her oldest shawl. "Robert, you'll stand watch to make sure we're not discovered. Can you do that?"

"Oh, I can't go back to that horrible place! I won't!" Hands on hips, he boldly met her gaze.

Robert's show of defiance didn't trouble Amice, though another mistress might have slapped the lad for his impudence.

"You don't have to go inside. Just whistle if you sense trouble."

"Very well." Robert practiced his whistle, a rather whispy wheeze.

"That will have to do. Come, we've lost too much time. It will soon be daylight. I can't wait another entire day to see how he fares or find out if I can help him get well."

Keeping close to the stone walls, the conspirators hurried to the infirmary. Robert poked his head in, confirming that the physicians were still engrossed in surgery. He pointed to Nicholas's bed, then crouched by the door.

Amice swallowed several times against a stomach that threatened to rebel, forcing herself to ignore the writhing men, wretched moans and pungent odors of blood and worse things. She breathed through her mouth as she crawled to the end of the row of cots, the wood floor cool beneath her palms.

A flailing arm hit her in the face. She bit back a scream of pain and continued on. At last, her cheek throbbing, she knelt by Nicholas.

His eyes were closed and he was frowning. She put her hand to his face, for the moment just glad to be with him, even if he was unaware of her presence. His skin was hot, too hot, and damp. He tossed and turned, revealing a leg swathed in a thick, brown-stained bandage.

Her heart sped and her grip tightened on the wineskin. How could she get him to drink? Would her tisane work?

She imagined that he calmed at her touch, as though he could sense her concern. As if he knew she was there and was glad.

Her breath stopped as he opened his eyes and shook his head.

He tried to sit up, but she pressed his shoulder back to the bed, afraid movement would draw attention.

"What?" he whispered, his voice scratchy. "Amice?"

He had regained his wits. Relief filled her, cool and fortifying. Amice yearned to tell him of her love, how miserable she'd been while he was away. How she'd feared for his life. This was not the place. He was safe, she was by his side. For now that was enough.

"Nicholas, you are at Clarendon. You're back with the king." *And me.*

⁂

"Amice," Nicholas breathed. "I saw you...." Was he still dreaming? He fought for the words through a thick haze.

"Shhh. You've been ill. Drink this if you can. They forbid me to see you, but I had to."

His mind cleared, sun shining through fog. Amice had come to him. She was so beautiful, her eyes so green. His heart filled with warmth he hadn't known he could feel again at her concern, the effort she'd gone to on his behalf. Until memories flooded him again.

Memories. The kind that ripped his soul to shreds.

Nicholas heard pounding cannon, saw clumps of earth shoot into the sky. Talbot went down. He fell, struggled to get up. William's rescue attempt and...William's death.

What could he tell Amice? She couldn't know how William had died. He hadn't told anyone the horrific details. Not spilled a word of how anguish tore at him like a vulture feeding on carrion for his part in it. The pain in his leg was nothing compared to that. If she knew, would she still be by his side?

"Nicholas, can you understand me? Are you all right?" Her whisper was filled with fear. Her nails dug into his arm.

"I will be well." He covered her hand with his. Her icy skin didn't relieve the heat of fever but sparked his worry. "Amice, you must go. You shouldn't be seen here or—" He didn't know what time of day it was, or what day, for that matter. "Go now. When I get out of here, we'll— Get under the bed, someone's coming!"

She dropped to the floor as he slid the wineskin beneath the coverlet. Sweat cooled on his brow in the wake of the physician's approach.

"You are awake at last." The physician wiped his hands on a piece of stained cloth. He lifted the coverlet and then unwound the bandage on Nicholas's thigh.

Nicholas clenched his jaw against stabbing pain. The occasional moan from other patients broke the silence.

"I've seen worse. How do you feel?" the physician asked.

"Ready to leave the infirmary."

"Not yet, with that leg of yours. You must keep it still a few more days, and we must watch your fever. Then we will see."

"I disagree. I wish to recover in my own quarters."

"Hmmph! I'll move on to another patient who might be more willing to follow my orders." He walked away.

Cautiously, Amice appeared from her hiding place under his cot. Her hat was askew. What was that red mark on her face?

"Who hit you?" he demanded.

"It's nothing. One of the injured flung out an arm by accident as I passed by." Her fingertips skimmed her cheek. He reached to take hold her hand, to reassure her all would be well, but thought better of it. "Get well quickly. Will you...will I see you when you're better?"

He wanted nothing more than a few moments in her company. To talk to her, see her smile. But the king would soon find her another groom. Why feed a slow-burning fire that could never burn bright?

Against his better judgment, he said, "Yes. I'll have Robert bring you a note."

"I'll look forward to it." She kissed her palm and laid it on his, then crawled away.

Nicholas steeled himself against the melting sensation that filled him at her light touch, just as he'd fought his concern for her a moment ago. If not for him, her betrothed would be alive.

How could he allow himself to care for her knowing that?

A week later, Nicholas had recovered enough to return to his quarters. Supported by a cane, his slow gait, bedeviling twinges with every step...he felt and knew he looked like an old man. But he was alive. So many were not.

He needed time alone to grieve. But though nothing could be the same as before Castillon, on the morrow he'd return to his duties. And he'd have to contact Amice. Memories of their time together had often soothed the harsh edges of his grief. Would talking with her make him feel better because he missed her or worse because of his unwillingness to share his role in William's death?

As if summoned by his thoughts, Robert arrived with a note. Amice was concerned because she hadn't heard from him. He wrote back that since the doctor had encouraged him to take walks, their paths could cross in the forest.

He couldn't wait to see her. Would he find the strength to tell her the truth?

Slivers of late afternoon sunlight filtered through the canopy of oak branches. Amice shivered, wishing she'd brought a shawl. The air so near the sea was cool even in August. But the scent of growing things, the crunch of leaves beneath her shoes revived her. She'd been cooped up too long. And it'd been far too long since she'd had a real conversation with Nicholas.

Her heart sped as she waited. How would he look? How would she feel?

Could they ever regain the closeness they'd shared at Castle Rising? Maybe that was too much to ask. To see him hale and whole, to spend even a few moments with him, would be enough. For certes it was more than she'd had for weeks.

Her spirit lifted. She couldn't hold back a smile as Nicholas came into view around a curve in the forest path. Sympathy tweaked her as he leaned heavily on a cane, but his dark hair, familiar handsome face and blue eyes sent joy soaring.

Amice ran to him, hopeful yet unsure of her welcome. She paused a few feet away.

He smiled and spread his arms. She hurried into his embrace, tears filling her eyes as she inhaled his pleasing scent and his strong arms held her against him.

At last. She was exactly where she wanted to be.

"Amice." He released her, then twined a finger in her curls. "It's so good to see you."

For a long moment, he stared at her. She stared back, noting every detail, familiar and new. She traced a small scar near his left ear. "I'm so glad you made it home."

He winced.

"Did I hurt you?"

"No." He took her hands. "No."

Yet she sensed she'd done something to dampen the pleasure of their reunion.

"Do you want to tell me about France?"

"Not just yet. Let me enjoy a few minutes of peace. Of the pleasure of seeing you."

Her heart warmed, but impatience nagged. "What happens now? Is there anything I can do? I don't want to wait for the king or queen to find me yet another groom."

"We're all at his command. At times I confess I begrudge the lack of control courtiers, knights and even lords have over their choices."

"But even kings can be swayed. Perhaps things have changed since Castillon. Perhaps if I offer coin once more, Henry will accept it. And then when I'm free, we can—" She couldn't go on. The words stuck in her throat, pricking like chicken bones.

How could she tell Nicholas what she wanted...a future with him? Difficult to say in any case, but when he didn't yet know about her work for York, and she didn't know if he felt as strongly for her, nearly impossible.

"We? Can what?" he prompted.

She burned to know if he wanted what she did, but fear of rejection burned brighter. "We can leave court. And return to Castle Rising."

He put a finger under her chin to tip her head up until their gazes locked. "We? Are you saying you want me to go with you?"

"Yes." The word was softer than a whisper, mingling with the breeze. "Yes, Nicholas. I want you to take me home." She wanted so much more, but couldn't ask. Not yet.

"I can ask for an audience with the king. We can speak with him. Together. Perhaps he'll permit me to escort you."

A long pause. She could see a struggle on his face. With what? "And then, I hope we can talk about what we want to do after that."

"I hope so, too."

We. He thought they were a team. Holding his hand, gaining strength from being with him, was wonderful. But not enough.

"Do you think we can have a future? Do you want one?" The questions were a risk, but after all that had passed she needed to know. Her heart pounded as she awaited his answer.

"What we want and what can be are often two different things. I don't know, Amice. Sometimes I think we can find a way, others...too many obstacles block our path."

"I'm tired of waiting, of being patient."

"As am I."

Even as he said words she wanted to hear, proving that she might have the chance to spend days or her future with him, her failure to be forthcoming combined with a hint of sorrow in his eyes chilled her to her fingertips. Was it because of something she hadn't said? Or something he hadn't told her?

If so, it would serve her right. For there was plenty she'd not told him. She'd handed off more letters for York to Belinda earlier that morning. How could they move ahead with their relationship until he knew it all?

❧ ❧

The forest meeting with Amice had frustrated Nicholas. Just like recent council meetings, which eroded his nerves faster than sand in a windstorm. Few of Henry's advisors seemed concerned with the good of the realm, but hungered for as much power as each could wrest.

Despite his loyalty to Henry and England, he'd hoped the catastrophic defeat would put an end to fighting with France. After a hundred years of war, after the great inroads Henry's father had made, Calais was the only bit that was left to England. Why didn't the king focus on the abundance of problems at home instead of draining his coffers to pursue a lost cause abroad?

Occasional twinges of discomfort in his leg served as nagging souvenirs of Castillon. How could he forget? Horrific sights, sounds and smells of battle, all centered around William's death, accompanied him each night and kept him from sleep.

The constant reminders incited him to avoid Amice. In the forest, they'd been so happy to see each other, to plan, he hadn't been able to bring himself to explain his role in William's death. He didn't want her to know of his guilt, to watch joy fade from her face as he told of his failure to save William. How could he face her again without doing so? Would he ever be ready to? He was cracking slowly, like pond ice in the spring. He'd allowed Amice into his heart, savored the elation of feeling so close to someone with whom he'd wanted to share his life.

Now he endured the agony of not deserving her. Because of William. And because he couldn't shake the belief that by offering coin for her freedom, she'd also be buying him. What man of honor allowed himself to be purchased like a trinket at a fair? But breaking his promise to arrange a meeting with the king made him feel worse than a coward.

He hardened his heart against her inquisitive looks. Once she'd walked up to him as they passed in a hallway. He'd forced himself to ignore her. Better that she hate him for abandoning her than because she knew the truth. Even if she could find it in her to forgive him, he didn't think he could forgive himself.

But there were fewer people at the smaller manor of Clarendon than at any of the king's castles. Avoiding her here was more difficult. So he had to find the strength, somehow, to tell her he hadn't yet spoken to the king. He owed her and himself that, at least.

A scream disturbed his musings. A page ran up to him. "My lord, my lord, you must come at once, at once!"

Nicholas was about to reprimand the page's imperiousness, but the boy's flushed face and bulging eyes stopped the rebuke. He jumped up from his chair, weight on his good leg. "What is it? Is it the queen, the babe?"

The page bent over and gasped for breath, resting his hands on his thighs. "No, no, no! To the king, the king!"

"Show me," Nicholas ordered.

As fast as the page's short legs and his injured one could carry them, they raced to the hall, where they were brought to an abrupt halt by the stillness of the tableau before them. No one moved a muscle, captured like a page torn from an illuminated manuscript.

Several advisors and attendants stood staring aghast at the king. Henry, dressed in his customary black, sat motionless on the throne. His eyes were glassy and unfocused. His head tilted slightly to the left, as if listening with mild interest to something no one else could hear. Even the outspoken Margaret was frozen, a beringed hand held to her chest.

All gaped at the king, as if focusing their energies on him would encourage him to move or speak.

"What happened?" Nicholas asked.

"One minute he was fine. The next, as he is now," explained the page.

He'd never seen anything like it. "Go find Hatclyf, the king's physician."

The boy ran off.

Several minutes later, after a brief look at the king, William Hatclyf proclaimed, "I've been called one of the most skilled in my field, but I can offer no immediate diagnosis."

Those waiting had gathered into small, whispering groups.

"Maybe he was poisoned," someone offered.

"Could it be the shock of losing all at Castillon?"

"Perhaps he has inherited the madness from his grandfather, Charles VI?" another suggested.

"No, no. Charles had frantic fits. This is different." Hatclyf said. "Though I have never seen symptoms such as these, I believe it's safe to move him to his chambers. Perhaps after purging him I'll know more."

Nicholas, Hatclyf and John Norris, an esquire of the household, carefully carried the king from the room.

Queen Margaret sank into a chair, hands over her bulging abdomen. Amice, worried that the shock of Henry's illness might induce early labor, hurried to her side.

"I'm fine, fine," Margaret breathed. "We needs wait. Maybe the king will recover soon...." She pushed herself to her feet and announced, "No one in this room is to discuss what they saw here."

Hours later, the physician and John Norris returned to the queen. Hatclyf reported, "King Henry cannot speak, does not appear to understand when spoken to, nor do his eyes or expression reflect awareness.

"Your Grace, I am most sorry to report that I can find no cause for King Henry's strange affliction." He wrung his hands. "I suggest we send for my colleagues, John Arundel and John Faceby. Perhaps they'll see something I do not, think of a treatment I have not."

"Agreed. I also propose that the king be moved, if it won't injure him further, to a larger holding, where he can rest more comfortably," said Norris.

The royal household moved back to Westminster as quickly and quietly as possible. Margaret made her wishes known to a small group of the king's advisors, including Nicholas.

"No one else is to know of his infirmity," she told the group, gathered around a large table. "No one. Not the people of England, and certainly not Parliament. Henry has no heir of his body. Should something happen to this child...." She didn't need to say more. Many babies failed to survive infancy. "If I have a son, he'll need a regent, like Henry when he became king at nine months old. And how should the regent be chosen amidst squabbling similar to that of a generation ago?"

No one could meet her gaze.

Long days passed. Each member of the king's and queen's household moved about in silence, trying to look busy. Each prayed fervently that the king would recover and life could continue as normal. Few words were spoken, and those that were came as hushed whispers filled with uncertainty. Henry's councilors met for hours on end, trying to come up with a feasible solution to a land without a king.

"Henry's condition hasn't changed. We can't go on behaving as though he'll miraculously recover," said Norris.

"The Lancastrian position was precarious enough before he took ill," a lord interrupted. "Our enemies can't learn Henry is incapacitated."

"We must decide who shall rule. And should Henry die, who will succeed."

As murmurs buzzed about the room, Nicholas worried about his king, queen, and country. Yet part of him rejoiced. Surely no one would think about finding Amice another groom now.

CHAPTER 11

mice had never been so miserable. Like everyone else, she was concerned about Henry's condition, not only for Henry, Margaret and their unborn child, but because of what it meant politically and personally. How long would she be forced to linger at court, unable to plan? Cyril's reports that all was well at Castle Rising made her miss home all the more.

Margaret's pregnancy advanced along with concern that Henry would never recover. The more time that passed, the more she feared Margaret might yet select another groom for her. Every day was spent in turmoil, wondering if anything would happen, if York would find out about Henry's ailment and try to take advantage of his indisposition, if Margaret would decide to send her ladies home. If.

Belinda delivered letters and parchment from York, Amice dutifully returned accurate copies. The latest batch had been to highly-ranked supporters, wondering why Henry had been absent of late. Knowing the reason, yet unwilling to go so far as to contribute information, heightened the war in her head between right and wrong. Her fear of discovery never abated.

She rarely saw Nicholas, who was constantly closeted with the council. When she did, lines of strain etched into his face discouraged her from conversation, from troubling him further with her concerns. He couldn't be avoiding her, could he? His customary tan had faded, stress adding to his pallor, she was sure. Dark circles under his eyes attested to long hours of arguing with the council and getting nowhere.

She wanted to tell him she thought of him often, that she couldn't put him from her mind, remembering his few kisses still made her yearn for more. That every time she saw him a rush of desire filled her. Even if she could bring herself to say the words, personal matters paled in importance to the king's illness and political problems.

Finally, in early October, out of concern for Nicholas's health and to escape the close atmosphere of the queen's lying-in chamber, Amice wrapped herself in her wool cape and waited by the stables. She knew he rode or visited his horse each morning.

She had to talk with him.

❧ ☙

Someone tugged on his sleeve as he came around the corner of the stables after feeding Merlin a few apples.

"Nicholas. You have to get some rest. I've been watching you...."

Amice. He was so tired he could barely convince his mouth to smile. In the early morning light, with the hood of her cloak outlining her face and a few curls wafting in the breeze, she'd never looked lovelier. Such a welcome sight. Though it seemed a lifetime ago, he recalled the feel of her lips on his, her soft body against his. And wanted to feel both again.

As glad as he was to see Amice, he still wasn't ready to tell her the truth. The passage of time hadn't eased his guilt over his role in William's death, nor could he think of the right words to say.

He hadn't told anyone, even Martin, the details of his escape from the Battle of Castillon. Memories still pounced upon him in the dark and chased him into his dreams. Night after night, he felt the shot pierce his thigh, heard thunderous cannon blasts and shouting as he and William argued, saw William's lifeless brown eyes staring at the smoky sky before Nicholas closed them, his fingers leaving a trail of smeared blood on William's face.

"Watching me, are you?"

Was it the brisk breeze that tinged her cheeks pink?

"You look awful," she said. "Have you been sleeping, eating? What is it you do in session all day? What can anyone do?"

"We're trying to save our country by keeping it in the hands of its rightful rulers. Without our king's guidance, we face an even more difficult task. Nothing like this has ever happened. We keep hoping a solution will surface. Concealing Henry's condition from the world gets harder each day."

"And if you or the other advisors take sick, what then?" Amice shivered and drew her cloak tight.

Nicholas avoided her question and the desire to take her in his arms and keep her warm. "How are you?"

"Well as I can be, helping Margaret. The baby should come any day now. Waiting for the baby coupled with waiting to see if Henry's condition changes…. I want to go home, Nicholas. I don't belong here anymore. Until the king recovers or someone else has authority and wherewithal to arrange marriages, I'm just an extra mouth to feed."

"What's one more in the midst of so many? Henry has over nine hundred on his staff now, from the chamberlain to his growing team of doctors to attendants paid to sit with him day and night lest there be a change in his condition."

His shoulders tightened. He had to broach the painful subject of Castillon. If he didn't, his nights might be haunted for the rest of his life. By the battle, and by Amice. For no matter how he tried to put her from his thoughts, no matter how he tried to focus with the others on a solution, somehow she found her way back in. Time apart hadn't lessened his interest, though he'd hoped and prayed it would. Talking with her now, looking into her lovely green eyes, his need for her companionship bubbled to the surface from the depths of his soul.

"Amice, I've been keeping an eye on you as well, and meant to talk with you sooner. I've feared telling you of this, but I can't continue as we have been. Now we see how short life can be, how quickly things can change. I could have died at Castillon, as…so many thousands did." He took her hands, chilled by the autumn air. "Even in these times of trial, I can't forget our kisses. How I wished we could do more. I don't want you to wed another."

Amice's mouth fell open. "You've felt this way but waited all this time to say something?"

"Before my journey, before Henry fell ill, I was determined to do what was best for my king and the kingdom, no matter what I wanted for myself. But our defeat in France, the sudden onset and the persistence of Henry's ailment show me I can't keep waiting for my own desires to be met. Only God knows how much time we have." Already Nicholas sensed his burden was lighter. Sharing his feelings, telling the truth, took less effort than keeping it all inside. "Who knows if Henry will recover, and if he does, whether the Lancasters will remain in power. If York and his followers gain control of England, will any of us be allowed to go free? They could seize all we own or put us to death.

"Our situation was delicate before. With Henry's illness, it's become so fragile it's as if we'd tripped while carrying a basket of eggs. Our lives could crack apart." A curl had dangled free of her hood. He twined it around his finger and was rewarded with a slight smile. Even that simple connection to her was better than none. "What does it matter what two people do when all of England is in an uproar?"

He continued, as if now that he'd started to speak words would spill until their source was spent. "I never thought I'd feel this way, never. We must take hold of whatever happiness we can, not knowing what the future will bring or if either of us even have one. I want to be with you, to enjoy you while I am able, before events beyond our control separate us."

The need to hold her, to kiss her overwhelmed him. He'd been a fool to wait so long. He'd thought to protect her and himself, but instead had wasted precious, precious time.

"Yes. Oh, yes, that's what I want, also."

The delight on Amice's face added a stone to the weight in Nicholas's heart. He'd thought to spare her pain by staying apart, but had caused her more instead.

"There's something else. I must tell you the rest, or whatever happens between us will be tainted. You may change your mind when you hear."

"What could make me change my mind about being with you? I've wanted that since before we left Castle Rising."

He wanted to smooth away the lines on her brow but knew

his reply would only deepen them. "William died because of me."

Amice gasped. "You bring up William's death now, in the midst of telling me that I matter to you? That you want me. Are you saying you killed him?"

"No. Not exactly. But he died trying to rescue me."

"What happened? Why didn't you tell me sooner?" Amice gripped his arms so hard her nails dug into his skin. The wind blew off her hood and he replaced it. "Don't leave anything out."

His focus blurred, his inner vision returning as it so often did to that horrible day. "After my leg was hit, I couldn't move quickly on my own. William wanted to help me leave the field. I tried to dissuade him, told him to press on alone, but he insisted. I would've died had he not saved me. The next cannon blast hit him in the head. Instead of me. If he hadn't been there, if he hadn't stayed, I'd probably be dead and he might still be alive.

"I couldn't help but believe my feelings for you, my wish to be with you, somehow contributed to his death, that I didn't try hard enough to send him away."

Each word was as difficult to say as if it were a cart stuck in the mud and he the horse pulling it out. When he finished, she didn't recoil. She didn't burst into tears.

She hugged him, then took his hands. "How you must have suffered, to add this to your burdens."

"Don't you see? I couldn't bring myself to tell you. I thought you'd blame me as I blame myself for being responsible for his death. I tried to forget about you. Now, as everything crumbles around us, I see my only salvation is in the truth."

"How could you keep this secret for so long?" Amice asked. "I thought we meant more to each other. I thought I knew you. Obviously, I was mistaken. When we talked in the woods you let me think…. You preferred my not knowing to coping with my response."

"It's because I do care for you that I remained silent. How could I tell you that I, who wanted you for myself, who burned with jealousy seeing you merely talk to William, caused him to die?"

He reached inside his tunic and pulled out Amice's necklace.

Amice's hands shook as she accepted it. Her eyes filled with tears.

Would she hate him? Or would she forgive? His future depended on her response. But he felt free. He'd done the right thing. At last.

"How did you get this?" She traced each amethyst.

"As I was crawling away from William, I saw it on his neck. I've worn it ever since, afraid to give it back because I'd have to tell you how I obtained it." And wearing the necklace had made him feel closer to her even as he burned with guilt.

Anger sparked in her eyes. "You didn't trust me to believe you if you said his death wasn't at your hand? How could you think such horrid thoughts, be so smitten with honor that you stayed away from me? You don't know if you'd have been hit by that next cannon blast, not he.

"You worried all this time that I cared more for a man I barely knew, whom I didn't ask to wed, than I cared for you. You, who befriended and helped me? For this, which was none of your doing, you avoided me for weeks. When we could have comforted each other, been there for each other. When I'm not bound to any man. Who knows how much time we have before we're separated forever, before Queen Margaret finds me another betrothed?"

The flame of her righteous anger was so bright he thought she'd heat the cool air. Nicholas grasped her shoulders to draw her near, but she remained stiff. He willed his gaze to pierce her fury and any shred of practicality that remained. He wanted to be with her, she wanted to be with him. How could something so simple be so complicated?

At last Amice melted against him. His arms enfolded her, drawing her into his warmth, dispelling the early morning chill.

"Holding you feels so good. So right," he said. "Ah, Amice, I have missed you."

She looked up at him. Her lips parted. Under the eaves of the stables, he bent his head and kissed her. Their breath frosted in a white puff as their lips met, filling him with a yearning he hadn't known possible. Her mouth, her tongue against his, so warm, so right.

At length, they parted.

"Well. That was…worth waiting for." Her cheeks were pink

and her lips an enticing red. From the cold? Embarrassment? Or desire? "I'm sorry you suffered guilt for so long. As to the other, I agree. There's such distress here and strife elsewhere. I want to spend time with you, be with you. It's as simple as that. No matter how long we have. Surely doing so can't be wrong. Let's find a way to meet each day."

His hands slipped inside her cloak to encircle her waist, drawing her against him.She felt so soft, tasted so sweet, he wished he could make her his right now.

"We can't spend too much time together in public. People will talk, and I don't want word to reach the queen," she said. "If you come to my room…we won't be alone. But Ginelle sleeps soundly."

"I'll come to you tonight. No matter what demands may be made of me. Until then." After a swift kiss, and a lingering touch on her face, he released her and walked toward the castle.

Despite the uncertainties to come, his heart felt lighter. And warmer.

❧ ☙

Nicholas and Amice had been too caught up in each other to notice him lurking on the opposite side of the stables. Lovesick fools. The disgusting kiss—he wouldn't think on that.

Harry pulled his black hood further over his face just in case Amice turned, then waited until she had made her way back to the castle before following her inside.

Getting here had been more difficult and taken much longer than he'd planned. But at last he'd found her.

"Smile while you can, my dear," he muttered, closing the castle door.

CHAPTER 12

Partaking of evening meals at Westminster had become like living in a monastery where monks were sworn to silence. Had pious King Henry been aware, he'd have appreciated the hall's hushed atmosphere. But Amice knew fear of the unknown prompted the quiet, not reverent respect.

When someone dropped a knife, everyone jumped as though a cannonball had smashed through the wall. When someone entered, everyone looked up in uncertain anticipation as though a horrendous announcement was forthcoming.

Amice's nerves were on edge as she pondered her evening plans. What had she done, throwing herself at Nicholas and kissing him? She was no better than Belinda, whom Amice knew had worked her way through many men serving Henry.

Had he been able to see the love she'd felt for him almost since the day they met?

This morning, she'd been exactly where she wanted to be. In Nicholas's embrace.

His hot mouth had moved on hers, tasting, teasing, then melding for a deeper kiss as he clutched her close. This was what she had been waiting for. From the tips of her fingers to her toes, she loved him.

But their differences were still too great because of her work for York and his for Henry. They might not have a future, but they could have right now.

Some of the strain had left his face after their kiss, perhaps because she didn't blame him for William's death. Perhaps because he knew she still cared. He'd told his truth at last, and now she had to reveal hers. But how? How could she blame him for not coming forward when she, too, had thought to protect him, protect their brief time together, by remaining silent? Even if England plunged into civil war, Nicholas had finally told her he cared. Though she'd stood in the cold, she'd felt warm and safe for the first time in a long while.

Yet while part of her heart rejoiced, part feared his reaction when she told the truth. And another part wept for the downfall of her country as she knew it.

What they were going to do was a sin. The Church proscribed lovemaking outside the bonds of marriage. Why was it more acceptable to make love to someone just because you agreed to marry him but felt nothing, yet wrong when you truly cared for a man, though no words had been spoken by a priest?

The answer had been drummed into her all her life. Because any fornication not for the purpose of creating children was wrong.

She knew the tingling in her body, the yearning in her blood should embarrass her, but it didn't. Wanting Nicholas was as natural to her as breathing.

Yet she couldn't meet his gaze during this meal, though she knew he often looked at her from his seat several tables away. Would he change his mind about meeting with her?

Could he read the struggle in her eyes? Did he fear she had second thoughts? She took a deep breath, concentrating on the rather bland fare on her plate.

Finally, without even a glance in Nicholas's direction, Amice excused herself. She knew Nicholas would return to his quarters to keep gossiping tongues from wondering why he headed off with her. Neither wanted their names bandied about.

The moon was high when Amice heard the soft knock at her door. Anticipation coursed through her as she opened it.

Nicholas walked in. Firelight brought out the red in his dark hair. His welcoming smile sent a thrill up her spine. Any lingering doubt melted.

Would he hold her? Kiss her?

"I'm so glad we have this time." He took her hand, running

his thumb over the backs of her fingers. A shiver more delicious than the food ran up her arm.

"As am I. I've missed our friendship. I've missed you." Challenge enough to confess that. How would she tell him more?

"I've missed you, too. I wish we were at Castle Rising."

She wished the same with all her might.

They sat in contented silence, as if they'd agreed traveling down this rocky path couldn't yet lead to a discussion of the future, their future, as if there could be one. There'd be too many questions with too few answers. For once, instead of worrying about what would be, they'd enjoy each other.

Amice mentioned the latest book she'd read. Nicholas replied, and put his arm around her. She leaned back, fitting perfectly against him. How wonderful to enjoy such closeness, share simple moments. But she wanted to be even closer to him.

The curtains on the high bed were open. She stood, facing him, motionless, her eyes wide. Boldly she started to untie the sash on her robe.

❧ ❧

Nicholas sucked in a breath. Holding her close had been appetizing torture. But this…he needed to touch her.

He moved to her, then touched her face, using only the light pressure of his fingers on her cheek to draw her closer. He bent nearer. Her head fell back, her lips slightly parted, waiting. How beautiful she was, how sensuous. After a few seconds passed, she opened her eyes in surprise. He bent still nearer, until his lips were a scant inch from hers, delaying the moment, knowing there could be no going back.

How he desired her. His erection pushed against his hose. But he had to find restraint, so he could enjoy every moment that was to come.

At last he kissed her, pressing her soft body against his muscled one, his arms pulling her tight against him. She put her arms around his neck, twining her fingers in his hair.

His tongue delved into her mouth. Her eager response sent need surging. She untied her robe, offering him access to what lay beneath, glowing underneath his heated gaze. She pushed the robe off her shoulders.

Nicholas drew in his breath as she revealed herself, admiring her white skin, the curve of her hip, the fullness of her breasts, the proud look in her eyes. He had to hold her, had to feel her flesh against his. He tugged off his tunic.

His anticipation was so great, his need for her so tangible, how could he wait another minute to have her?

"I want to do that," Amice breathed. Sliding her hands under his shirt, she smoothed her palms against the heat of his chest, exploring the contours of his muscles and following the path of his hair from his chest to….

He stilled her hand, desiring her touch but knowing in his present state it might be his undoing. After helping her remove his shirt, he tossed it to the floor. She put her nose to his chest, inhaling deeply, then kissed him, pressing her body to his.

She sat on the bed, at just the right level for him to explore the wonders of her breasts.

"Ah, yes," he breathed.

He lowered his head and relished her gasp as his mouth found her nipple. Her hands grasped his hair, drawing him closer. As he proceeded to lavish kisses on her other side, a loud growling noise rumbled in his ears.

"What was that?"

❦ ❧

Embarrassment flooded her. Amice tried to hide it with a nervous giggle. "My stomach. I hardly ate anything at dinner, so I had this tray sent. I thought I could eat, but…."

He smiled, a cunning look in his eye. "We'll eat something now, then."

"Now?" she cried, fearing the mood broken, fearing he wouldn't continue to make love to her.

When he kissed her breasts, the power of his desire poured into her. She'd never felt anything but mild distaste with Edwin. Now she knew she was on the verge of experiencing the heights of passion. She'd hoped so long for this moment only to eat cheese?

He smiled, reaching for the large platter of bread, cheese and fruit on the table beside a jug of wine and two cups.

"What have you been doing while we've been apart?" Nicholas asked as he tore off a piece of fresh white bread.

Amice started, her haze of desire fading. She felt exposed, and had a sudden urge to cover herself.

"Waiting with Margaret." Copying documents for the king's rival. Furthering York's cause, easing his way to power, she thought as he cut a slice of cheese.

She couldn't tell him that. Guilt sopped up her appetite. Though it had taken a while, he'd been honest to a fault with her, yet she concealed her involvement with York.

She swallowed. She'd tell him, soon. Selfish, perhaps, but she wanted a few hours with him. Nothing, nothing, would come between them this night. Not her omissions, not concern for the king.

This night was for her and Nicholas to share.

Gently, he pushed her back on the bed. Tearing off a small piece of bread and one of cheese, he placed the remainder of the food on her stomach.

"Open your mouth."

Gazing at him, she complied. He placed the morsel of bread and cheese on her tongue. She chewed, licking her lips, not the least bit shy in front of the man she loved. There was no denying it, she loved Nicholas and would give him and take from him as much happiness she could. She swallowed, then smiled. A sensuous smile, she hoped. A smile of love.

❦ ❧

Nicholas enjoyed this test of his will. Clearly Amice was aware of how the sweep of her tongue affected him. He'd see how long he could hold out.

He took another piece of cheese and fed it to her. She closed her lips around his finger and proceeded to lick off the remnants. The rhythmic, sucking motion of her warm, wet mouth augmented his already intense desire.

"Now I'm thirsty." Smiling, she sat up and reached for the

jug of wine, pouring some into a cup. Her curls slid seductively over her shoulder as she handed it to him.

Taking a sip, he bent toward her, letting the liquid trickle into her mouth. When it was gone, his lips replaced the wine and they shared a deep kiss. He gave her the cup, and they repeated the intimate drink.

Next he stroked her from the inside of her pretty thigh upward, enjoying her body's soft yet firm feel, admiring the undulations of her breasts as he caressed them. She arched against his hand, silently urging it lower. He trailed his fingers across the dark triangle, venturing into the folds of her heated flesh. The wetness that greeted his probing sent a surge of need to his erection. She was ready, too.

His desire reached a fevered pitch.

Amice gasped with pleasure as his fingers found her. "More. I want more. All of you. Nicholas, now."

He was happy to comply. As he adjusting his position, her gaze raked his body, from his chest to his flat stomach, then lower still. As her eyes widened at the sight of his hardness, need consumed him. He wanted to go slowly, to savor their first joining, but the instant he felt his flesh meet hers he lost control. He slid into her, deep and smooth. Both gasped. A powerful thrill coursed through him.

Amice gasped again and again, her pleasure increasing his as he joined her at the height of sensation.

They lay entwined as their breathing slowed, neither wanting to break the mood by speaking. What words could describe the passion they felt for each other, the overwhelming need, the incredible surge of feeling?

"I love you."

"I love you too, Nicholas."

He propped himself up on his elbow and stroked her face. One by one, he arranged her long curls into a fan on the sheets. There was no reason to say anything else. Further words would inevitably lead to a discussion of the future, their future, if there could even be one. There'd be too many questions with too few answers.

Had his heart ever been so full? He wasn't the writer Amice was, and lacked eloquent words to express his sentiments. But he knew he wanted to look at her until his eyes were tired and then look at her some more. And then stop looking and start touching. He wanted to make love to her, help her, just be with her. No other woman had ever made him feel this way, satisfied beyond release, so at peace. And to feel at peace even in a time of turmoil was a great thing.

He wouldn't let his awakening into love be marred by thoughts that she might be given to another man.

"Ah, Amice, I must go. It's too late already," he said.

❧ ☙

Amice clutched him. She hadn't had nearly enough.

She'd clenched his shoulders, overjoyed at his intensity, feeling bereft each time he temporarily left her, only to be renewed each time she was filled. Excitement vibrated through her. She didn't want the waves to end. She'd spiraled ever higher, holding her breath as the peak washed over her. How would once be enough?

"Stay a little longer. How can I go on as though everything is the same? Everyone who looks at me will surely see the way I feel for you shining in my eyes. They'll know. I can't dissemble as they do."

Slowly, with obvious reluctance, he eased himself out of her grasp. "Fortunately, everyone has other things to worry about."

"Yes and no," Amice said. "Of course they're worried about Henry. But he's been ill so long, people are starting to grasp at any diversion. The gossip would be worse than before."

"We mustn't give them anything to gossip about," Nicholas decided. "We'll have to take things a day at a time. Henry could recover, and then there will certainly be war."

"Do you really think he'll be himself again?" Amice asked.

"I have to."

As he left her with a lingering kiss, as the moon waned, she couldn't stop smiling. She'd finally brought some of her feelings for Nicholas out in the open, and they were returned. This was better than she, Joan and Maud had imagined all those years ago when they played at being married. A shadow dimmed her smile, because of course she and Nicholas weren't married, and it was highly unlikely they'd ever be. She felt married to him in her heart. And knew she would love no other.

The thorn in her roses was her work for York. She'd have to stop, giving up something she enjoyed that made her feel valuable, and that served a great cause, or bring herself to tell Nicholas the whole truth.

On his way to break his fast, Nicholas recalled how Amice's scent had washed over him as he entered her room last night. How beautiful she'd looked in the moonlight, in that thick robe that masked her lithe figure, motionless, eyes wide. Her hair had been down, tiny ringlets tumbling past her waist gleaming red in the glow of the many candles augmenting the firelight. If only they could be together more often.

Whispers and giggles from several women grouped in the corridor ahead caught his attention.

"I wonder when she'll tell Amice. It's about time something interesting happened around here," one said softly. Margaret's attendant, Eleanor Roos, he thought, but couldn't be certain.

He tucked himself behind an open door.

"The queen said she couldn't endure the somber atmosphere one more day," whispered a second woman, Rose Merston. "She's been lying-in for weeks. Though the baby could…any time, she is so bored, so frustrated. Even though she can't attend, what better than a wedding to liven things up? To give people hope."

Nicholas strained to listen, but could barely hear her. Had he missed anything of value?

"How fortunate we were to be in the room when Margaret made up her mind." He recognized the third voice instantly. Belinda's. "We're the first to know! Who else shall we tell? Shall we go tell her now?"

Nicholas's heart raced. Amice to wed, so soon. He'd lose her if they couldn't find a solution, fast.

They'd been lax, thinking the queen had a lengthy list of far more important issues to handle before finding Amice another husband. Impending childbirth, Henry's illness, deciding who should govern, to name a few.

The footsteps stopped in front of his hiding place.

"No, let's relish our secret," the first woman said.

"Besides, Margaret would be furious if we told, and she'd know it was us because we were the only ones there," Rose added. "I know! We could tell some of our friends...and tell them not to tell."

Another series of giggles.

"We must find out when the announcement will be." Belinda again. "And be in attendance. I don't want to miss the look on Amice's face when she finds out who it is!"

Still more shrill giggling. Margaret's ladies were so exasperating.

Nicholas clenched his fingers and tried to breathe quietly, fighting the urge to move. *Go away.... I don't want to know any more! If you say his name—*

"A member of the House of York, no less. Margaret will do whatever she can to stay in power, even if it means pacifying a few enemies."

"Such urgency, to hold the wedding in a week. I think she worries Amice will try to run away like I heard she did when her first husband's cousin wanted to marry her, if you can believe that."

The voices faded as the three continued on their way.

Nicholas let out his frustration in a loud grunt. He leaned his back against the cold stone wall. Amice was to marry a Yorkist...in a week. Margaret must have gotten a dispensation to move things along so fast.

How could he go to Amice now, knowing what he knew? How could he tell her? How could he not? He'd thought they had more time to work out a solution, but Margaret had surprised him.

Nothing had really changed, not yet.

This new knowledge shattered the contentment that had been his only moments before.

Now that he'd admitted his feelings to her and more to himself, losing her would be all the more painful. Jealousy had soared when he watched her with William. How would he handle the agony of seeing her with this new betrothed...and wed within a week?

A vision of her lying in bed washed over him. Memories of making love were wonderful, but not as good as the real thing. Nor were they enough. But memories might be all he would have.

❧ ☙

Amice couldn't stop smiling. Her time with Nicholas was the best thing that had happened to her. The comfort of his heat remained with her and her body still tingled from his touch. *So this is happiness, this is love.* Even a summons to visit Queen Margaret in her lying-in chamber didn't dampen her good mood. Surely the queen was too focused on the birth of her first child to think of arranging marriages.

She curtseyed to Margaret, who was propped up by piles of pillows and dressed in long robes. Perhaps Margaret wished to while away the time discussing Christine de Pizan or to recommend another book for her to read. Or maybe she was ready to enlist Amice as her scribe, as she'd suggested. If so, there was no way to refuse. But how would she handle working for York and Margaret, hostile, bitter opponents?

"I have news for you. I have found you another groom. Your third, is it not?" Margaret wasted no time on pleasantries, clearly uncomfortable in her final days of pregnancy and bored with her long lying-in.

Amice looked at her shoes, flushing as other ladies hid laughter or snide whispers behind their hands. Chilling fear wiped away her smile. What could she say? She was supposed to appear pleased that Queen Margaret had not only thought of her yet again, but had gone to such trouble on her behalf at such a time.

"You'll wed in a week's time, that the event might take place before the prince or princess arrives," the queen added, patting her large midsection. "Well, Lady Amice? Have you nothing to say? Aren't you curious about his name and standing?"

Margaret didn't wait for Amice to answer, which was a good thing, for her throat had gone dry and her imagination had fled.

"He's of the House of York, and highly ranked. Sir James Bourchier is his name. He's one of York's closest advisors as well as a relation of the Duke of Norfolk. This marriage is to show our good faith, to attempt to bind our factions. I wasn't the proponent of this union, but others on the privy council persuaded me it would be for the best."

Amice flushed again. Guilt washed over her like a cold rain, knowing that Margaret's hope for unity through her marriage was a sham. She might reside with the Lancasters at their command, appear to be one of them, but her political heart was with the Yorkists. By now the duke himself knew this, too.

How had she ended up in such a quagmire? She hadn't meant to be duplicitous. Each small step seemed the right choice. For her country. She and Nicholas didn't see eye to eye, but she believed as he did that each had a duty to serve England. The sticking point was who to follow.

Men often used women as powerless pawns in their need for power, money and land. But Amice knew her situation placed her below even the lowliest piece in a chess game. The Yorkists would be laughing behind Margaret's back, claiming another victory. One of their own would be viewed as a symbol of the Lancasters.

Amice was trapped. If she told Margaret she'd aided York, she could be punished and likely found guilty of treason. A vision of herself about to be hanged, drawn and quartered flashed in her mind, causing an unwelcome shudder. If she said nothing and Margaret found out, all would be lost. Would York and his supporters come to *her* aid then?

If her secret remained hidden, she'd suffer nonetheless, for she'd live with remorse. Amice would know that by aiding the queen in going through with this marriage, she was also deceiving her. Belinda would know, too. She could be trusted only because if Amice's involvement were revealed, so would hers.

The good of the country was more important than offending the queen. Amice had to do as she thought best. And support those she believed in.

Margaret gasped, then brushed away the women who rushed to her side. "It's nothing. Now, Amice, what have you to say?"

Nicholas, are you lost to me forever?

Amice stood tall, hands folded before her as if she were calm.

She'd made up her mind. There was only one course of action she could take.

"Your Grace, though I thank you for your many kindnesses to me, I cannot marry Sir James."

The silence in the room weighed heavily on her shoulders. No one moved, or breathed. Not even a gem dared to sparkle in the face of such outrageous defiance.

Margaret tilted her head. "Did I hear aright? You dare to refuse a royal command?"

The other women stared at her as if she were the newest addition to the menagerie.

"I'm truly sorry, Your Grace. But I must refuse." Her insides churned.

What had she done? Amice stood her ground, despite the urge to fall to her knees and beg forgiveness. Lacking time to consider her options fully, she'd chosen the middle road. She wouldn't reveal her Yorkist ties or leanings, but wouldn't accept the marriage either. It was the only way Amice knew to be true to herself, York and the queen. She raised her chin, desperately forcing away nervousness and fear as the queen's beautiful face blotched red.

"You're too intelligent for your own good," Margaret snapped. "I know you've read every book we possess. What, pray tell, is your reason for such defiance?"

If she knew what I'd done.... Amice hadn't thought far enough ahead to come up with an explanation. Her knees shook beneath her thick skirts, but she wouldn't show the queen how afraid she was.

The circle of women was silent and motionless.

"I simply do not wish to wed again, Your Grace. I have, as you know, lost two men. I remain willing to pay a fine to make up for your loss of an alliance. I've heard the royal treasury has suffered significant losses. It would be an honor to provide additional revenues for your coffers."

Margaret's face turned redder. She sat up straight. "You have the nerve to cite the crown's financial difficulties? Lady Amice, I shall grant you two choices, neither of which you deserve. You will marry Sir James in one week, or stay locked up in the Tower until I decide what else to do with you or you come to your senses," the queen proclaimed.

Amice couldn't speak. Her worst fears had come to pass. Thrown into the Tower like a traitor, when she'd only wanted to serve her country. How could doing what she felt was right turn out so wrong? Could she truly go against the direct order of her sovereign?

"In the meantime, like the misbehaving child you resemble, you'll be refused all food and water," Margaret added.

Gasps echoed through the room, but no one dared speak in Amice's defense. The Tower was bad enough, but to deny sustenance? Few women had been imprisoned in the Tower for any reason. None had heard of such a punishment for a woman, but then again, none had seen such open defiance of the queen's wishes.

Amice swallowed. What to do? She could make no other choice.

Margaret waved two women toward Amice. Belinda and Rose each grasped an arm to lead her out of the queen's private lying-in chamber, where no men were allowed, so she could be turned over to the guards. Amice met Belinda's gaze, surprised to see unfeigned concern. She must fear for her own safety if Amice decided to unburden her tale.

As they led her away, Amice held her head high. *Please don't let Nicholas see this.* Even as the words passed through her mind, there he was, close enough to overhear one of the women telling a man-at-arms where to take her. Had Nicholas been waiting for her? Had he known what Margaret was going to say? Her heart sank further at the thought that he might have known the queen's intent, even as early as last night. Their sole night of shared passion.

Amice could see rage growing inside Nicholas like a living thing, but he didn't stop the man-at-arms from taking Amice's arm.

"What has she done to deserve the Tower?" he demanded.

Rose answered with a smug smile. "She refuses to marry the latest man the queen orders her to wed. She's being sent to the Tower to consider her options."

Amice twisted to glance at him as the guard pushed her toward the door. Nicholas looked on helplessly.

CHAPTER 13

ours later, Amice paced her damp, cold Tower room. It was narrow, with sparse furnishings and one tiny window set high and deep into the stone wall. If she were allowed, as some prisoners were, she'd pay to have some of her own possessions brought. If she had to stay here long enough to need them.

She sighed. All she'd wanted was a family to cherish because hers had been taken away, to watch Castle Rising prosper under her care, and the opportunity to write. She hadn't sought out court or political intrigue, yet was steeped in it literally up to her neck.

A bitter smile lifted her lips. Only a few short months ago Harry tried to force her to marry him by starving her in a locked room. Now, here she was, locked up and denied food once again because she didn't want to marry. Before, she'd escaped. There was no escaping the Tower. Even if she could get free, there was nowhere to run from the queen's wrath.

Darkness descended. Already it seemed she'd been imprisoned for a week. The walls closed in more and more every minute, the damp air hard to breathe. She lit the candle, then stared at the flickering light.

One candle wouldn't last very long. Was she expected to sit in the dark, without even a glimmer of light and hope? A shudder raced through her at the thought of the disgusting creatures that might crawl out of the ancient Tower without light to keep them at bay.

"Guard!"

No answer. Very likely he hadn't heard her through the thick walls.

"Guard!" Yelling as loud as she could strained her throat. "Another candle, please. Please."

No answer.

She sat on the stool in defeat. Oh, for some frumenty pudding, sweetened with cinnamon and almonds. Maia's fresh white bread. Her mouth watered.

What if Margaret had her baby and forgot about her? Maybe hunger and thirst would force her to submit. She was helpless, unless Nicholas chose to and could find some way out.

There was nothing she could do but starve for her honor or give in and live with deception. She struggled to keep back taunting tears of self-pity, but a few spilled down her cheeks before she regained control. Never before had she so needed comfort, but she was well and truly alone. She closed her eyes, remembering the comfort and warmth of being in Nicholas's arms. For a brief moment, she thought she felt him. Finally, tears still damp on her skin, she lay on the narrow cot and fell into a troubled sleep.

The next morning, Amice combed her hair as best she could with her fingers, taking great care with each tangled curl. After all, she had nothing but time. They hadn't brought water for washing, probably for fear she'd defy Margaret's orders by drinking it. She'd tried again—just as unsuccessfully—to have the Tower guard attend her, shouting her throat raw with her pleas. Four days had passed, she noted from small marks she'd scraped on the wall with her fingernail. She tried to save her strength, though for what she didn't know. Hunger was her only companion, her throat was beyond parched. When dizziness overcame her, she slept, no matter if it was day or night.

Had she wanted to capitulate, there was no one to tell. The chamber pot had long ago filled and smelled so bad she had to breathe through her mouth. She'd thought to fling its contents out the window, but it was too high to reach and she lacked the energy. At night she lay in the darkest dark, steeling herself not to jump at every scratch and squeak.

She had no way to contact her cousin Cromwell and ask if

he'd use his influence to free her. The only other true friend close to the king she had was Nicholas. If he'd been able to or wanted to help she wouldn't be here still. But despite his apparent abandonment, she had nothing else to think of.

Was she being punished for wanting other than what she had, or was this her penalty for loving Nicholas? Was it wrong to want her life at Castle Rising instead of being grateful for the king's and queen's interest in her marriage?

Castle Rising. Just the thought of her wonderful home lightened her mood a little. It would be well past harvest by now, the first she'd missed. She loved this time of year, when villagers and tenants reaped the benefits of their hard work.

She hadn't even marked the passing of Michaelmas on September 29. Everyone at Castle Rising was so happy then, with all sorts of fairs and games. The end of one farming year and the start of the next had been her favorite.

Amice envisioned herself at Castle Rising, writing at her desk, contented. Late afternoon sun on a crisp autumn day shone through the glass windows. Nicholas was there. They were happily married, of course. She'd spent so many imprisoned hours imagining their wedding day she was beginning to believe it had happened.

As her husband, in her imagination, Nicholas was free to show his affection for her. He was so handsome, and deeply tanned again from working in the sun. His shirt was unlaced so she could glimpse the muscles on his chest. Her heart contracted with love at the sight of him.

A smile lit his brilliant blue eyes. He bent over her and kissed her neck, right in the crook where it met her shoulder. She concentrated harder on the image, and a shiver ran through her at his touch. He told her to close her eyes, and because she trusted him, she did. Robert was nearby, laughing, obviously in on the surprise.

Suddenly there was a scratchy wetness on her hands. She opened her eyes to see a tiny greyhound puppy marching about in her lap, seeking a comfortable spot as it licked her fingers. She laughed delightedly, hugging it close. Her eyes filled with tears of happiness that she'd be so lucky to have so thoughtful a husband. That she was in love. She jumped up to thank him with a hug, trying not to squish the pup between them as it scrabbled to gain hold on her gown. Their lips met....

The wonderful image popped like a soap bubble with loud pounding at the door, returning her to grim reality. Why bother to knock? She was a prisoner. They'd come to question her at last. She pushed off the cot with her hands, tried to stand, but her legs were too weak. She couldn't have risen if her visitor were the king himself. But then, these days he couldn't walk unassisted, either.

The heavy wooden door opened with the high-pitched creak of disuse.

A tall figure entered her cell. She couldn't breathe. Nicholas. Her mouth was too dry for words, but tearless sobs of relief shook her.

He looked almost as awful as she must. His hair was tousled, his skin taut over his cheekbones. "Amice, I'm so sorry it took me so long to free you. All will be well soon, you'll see."

The sound of his voice was more welcome than water for her parched throat. Effortlessly lifting her from the narrow, straw-filled cot, he carried her down the spiral stairs and into the sunshine. When she recoiled at the bright light, he turned her face into his chest and smoothed her hair, making soft, shushing sounds. She was tired, so tired she couldn't even bring herself to ask how he'd saved her.

When she awoke in her room at Westminster, Nicholas was by her side. She tried to speak, but no sound came out. Her eyes filled with tears.

"I'm here. You're safe." Nicholas touched her cheek, calming her. "Don't talk yet. Have some broth first."

He uncovered a bowl on a nearby table, then fed her spoon by spoon until she had finished. She drank in the sight of him as she drank the healing soup.

She squeaked out a question. "How?"

"I tried to convince the queen to let you go," he said, setting the bowl aside. "We had to communicate through messengers, of course, because of her lying-in. Since I couldn't go to her, it took more time. She refused to help. Finally I thought to send word to your cousin Cromwell. Reaching him took more time. He was appalled at the way you had been treated and was able to secure your freedom through his influence with the council. Margaret wouldn't apologize to him and won't to you. Obviously she doesn't like having her word countermanded, but I do think she regrets the harshness of her sentence. When you recover, all will be well."

He'd gone to great lengths to save her. If Nicholas found out what she had been doing, would he still care for her?

It had started out so simply when she overheard Belinda reading that letter. All she'd wanted to do was assist the cause she believed in. What harm could there be in copying a few documents for York? But there had been another request, and another.

Nicholas would be horrified if he knew. Nicholas, who had rescued her. Who cared for her. Who believed what she did not, both in his faith and his politics.

"How did you manage this?"

"Cromwell did it. He sent Margaret a message saying she had no right to force you to wed as you aren't the king's ward but a widow with properties in your own right. In addition, he convinced her that she and Henry need the money you'd pay as much or more as they need the alliance. He stated the obvious, that they could find Bourchier another bride to bind the houses. In a way, I think Margaret was impressed that you dared defy her will. Not many people risk going against the wishes of the king and queen."

Amice wasn't proud, just so very relieved that she wouldn't have to marry, at least the latest candidate. She'd bought some time. But she owed her cousin yet another debt. And she owed Nicholas.

"You're here…with me."

He smiled and took her hand. Any connection to him was welcome. Too welcome.

"I'm still your protector. Your champion," he said.

Amice pulled her hand free and turned her head. She couldn't face the goodness in his eyes. But she lacked the strength to explain. Lacked the courage. "What happens now?"

"When you feel up to it, you're to have another meeting with the queen. That is, if she doesn't give birth; the babe is expected at any time. The queen has returned you to your former status. Things are as they were."

She couldn't agree. The days of utter solitude, darkness and silence except for the rats had changed her. Hardened her. She knew what it was to have absolutely nothing, to suffer deprivation, which made her more determined than ever to achieve her dreams.

The aid to York would stop. England mattered naught to her now. The huge causes Nicholas espoused and in which she'd come to believe couldn't help her gain what she desired. Peace. She could battle herself, fight her own civil war, no longer.

"Nicholas. I can't thank you enough for your assistance. But we mustn't be alone again." She drew in a slow breath to keep from crying. "Being with you makes me want things we can't have. Makes me want…. But we have no future."

"I thought we agreed that life is too short—"

"We did. You know how much I want to be with you, how much I care for you. Yet at the same time, it's torture. Too hard." She had to be strong, even as she looked him in the eye, saw the hurt on his face. "The queen has restored my position, I think in part to save face. So I'm going to build on my disgrace and ask to be sent home. I won't be a reminder to her of all that has happened. My hope is that Margaret will accept some of my lands as the fine for my freedom."

Margaret would gain some of Edwin's properties and revenues, which England sorely needed but meant nothing to Amice. She'd never seen most of them. All she wanted was to live at and care for Castle Rising. Her personal peace of mind and the welfare of the villagers were all that mattered to her now.

"I see." His face was hard. "I hope you feel better soon. Godspeed."

He rose and walked out of her room, closing the door behind him.

"Farewell," she whispered.

What had she done? She had sent away the man she loved. For his own good, so he wouldn't fail his duty to Henry.

A few days ago, she wouldn't have been able to leave him, the heart of her heart. Now, embittered by her unjust punishment, she could no longer succumb to feelings. Those who loved were weak, opening themselves to hurt and anguish. She was a woman with responsibilities, who no longer harbored fantasies of romance. She would depend on herself from now on.

The constant ache in her chest now was far worse than the pain of making the most of every stolen moment, of wondering when she might see him again…. How would she bear not seeing him?

As Chaucer had said in *Troilus and Criseyde*, "As tyme hem hurt, a tyme doth hem cure." She had to believe that.

The next day, she felt well enough to spend some time writing. But she didn't want to finish the letter due to York about why he hadn't been called to attend council meetings. The stakes were getting higher and higher the longer Henry remained ill.

But after setting out her ink and quills, she opened the small chest which contained her manuscript. Reaching in to pull out the pages, she grasped hundreds of scraps instead. They slipped through her fingers. Someone had destroyed her work.

"No!" As tears splashed on the tiny, useless snippets, she noticed they were all of a size. Whoever had ripped the vellum had taken the time to tear countless hours of her labor into neat little squares. Who would do such a hateful thing? Who could invade her privacy, open her chests?

All the more reason to go home, away from gossip, rumor, and evil deeds. From the man she couldn't have.

Even in those darkest of hours in the Tower, she'd held back all but a few tears. Now, it seemed as though a river surged from her eyes. She cried for every problem she faced, from her hopeless feelings for Nicholas, being away from Castle Rising, York against Lancaster, to the uncertainty of her future.

And the ruination of her writing. How would she find out? She'd only mentioned once to Nicholas that she wrote, but he wouldn't do this. She wasn't aware anyone else knew. How would she walk the halls, go to meals, without wondering if every glance, every smirk in her direction was the perpetrator? She shuddered.

Worse, if someone had discovered her personal writing, could they uncover her work for York?

❧ ☙

Two days later, chaos reigned in the queen's lying-in chamber. Fluttering matrons surrounded the queen, who gasped with her pains.

Amice had lost her chance to speak with Margaret. For now.

The midwife, tall, thin and grey haired, elbowed her way through the throng. Matrons offered bits of advice as she bent over her patient.

"Silence. Don't you know loud noises can bother the baby? Where are the musicians I asked for? Where is the honey, the hot water?"

Various women jumped to do her bidding as she barked assignments.

Amice huddled in the back of the room. She'd attended to prove all was as it had been. She so wanted her own children. Nicholas's children. No. She wouldn't wish for a future that couldn't be. But how to stop?

As the hours passed, Margaret grew increasingly restless and fretful. The women, tasks completed long ago, now waited silently. They wouldn't allow themselves to even consider what would happen if the baby didn't survive. Margaret's pregnancy had been the only hope for months. England with an incapacitated king and no heir? A possibility too horrible to discuss. A land without a king. Just like the story of King Arthur, when he took ill after discovering Guinevere's infidelity with Lancelot.

At last the babe was born. England had a prince.

After cutting the cord, the midwife held the baby high before clearing its nose and mouth. Cheers and laughter filled the room, squelched by the midwife's loud "SSSSHHHHH!" She quickly bathed the boy. All watched in silence, as, following an ancient tradition, she rubbed the newborn's palate with honey and wiped its tongue with hot water so it would grow up to be well spoken.

The godmother, Anne, duchess of Buckingham, stood ready to take the baby to be baptized. With the high rate of infant mortality, even seemingly healthy babies were baptized as soon as possible. As the midwife tended to Margaret, Anne led the procession.

Pages ran ahead to summon the godfather and the rest of the men. The ladies followed, eager to spread the joyful news.

Church bells rang, a Te Deum was sung. Edward was wrapped in a mantle studded with pearls and precious stones with soft linen lining to protect his delicate skin.

Amice forced herself to focus on the baptism by Henry's confessor and not meet Nicholas's gaze. After the ceremony, all except the queen attended a feast held in his honor.

In the midst of the celebration, a page approached. With a summons from the queen. She could feel Nicholas watching her as she exited the hall, but didn't look back.

On her way back to Margaret's chamber, she wished she'd eaten something to quell her jumping stomach.

Her heart thudded in her chest. She curtseyed. "You sent for me, Your Grace?"

"How was the feast?" Queen Margaret sat in her bed, dressed in a fresh robe, propped amidst a pile of pillows. The room felt as oppressive and close as it had during the long childbirth.

Surely Margaret hadn't summoned her, the day of her child's long-awaited birth, for a rendition of the foodstuffs served. "Very joyous, Your Grace. And filled with good wishes for you and the prince."

"I doubt 'twas as grand as befits a royal birth, but it was no doubt an improvement over recent fare." Margaret stirred and grimaced. "Sit." She indicated a stool near the bed.

When Amice complied, Margaret continued, "I called you here to discuss duty, which you clearly don't understand. Your stubbornness is inexcusable. Who do you think you are? I thought to leave you to rot in the Tower, but was persuaded otherwise by your friends.

"I have a son, someone new to fight for. The people refuse to accept me as one of them though I've appealed to them time and again. They remain convinced that I think only of my native land, France."

Amice twisted her fingers in her lap, then stopped because she didn't want to seem nervous. She had no idea what she was expected to do or say.

"I want you to listen carefully. Due to my father's sorry finances, I served as my own dowry." Margaret sighed, clearly pained by the memory. "Which was a two-year truce between

England and France. I had to wait nearly a year for the wedding. A wedding by proxy, where the Duke of Suffolk, my first English friend, stood in for Henry.

"Did you know Henry was once engaged to another woman?"

Amice couldn't contain a gasp of surprise. She could see where this was going but couldn't stop the queen from driving her point home. "No, Your Grace, I didn't know."

"His first betrothed, the Count of Armagnac's daughter, would have brought significant wealth and two French provinces. Henry and his advisors decided he should marry me instead, convinced that my personality and relationship to the king of France were more important than money, no matter how sorely needed. Henry had to pawn his jewels and household plate to pay for the marriage and the coronation.

"I had to leave my country. The life I'd known and wanted. When my ship reached England, I was so sick Suffolk had to carry me to shore. I wondered if God had tried to send me a message through illness and horrid weather that I should return to France."

Amice squirmed. Each word pounded her head like a hammer.

The queen stared at Amice for an interminable moment. "Do you understand?"

"Your Grace, I...."

"Tell me why I bothered to divulge my private tale to you."

Amice's heart sank so hard she thought she could feel it land in her stomach. She knew, and the message ate holes of guilt in her soul the way moths devoured woolens. What reply wouldn't make her seem spoiled and incredibly selfish? What reply would commend the queen's sacrifices, yet free her from the need to make her own?

"I believe you want me to see that we don't always get to choose our course," she said. "That others have the power to choose the path we follow, even a queen's, and we must make the best of whatever follows."

"An excellent start. Go on." Queen Margaret nodded.

She knew her cheeks burned. Hadn't she suffered enough already? Her voice came out as a whisper. "And who am I to refuse to marry when those so far above me have had to endure so much?"

"Think on that. Now, what I need is a goodly amount of rest. You may go."

Amice curtseyed and left, her heart heavy as lead.

CHAPTER 14

With a shake of his head, Nicholas ripped down another of the hateful poems impugning the prince's birth that had been posted in many public places. His cadre of men roaming the streets couldn't remove the missives fast enough to keep vicious gossip from flying through castles and countryside. As soon as he learned who was behind them, the queen would toss the culprits into the Tower and throw away the key.

As he passed the kitchen after leaving the stables, Nicholas overheard the cook talking with the ale supplier. The dark grey sky matched his mood.

"I hear tell it's not Henry's babe. The father be Somerset." The supplier shook his bald head as he hauled a barrel off his cart.

"No, no, no." The portly cook wiped his hands on his apron and leaned forward. "The real prince died in childbirth and they put some other brat in his place, so England would 'ave an heir."

The alemonger unloaded another barrel. "Well, I was at St. Paul's Cross when the Earl of Warwick spoke. He said Margaret's adultery produced this baby, and he should know. Henry should have married one of his own. Nothing good comes of dealings with the French."

Cook nodded. "Either way we're ta 'ave some unknown bastard as heir to the throne. I doubt Parliament will stand for that."

Nicholas could stand no more. Putting an end to one

conversation wouldn't stop the rumors, but he had to do what little he could.

Maybe the truth could become its own rumor.

"You there, what kind of talk is that?" he asked. "You know nothing of it. Margaret's women witnessed the birth of the true prince."

The alemonger must not have known who Nicholas was or he'd have remained silent. "Aw, they'd say whatever the queen told 'em to. They want to keep their places and their heads, don't they? Who do you think be the father?"

The cook hastily turned back toward the kitchens without a farewell.

Nicholas sighed. If he couldn't even convince one Englishman, how were they to persuade the whole country that Edward was the true prince, born of Henry and Margaret?

"They say the king refuses to recognize the baby." The alemonger heaved a third barrel. "Wouldn't even look at 'im! Can't be the real prince, not if 'e be not known by the king himself."

Nicholas wasn't about to tell the man the king didn't recognize anyone at all, and for that reason the baby hadn't even been presented yet. Or that fears the king wouldn't be able to fulfill the long-standing tradition of acknowledging the child as his own were very real. No official announcement of the king's illness had been made.

"Be on your way. If I hear you spreading more tales, your position will be in danger," Nicholas said.

The man seemed unconvinced, but moved on with his clattering cart of barrels.

Things were no better among Henry's nobles. Margaret had possession of England's heir. They couldn't let her keep him for long, for that would give her too much power. They didn't want her ruling through her son as regent.

Nicholas wished he and Amice could leave court behind and live in peace at Castle Rising. But the way events were progressing, he'd be fortunate if anything he desired came to pass.

❧ ☙

Amice spent the week after Edward's birth in a frenzy of activity waiting on the queen. She'd seen Nicholas in passing, but they hadn't spoken. Each time, she pushed aside the ache in her heart. The ache of missing him and wanting to be with him, as much a part of her as the need to breathe. She couldn't free herself of the longing. Whenever she had time, she threw herself into her writing with renewed vigor.

"Amice, you've been cooped up in here for hours," Ginelle said as she entered the tiny sitting room. "It's late. And freezing. You've forgotten to have firewood sent up again." She carried a stack of freshly washed linens into the bedroom.

Amice stretched, easing her stiff back. She blew on her fingers and rubbed her hands together. "I don't notice the time or cold when I write."

Ginelle stood in the doorway. "When will you finish?"

"Soon. Fortunately, I remember enough of what was destroyed to recreate large portions. Rewriting helped me improve some sections. You'll appreciate the chapter on recipes." She re-inked her pen and began to write.

Amice wouldn't discuss her other project with Ginelle— copying documents for York. Despite her recent resolve to focus on her own needs, she'd realized if the wrong group was in power, her properties and people would suffer. There might be heavier tithes, higher food costs or worse, the loss of many of her able-bodied men to war. So when Belinda appeared at her door with another assignment, she hadn't refused as planned and had quickly delivered the letter she hadn't wanted to finish.

Amice was glad she'd broken off her friendship with Nicholas. Glad he was out of her life. Yes, she was.

"You should get out more. You work for the queen, then sit here thinking about home and Sir Nicholas." Ginelle crossed her arms.

Amice opened her mouth to reply.

"Don't deny it."

She couldn't. She had to repair the tears imprisonment had made in her heart and soul.

"I'm worried about you. It's as though you make your way through each day without really living it. When do you think

Margaret will decide whether to choose another husband for you or accept your coin?"

Amice cringed. "I hope before the end of the forty days she, as a new mother, must spend in her chambers."

If she had to wait until the churching ceremony scheduled for November 18, she wouldn't be able to endure the uncertainty. The suspense.

"Have you spoken to Sir Nicholas?"

Amice walked to the window, looking down on the few who'd braved the cold. She didn't know how to express her feelings, they made no sense. When she was with him, even just glancing at him in a crowded room, a life without him in it seemed impossible and unbearable. But if she could manage to stay away, she could relish her memories without worrying if each time together would be their last. Or feel guilt over keeping secret her work for York. She hadn't lied to Nicholas, nor had she told him the whole truth.

"Nothing can come of it, were I free to choose." How could she love someone so different? Despite her need for him, she wouldn't want him to suffer or live less of a life than he dreamed. "He remains Henry's man. I support York."

More with each passing day. Henry had been incapacitated too long. To avoid civil war, the country needed a strong, decisive king. By birth, wealth and power, York was the logical choice. Yet the queen wanted her son to rule. But many a babe died in infancy. Even if he thrived, he'd need a regent, as his father had.

Being on opposite sides could result in disaster for her or Nicholas. At the moment, she was on the dangerous side. She could be imprisoned again, for good this time. If York prevailed, would he punish Henry's staunch supporters?

"It's clear you care for each other."

"So we do." The thought of Nicholas confessing his feelings warmed her. "But how can what we share surmount our differences?" She shook her head.

"There you go again, gnawing over things you cannot change, things that may never come to pass. Mayhap you should devote your thoughts to things you can change." Ginelle heaved a huge sigh. "If you wish to remain in here and sulk, that's your choice. I can bring you a tray."

Focus on the things you can change. Perhaps that was the solution.

"No, I'll come down for the meal." If Nicholas was there, at least she could see him. Maybe exchange a few words. Maybe arrange a time to meet, though the parting would be painful as ripping a dressing off a wound.

She forced herself to return to work, making an exact copy of the map Belinda had brought. The pen made scratching noises as she carefully outlined a road on the parchment. Amice didn't know what the documents were for, nor did she want to. She was content, for the moment, to work alone, on the outskirts of York's plans.

Belinda came to pick up the map and copy, her fair skin flushed pink and she bounced on her toes. "Amice, Amice! You won't believe what York wants you to do now, right away. He wants you to write a poem."

Amice paused in the midst of handing over the rolled parchments. "What?" she asked, incredulous. "York wants me to write one of those scandalous poems everyone is talking about?"

Belinda sat on the edge of Amice's table and spread her brocade skirts with one long-fingered hand. "Yes. He gave me some examples. Quite shocking, this about Edward not being the true prince. And look at this one, 'On Popular Discontent at Disasters in France.'"

Amice was confused. "How did York find out I could write original material?"

"Well, I told him, of course." She leaned close, as if to share a confidence. "He mentioned that he sought a new writer, and I thought of you. Aren't you pleased? If York approves, his men will distribute and post yours. Just think of how many will read your words. This is your chance to be a real writer."

Amice tapped her fingers on the desk. This would mean greater involvement in York's affairs. Thus far, she had been more scribe than traitor, though others might not agree. Writing her own material in opposition to the throne would prove a greater risk. Yet having original work she believed in disseminated was one of her fondest dreams.

Focus on what you can change.

She couldn't have Nicholas. She couldn't go home. But she could have this.

She could no longer walk the fine line separating king and duke. It was time to take a stand, though a cautious one. To do so, she'd have to trust Belinda even more.

"I'll do it. But no one else can know I'm the author. The poems must be anonymous." It was enough for her to know her work was read. That she aided the cause in which she believed.

She needed a new challenge, something to focus on. So she'd write some poems. Those she'd heard of and seen were full of lies and half-truths. But hers would be different. Hers would tell the truth.

"Very well," Belinda agreed with a sly smile, making Amice wonder how she planned to use this to her advantage. "How soon can you have the first one ready?"

"I'll work on it now. Though I've never tried poetry." Amice indicated the examples Belinda had brought. "'Ballad on the Death of the Duke of Suffolk,'" she read. "Return tomorrow afternoon. I'll complete at least one by then."

Belinda left, still smiling.

Amice picked up her quill, idly caressing the soft feather. Instead of rhymes about Edward or the king, Nicholas worked his way back into her thoughts. What would he do if he found out? Her involvement widened the gap between them. She didn't know if even the power of love could build a bridge over it.

She couldn't gnaw on that now. York needed her help.

She began to write.

England's babe, or is he yet
Proof of someone else's get?
Just who is his mother sweet?
Surely not our Marguerite.

York laughed with what seemed like genuine enthusiasm as he read the final lines of the poem to the others in his great hall. All were finishing a sumptuous meal of suckling pig and cherry pottage.

"Tiny daisies in his hair

Do not mean he came from there.
Perhaps we should ask the source
Who'd tell lies of her own, of course."

After the laughter died down, he said, "Belinda, this is wonderful. To the point, yet with humor. No one can accuse us of lying with this one, either. Clever approach.

"I had no idea you were so talented. Quite astute, to incorporate Margaret's badge, the marguerite."

Belinda preened. Her gamble was paying off. Why shouldn't she take the credit and increase her worth to York? Amice had requested anonymity, after all.

She smiled her slow, cat-like smile. "The marguerite represents fidelity in love. I'm so pleased you like my words, milord."

"You can be sure I'll have more work for you."

"I look forward to serving you," she replied. "In any way I can."

❧ ☙

Harry hoped he, the new scullion, appeared to be working diligently. Washing dishes, at his age and rank. The clatter of the kitchen made his head ache.

"Are you trying to rub a hole in that? You've been here for hours...look at that pile yet undone," the Steward of the Kitchen reprimanded.

Harry bit back a sharp retort and plunged the platter into the barrel of water in front of him. "My pardon, sir!" He bowed his head to hide the non-subservient gleam in his eye.

"I can find another to fill your place soon enough if you don't work hard. Hmph."

The steward went back to supervising the cook's preparation of the main meal of the day, featuring aigredouncy. The honey-glazed sliced chicken rolled in mustard, rosemary and pine nuts would follow a pastry tart filled with plum, quince, apple, pear, basil and rue. Not that he'd get to eat any of that fine fare. Not a lowly scullion such as he.

Harry tossed a bowl into the water with a satisfying splash and grabbed another.

"By marrying Amice I could get Edwin's lands for my life, at least, if not for our children. Why wouldn't she have me?"

The bowl in his hand did not respond. "She'd never go against the Church, that's why, because we share a forbidden bond of affinity. It pained me to lock her up, but how else could I persuade her? I trusted her when she agreed to marry me. But she betrayed me."

Freedom, even as a servant, was better than prison. "I took a horse, and followed Amice."

Did the drying cloth dare reproach him?

"No, that wasn't stealing. Amice's property should be mine, too."

But how to get her to consent to wed? A forced marriage could be annulled.

He'd heard of a drug that would dull the senses. If that drug worked, he could control her.

The repetitive, lowly, backache-inducing labors of the only job he could get tested his mettle and his temper. It would be worth it. Soon.

"I've only seen her once since I got here." He closed his eyes. "Like a miracle…a vision in the early morning mist. The way she looked at Sir Nicholas by the stables…."

That afternoon, he'd decided to surprise her. At first he was disappointed that she wasn't in her room. Then he noticed a writing desk with a carved metal latch on a large coffer. Excited and afraid at the possibility of discovery, he opened the lid. He tried to read the pages, but could pick out only a few words. That she could write better than he!

Page by page, he'd ripped her writings into tiny squares. After piling the scraps in the desk, he hurried back to the kitchen. When Amice was his, she wouldn't have time to write.

Despite all his plans, nothing had changed for the better. Soon he'd be back in a corner of the king's kitchen with his pile of filthy bowls.

He'd work harder. He had to succeed.

CHAPTER 15

January 1454

Today the queen would show the prince to the king, whose condition hadn't changed.

Margaret held her head high. She wore a robe with the verse of a psalm embroidered around the hem. A shimmering gold net headdress completely hid her pale blond hair. Her ruby wedding ring gleamed on her finger.

Amice knew Margaret and her supporters had delayed the event as long as possible, praying fervently that Henry would recover, would recognize Edward as his son and heir as tradition required and put the rumors to rest.

All waited in breathless anticipation as Henry was brought in, supported by two men. He couldn't bear his own weight. Amice hid her shock at his wasted appearance. Jewels flashed as nobles whispered amongst themselves.

The Duke of Buckingham stepped forward to present the prince to the king. Henry had been placed in a large chair, padded with colorful cushions. His head listed slightly to the side, resting on an embroidery of the Holy Mother. His eyes were cast down.

Obviously the purges, unusual ointments and potions administered by the physicians had failed. Bright red and blue velvet and brocade robes, colors he wouldn't have chosen himself, served to make his pallor more obvious. He was so thin his bony knees poked at the velvet and brocade robes he wore. For some reason, they had even shaved his head, now covered with a black felt hat studded with jewels.

Unexpected tears gathered. She didn't have to think Henry was a good king to feel sorry for the man.

"Your Grace, may I present your son, Prince Edward of Westminster, soon to be made Prince of Wales, Duke of Cornwall and Earl of Chester. I, and those here today, ask your blessing," the duke said.

There was no response.

"King Henry, the sixth of that name, I present your son, the prince, Edward." The duke tried again, as if more volume could guarantee a result.

A collective gasp sounded as Henry's lids flickered. Had he glanced at the baby? But he didn't speak or move.

Each held his or her breath, hoping or not hoping that the king would do something. Anything. Slowly each exhaled as the king remained exactly as he had been.

Margaret said, "Let me try." Sweat beaded on her forehead, though the room was cool. She scooped her son from the duke's arms. "My lord, I beseech you to recognize your son and mine, your heir, Prince Edward."

Once more all waited breathlessly. Still nothing. Slowly, silently, they left the king to the continuing, unsuccessful ministrations of his physicians.

Margaret's despair was clear to all.

What would the privy council do now?

❧ ☙

"Amice!" Nicholas hissed. "Here!"

His heartbeat sped as she glanced both ways down the hall to ensure that no one was watching. She hastened toward the room he'd poked his head out of.

He reached for her the instant she passed through the door. She sneezed. And sneezed again. They stood in a barely furnished room so dusty it looked as though no one had been inside for years. Faded curtains partially covered the windows, letting in a few stripes of light.

"Bless you," he said. "It may be dusty, but it's private as one can be in this castle. I've been hoping to get you alone for days. Despite our last conversation, I've missed you. How do you fare?"

"Well, now that I'm with you," she confessed.

Nicholas agreed. That was the annoying truth. Her smile, being close to her, were welcome as the sun on her fields after a storm.

"How did you know I'd come this way?"

"I didn't. I waited when I could, knowing you'd eventually need more parchment or ink. I had to see you."

"I've wanted to see you, too. But what's the point? I can't think of any way to change our situation for the better."

"Neither can I. Yet."

"Seeing you, being with you like this, is so…bittersweet. It's harder than I'd thought."

Nicholas cupped her face with his hands. "So beautiful." He bent toward her. "I couldn't stay away." His mouth closed over hers. She sighed into him, returning his kiss like a thirsty traveler given water.

He slid one arm beneath her knees without breaking the kiss, and carried her to a padded bench. He sat with her on his lap.

"Can you feel how I want you?" He slid his hand into her low neckline to caress her.

"Yes." Her head fell back against his shoulder. "Yes."

"I'll come to you tonight."

"No."

"No?"

"I want you now. Here." She rose, then undid her belt and slid off her overgown. She removed her mesh headdress and shook her hair free. "Tell me how to please you."

"Ah, Amice," he breathed. He removed his boots and hose. His tunic fell to his knees, concealing evidence of his desire. "Come to me." He sat again, holding his arms to her. "Sit upon me."

He helped her straddle him, pulling up her gown and pushing his velvet out of the way until no fabric separated them. Hot flesh met hot flesh, soft and wet met hard.

Amice guided him inside her. Slowly, slowly she moved her

hips. She moaned, settling into a measured, sensual cadence. She grasped his shoulders and dropped her head onto his shoulder, sending her hair spilling down his back. Need built within, but he wouldn't give in to the urgency, savoring each sensation.

Nicholas kissed her neck, and worked his way toward her mouth with a dozen more kisses. He ground out, "I can't take much more of this. I want you with me...now, Amice, now...."

"Patience, my lord," was her soft reply. "I want this to last."

She took him deep, then moved away. Again and again. "Ah, yes. Just like this," she whispered in his ear.

"Can't wait...." He grabbed her hips and pushed into her with a groan.

The jolt of their bodies meeting broke his control. He soared into release as she found hers.

Nicholas wrapped his arms around her. Her softness, her sweet scent permeated him. She combed his hair from his face and kissed him.

They remained together for a few moments.

"That was...." he began.

"...amazing." She smiled, climbing off him and reaching for her overgown.

Nicholas dressed. They sat, and he took her hands. "Have you been writing?"

"Yes. Writing and waiting with bated breath for the queen to tell me whether I can go home or if she's going to decide to foist another husband on me. And you? What's the latest news?"

"The king's council decided Henry's failure to recognize his own son was the final straw. The council expanded the medications and treatments that could be tried on him. They can no longer pretend he'll recover and are forced to admit something has to be done. The time has come to make changes all knew were necessary. The time has come. The council sent for the Duke of York."

Amice's jaw dropped. Satisfaction washed over her, warm and welcome. She felt vindicated. She, a mere woman, had played a small part in this. She'd done the right thing for her country and for herself.

Even better, now she'd be able to tell Nicholas all she'd done. "I'm glad. What do you think?"

"I don't have a vote. But Henry isn't capable of being king now, nor is an infant prince. Someone with authority and the ability to control the factions must take charge. The long-postponed Parliament finally met. Margaret, as expected, declared that she wanted to be regent. York demanded the same."

"Surely I'd have heard about that."

Nicholas shifted slightly on the bench, turning toward her. "You would have, had a decision been reached. The question remains, who will take charge?"

Such decisions were so far above her, yet all would be impacted. But she could think of nothing else except where she stood with him.

Amice slid closer to Nicholas, catching a hint of his inviting herbal scent. "And what of us? Do you still care for me?"

He took her hands again, warming them. How she'd missed his touch. The sound of his voice. The way he looked at her when he smiled. Just…him.

"I've tried not to," he said. "But, yes, I still do."

A rush of joy filled her. "I'm glad to hear that. What does this news mean for us? Have recent events cleared a path?"

"Not until the queen or whoever is permitted to rule allows you to wed as you will. All we can have is a few moments now and again. That's not enough for me, but at least it's something. If you returned to Castle Rising, I'd never see you."

"I know." That was one reason she hadn't made additional efforts to be free of court. "I thought seeing you was worse, because every time we part a bit of me goes with you. But not seeing you at all hurts more."

She yearned for him when they were apart and ached for all they couldn't have when they were together. How much longer could they go on like this?

❧❧ ❧❧

As before, almost all were abed when Nicholas stole silently through the halls toward Amice's room. He'd been unable to sleep.

He knocked softly on her door.

The expression of joy that instantly lighted her face when she opened it assured him of his welcome. She looked stunning, her hair tumbling past her shoulders in wild curls.

"Nicholas. Please, come in." She took his hand and led him into her room. "I'm glad to see you, but what are you doing here? Is something wrong?"

"No." He'd simply needed to see her, but found it hard to share the words. "I was thinking of you." Her beautiful face made him more at ease. Gave his day more meaning and hope.

They sat side by side on the window seat, in the moon's glow.

"And I you." She turned to face him, her expression serious. "Nicholas, there's something I've been meaning to tell you.... Either the time didn't seem right, or I just couldn't bring myself to do so because I feared your reaction. But now that we've grown closer, I think you need to know. "

He sighed and leaned his head against the blue velvet cushions. "Can the tale wait another day? I just want to hold you tonight. And kiss and touch you. Maybe we can play chess. For once, let's not dwell on anything serious…not politics, the king, England's future or ours. Can we do that, put our problems behind us and be in this moment?"

"Very well." Amice smiled, though he could tell by the look in her eyes that something yet troubled her. "I'd like that, too."

Nicholas opened his arms. She slid along the seat and nestled against his chest. As he held her close, and gently stroked her hair, he took a deep breath of her rose scent.

And was shocked to find that being with her was all he needed. He hadn't felt so content in months, since they left Castle Rising. He felt more at home in the king's castle, with her, than ever before. Never had his heart filled with such warmth and tenderness. He imagined he could feel it creaking, expanding beyond the boundaries of his past.

Could something that felt so wondrous be wrong? Was Amice a temptation to stray from his true path?

He'd thought a woman he could truly care for rarer and harder to find than diamonds.

He started. Amice looked at him questioningly but settled against him when he shook his head.

He'd never stop loving her.

❦ ❦

Good news, at last. Belinda couldn't wait to share her exciting information with Amice. York was to be named protector of the realm. They, women, had made a contribution in a world where men had most of the power. They need work in secret no longer, nor fear being discovered.

Despite the late hour, she hurried to Amice's chamber but hesitated at the door. If she knocked, Amice might be frightened by being awoken at such an hour. Worse, someone else might hear, and who knew what gossip would sprout. Maybe she'd been hasty and should wait until morning.

No, Amice would want to know. This news was too good to keep to herself for another minute. Belinda carefully eased open the heavy wood door, fortunately unlocked, hoping it wouldn't squeak. She tiptoed into the small outer chamber.

What she saw stole her breath. She clapped her hands over her open mouth but couldn't stop the tears that rushed to her eyes.

There, dimly lit by the dwindling fire, lay Amice and Nicholas, nestled in the high bed. Belinda blinked several times, as though she'd see something different.

The two were entwined like clinging vines. The bedcovers dangled off the side of the bed, revealing that their legs were entangled too. As if their combined warmth made quilts unnecessary.

Belinda closed her eyes, spilling tears down her cheeks and onto her dark cloak. Nicholas had never held her like that while they slept. In fact, most of the time he'd left shortly afterward, rarely indulging in cozy, sleepy aftermath.

Her worst nightmare had come true.

She'd waited for him so patiently, for so long, but he'd turned elsewhere. Almost as bad, Amice, who acted like a friend, hadn't told Belinda of her feelings for Nicholas.

They'd pay for hurting her. But she'd have to act with care. Nicholas wouldn't return to her otherwise.

She knew what she had to do.

Even if she was discovered, even if she couldn't get him back, keeping them from each other would be far better than knowing they were together. Knowing they'd continue to spend time together, perhaps even make their feelings known and get permission to wed, made her nauseous. Causing them pain might alleviate some of her own.

Amazing how quickly a friend could become an enemy.

CHAPTER 16

icholas held his breath, fighting for control. It was true. Amice was secretly consorting with Yorkists. He wouldn't have believed it if he weren't watching her do so.

If he hadn't found the note slipped under his door. *By the postern gate, there you will see. Amice cannot be trusted, so trust in me.*

Who'd want to incriminate Amice? At first he'd ignored the missive, tossing it onto his carved table, thinking it some far-fetched courtier's game. But as he washed and dressed, the scrap of parchment seemed to call to him *cannot be trusted, cannot be trusted.*

Finally, with a sigh, instead of heading to the stables for his morning visit with Merlin, he'd hurried to the designated destination. He'd berated himself every step of the way for allowing an anonymous note to sprout seeds of doubt, for succumbing to its advice, but he went nonetheless.

No. He was being thorough. In a few moments, he'd laugh at his own stupidity.

He was laughing, but in bitterness and disbelief that he'd foolishly trusted Amice. There she stood with a young man, a messenger or fellow spy, her traitorous face partially hidden beneath the hood of a fustian cape. In her hand, the hand he'd brought to his own lips and kissed, she held a letter. He could see the seal was York's. She said something, shaking her head. The man took the document, nodded and left. Looking around with a frown, as if she could feel his gaze on her, Amice carefully made her way back inside.

Nicholas's empty stomach roiled. How could she do this, after all they'd shared? How long had this been going on? He'd given her his trust, opened his heart as with no other woman. After their interlude in the dusty chamber, he'd wanted her all the more. Last night had reinforced his love for her. Back in his room after sharing wonderful lovemaking, such closeness, he'd allowed himself the luxury of enjoying his good fortune.

That's what made this morning's note all the more compelling. More fool he. That a woman he so cared for could seemingly reveal her heart to him, look him straight in the eye, hold him close, all the while betraying and violating everything he represented. Smile sweetly in the dark and slap him in the face in the light. Had he been blinded by her beauty, his need for her?

He froze, contemplating a new possibility. What if she'd never cared for him at all? What if luring him in was part of her plan? Maybe part of her assignment was to procure information. If he was happy spending time with her, he'd be less likely to suspect her interest in his knowledge of the king. Could she be that mercenary? Was she capable of masking her deceit with feigned, yet convincing, feelings?

But she'd pushed him away after her imprisonment. Had he been a far greater fool to renew their friendship, thinking he'd seen longing in her gaze? Last night, she'd said she had something important to tell him. He'd brushed off serious talk in favor of romance. Why hadn't he listened? Had she been about to reveal the truth, or baste her secrets with lies?

Even in the heat of battle he'd never experienced such turmoil. On the field, things were clear. Defend yourself and kill any enemies standing in your way. Fight for what you believed in and knew to be right. Live or die by the grace of God.

If he followed that logic now, he'd have to turn in to the privy council the woman he thought he loved, thought he knew. Nicholas was the king's man, obligated to punish wrongdoing and any hint of treason. He'd have to tell the council she'd used her position in the queen's household to pass information to the duke. York was protector now, but as hard as he tried to give Amice the benefit of the doubt, he couldn't think of any reason why she'd need to meet in secret with his messenger. And why she hadn't breathed a word about whatever she was doing.

On the other hand, who knew of Amice's activities and wanted to cause trouble for her by leaving him a note?

He realized he'd been standing in the bushes while his thoughts swirled and he struggled with unfamiliar indecision. As he strode into the morning light, he knew he had to investigate, to talk to Amice before he acted rashly. Before he did something that couldn't be undone.

Struggling to stem piercing anger and burying his hurt as deep as it would go, he approached Amice in the solar. She looked up with a questioning smile, pen in hand, beautiful as usual in a simple, high-waisted gown of red wool. They rarely spoke in front of others, to lessen any gossip or suspicion about their friendship, which had again blossomed into so much more. They'd thought to protect Amice's reputation. He wanted to laugh at the irony. Protect her from him discovering she was a spy?

He searched for a sign that she was hiding something, that she had forbidden knowledge. To his surprise, he saw nothing suspicious in those clear green eyes, only warm welcome. Either she wasn't doing anything wrong or didn't think she was.

Her expression changed to concern. "Nicholas, what's the matter? I thought we'd agreed to wait a few days before being alone again, to avoid gossip?"

He'd pry the truth out of her. If she truly loved him, she'd be honest. And then they could deal with it somehow, couldn't they? If she lied, he'd have to hate her as he hated all liars.

Clenching his fists behind his back, he struggled to keep the strain from his voice. "So what have you done thus far on this fine day?"

❧ ❧

What could've happened in the few hours since he'd been with her to so change his mood? A thrill passed through Amice as she remembered their night together, the passion his caresses had aroused, followed by such glorious release. Would their lovemaking continue to improve, or had they reached their pinnacle? She couldn't wait to find out. The new feelings he awakened in her needed further exploration.

Her cheeks blushed anew. The feelings he awakened in her couldn't be explored further. He wasn't her husband.

She put her pen down slowly, her gaze on the vellum, stalling. Did he somehow know of her early morning encounter?

She'd been sound asleep, exhausted from the joys of lovemaking and staying up so late with Nicholas, when a knock and fervent whisper had woken her. Robert claimed a man had told him he must fetch her straightaway to the postern gate. Though surprised by such a secretive request from an unknown source, she'd gone, thinking perhaps Nicholas needed to meet with her.

Surprise changed to suspicion when a cloaked man she didn't recognize stated the Duke of York had sent him. Never had anyone but Belinda brought word from York. Amice had replied that if York had reason to communicate with her, he could do so in public. Now that he was protector, he didn't have to resort to clandestine deliveries. She'd handed the note back without reading it and returned to the castle.

As she neared her room, her hand had flown to her mouth in shock. What had she done? Told a stranger she supported York simply because he wore the duke's livery. Was the messenger true, or a spy sent to lure a confession from her?

If she told Nicholas of the incident, he'd ask why York's messenger would send for her at all. She'd have to tell him she'd been working for York's cause for months. He'd feel betrayed because she had aided what had been, and could be again, the opposition to his own cause. Of course she hadn't done so to hurt or deceive him, but to support her own beliefs and do what she could to help her people by helping them to a better ruler.

What was she to do now? She couldn't lie, yet she couldn't tell the truth. Never had she felt so torn in two. Either way, she felt certain Nicholas's opinion of her would worsen.

She heard her mother say, "You're too honest for your own good. Someday that tongue of yours will get you in trouble."

Amice knew she could do nothing but tell the truth as she knew it. Better to deal with the consequences of honesty than suffer the reprimands of her conscience. How could she sleep knowing she'd outwardly lied to anyone? Well, except someone like Harry. She wouldn't lie to the man she loved.

Nicholas's concern had deepened to a frown. Her prolonged silence wasn't helping the situation. She proudly met his gaze.

"This morning Robert told me a man had to speak with me. The man said he was the Duke of York's messenger. I told the supposed messenger that if the duke wished to communicate with me he could do so publicly, not through a secret missive at dawn. I gave him back the message."

Perhaps he'd ask the wrong questions, and through omission she could hide her recent past. Wasn't that just as dishonest as a lie? She'd intended to tell him last night, but he'd put her off. Now that the topic had come up, she couldn't prevaricate. She had to find a way to ease the blow.

"What would York's messenger want with you in the first place? Have any contacted you before today?" Never had she seen Nicholas so intense. His voice was low, his words measured.

"Yes." There was nothing else she could say. Her heart beat so rapidly she feared it would explode. She studied a scratch in the table top.

"Why?"

"Because I was doing what little I could to aid York's cause." Her voice came out a whisper, despite her esteem for her efforts.

As wrenchingly painful as it would be, she'd rather lose Nicholas than hold him with an omission or a partial untruth. Than live with secrets between them.

Was her work more important to her than Nicholas? Real contributions she could make to the cause she believed in to help her country, or real love for a man she couldn't marry, with whom she could only garner stolen moments now and again?

Yet how could one say to the most important man in her life, to her lover, "By the bye, today I wrote a poem criticizing the king you serve and his queen. It was posted everywhere, and people will talk."

"Why?" he repeated.

"You know why, you just choose not to admit it." Anger heated her from within.

Several ladies passed through the solar, heads bent close. She was surprised their headdresses didn't tangle and trip them.

When they'd gone, she said, "You know I come from Norfolk, where York has always been favored. You know I think he should be king, that Henry wasn't strong enough to provide what our country needs even when he was well. And now…he's been ill for so many months. Our king can't even talk, much less make decisions. York, with his vast wealth and power, would be a better ruler. He suggests reforms I think we need, including reducing Somerset's power and creating a council with more power. And his heritage through Edward III's second son puts him closer to the throne than Henry, who is descended from the third son." She stood and walked around the table.

"I can't go to war. Nor do I have scores of men who serve me to fight in my stead. My mind is my sword, and when the opportunity to use it presented itself, I accepted. The chance to help England, which you've told me over and over is our duty, was too great to resist."

She put a hand on his arm. "I wanted to bask in our time together. Because it could come to an end at any moment. That's why I didn't tell you. I thought about doing so a number of times. I'm sorry. Maybe I was selfish, but despite our differences, you know I truly care for you. Believe it or not, I'd summoned the nerve to tell you last night, but you didn't want to listen. Can you understand?"

❧ ☙

Amice's answers worsened Nicholas's foul mood, made fouler for having been so incredibly pleasant only a few hours before. He pushed himself away from the table and turned his back on her. Inhaling deeply, he tried to temper fury and disappointment. Trust drained from him like water from a cracked pitcher.

"What does it matter now?" Amice said. "York is protector of the realm, selected by Parliament. There need be no more secret messengers. His cause—being named heir, to serve—is just and has been recognized by all."

He whirled to face her, flames of fury singeing his gut. "But he is not the king, nor can he be God's anointed. He's simply the most powerful, wealthiest man. Yes, with Henry ill we do need those qualities. But when Henry recovers, what will York do? If he rebels against the true king as he has before, what will you do?

You can't fight with your body, but your neck will dangle from the hangman's noose as easily as any traitor's.

"Ah, Amice, can't you see I fear for you? Despite how much I care for you, how could I protect you if you defy the realm?"

"What if Henry never recovers?" she countered. "Months have passed with no change. How can you still believe? I must do what I think is right. My feelings for you don't stop me from offering what contributions I can, though you may disagree with the choices I make. Can you accept that we disagree?"

Tears gathered, but she fought not to cry. "In the light of day, are we just too different? I've been truly happy during our times together, when nothing else matters but us. Happier, more whole, than I've ever been. Can our feelings for each other withstand the strain of being tugged in opposite directions?"

Nicholas closed his eyes and breathed deeply. As much as he wanted to heal the rift between them, it existed and wouldn't be denied. "I don't know, Amice. I still believe York wants to be king for himself and his heirs, not merely made heir until the prince is of age."

"And I believe he wants what is best for England. We need someone who can rule." She needed to tell him the rest, about the poems. "I also—"

Nicholas held up a hand to stop her flow of words. "I remain Henry's sworn man. A member of the House of Lancaster. You support the House of York. In my view, that still makes us enemies. I can't see it any other way. If you were a man, I'd not willingly consort with you. But you're the woman I love."

Amice's heart lifted. Nicholas still loved her. How she cherished hearing those words. She started toward him with a joyous smile. Finally the time had come to remind him that she loved him, too. She reached for him, but he stepped back.

His blue eyes were dark and dull. "The woman I thought I loved. Now I'm not so certain."

Amice stopped in her tracks. Following her heart had ruined everything.

Nicholas walked away. His broad back had never looked more forbidding. His heart had never been more unreachable.

Amice frantically sought words to call him back. But she couldn't think of any. Her heart pounded, yet ached with despair. Never had she thought to hear such hostility in his voice, each word slicing her like the blade of a finely honed sword.

What could she say to make things right? Would he want to repair the breach, too, before it grew too wide to mend? Was love strong enough to survive such dissension? He still didn't know exactly what she'd done. If he knew, he might never forgive her. Had she been a fool to choose her country over a man she couldn't have?

Amice packed up her writing materials. No more words would flow from her pen today.

She searched within for a positive thought. Perhaps Nicholas was only upset, and would return later with an apology. Couples often quarreled and forgave each other.

This was different. This wasn't a squabble about the best way to run a manor or how much to spend on flour.

It went to the depths of their souls.

❧ ☙

As he squirreled away coin after precious coin, Harry made discreet inquiries to locate an herbalist or apothecary in London. He'd heard that city was so crowded he'd go unnoticed. After much searching, he had a name. After much saving, he could finally afford his plan.

At last he made the trip to London. It was all he could do not to gape like a fool. More people, more buildings, more wares than he'd thought possible. He resisted the temptation to spend hard-earned coin on meat pies hawked by vendors, though his stomach rumbled at the smells. The sour stench of refuse turned his stomach the next moment.

He passed goldsmiths and cobblers, markets, taverns, inns, until his head spun. Finally, his destination on Aldrichgate Street was before him.

Behind a counter covered with bottles, pots and jars stood the tallest woman Harry had ever seen, barely visible in the dim light. Her hair was completely white, though she didn't appear to be old. Wise silver eyes watched him approach.

"I hear there is a way to dull the senses," he said. "You see, my wife raves all day. I cannot control her." He hung his head for effect, trying to evoke the woman's sympathy. "I love her, and couldn't bear to put her aside. I just want to calm her. Can you help me?"

Her gaze bored through him. "You lie. But that matters not as long as you can pay."

"I can pay." He hoped he hid his surprise at being caught out.

"We might try mandragora officiarum," she said, her voice rich and full.

He liked that she said "we," as though they were partners. "How do you use it?"

"It must be smelled or spread on the skin."

How would he get close enough to Amice to accomplish that? "No, no, no! I need something she can eat."

"It is the best substance I know to do what you require. It is not meant to be eaten. I can prepare a lovely, sweet-smelling cream."

"Hmm. What will happen if she uses it?"

"She will become sleepy. But I warn you, take care. If she uses too much, she'll fall asleep...or die. And if she uses it too often, she will die."

He waved her concerns away with a swipe of his hand. "When will it be ready?"

"Mandragora, otherwise known as mandrake, is not easy to obtain at this time of year."

"Did you say mandrake, as in mandrake root?" Harry shuddered. "I've heard that's dangerous. The root looks like a person, legs and all. They say the plant screams when uprooted, and if you hear it you can lose your mind."

"That does not concern you. I have means to obtain what I need," she said. "Come back in four weeks."

Harry regained his composure and adjusted his hat. "I'll double what you ask if you make it two." If only Edwin could hear him bargain.

She raised a white eyebrow. "Done. If something goes wrong, I never saw you before."

"What could go wrong?" He liked to believe he had the ability to see several steps ahead. But he always lost at chess.

The apothecary frowned. "What could go wrong? If the

person dies because you lack the skill to administer the drug properly. If this person happened to be of sufficient importance that an investigation ensued."

"Oh, I assure you I will use utmost care." He knew how to be humble when it was required. "I appreciate your advice."

He smiled. At last, things were progressing smoothly.

CHAPTER 17

April 1454

mice was in the midst of packing when she heard a knock. She gasped with hope. Nicholas? If only he had come to her. But she hadn't spoken to him since their quarrel. Nor had she spoken to Belinda since York was named protector.

She had alienated her closest friends, so it seemed a good time for short visits to her uncle's home in Lincolnshire and Castle Rising.

Her visitor was Belinda, elaborately gowned as always, with delicate embroidery and beads for trim and a fur hemline. A heart-shaped headdress with a long veil made her seem regal.

"I'm glad to see you," Amice began.

Belinda had a bitter look in her eye as she indicated the piles of clothing on Amice's bed. "Running away, are you?"

"I beg your pardon?" She stopped folding a pile of underclothes.

"The disgrace with Margaret. She's said she's forgiven you, but how could she, really, after what you've done? I understand why you'd want to flee. Having to hold your head up after being tossed into the Tower can't be easy."

Amice had heard others tell of Belinda's scathing tongue. Since she'd never fallen prey to it, she'd thought the tales mere fodder for gossip.

"Still, your travel plans are the topic of choice," Belinda continued. "I came to bid you farewell."

"Really?" Why would anyone care where she went?

"Yes, as I was breaking the fast with Nicholas this morning, I heard several people discussing your journey. They think you're leaving in disgrace."

So that was her game. Had Nicholas resumed his friendship with Belinda, or was Belinda hoping to make her jealous? Did she know Nicholas had said he loved her? That they'd quarreled?

Well. She wasn't sure if Nicholas still felt the same, but she did. Despite their differences, despite everything, she felt more at peace with him than without him.

Amice continued packing with a calm she didn't feel. "Have you been spending a lot of time with Nicholas?"

"He seems more receptive of late. A shame he'll never marry."

As though he'd marry you? But the comment had gotten her attention. "Why do you say that?"

"Ah, so he hasn't told you about his parents?"

Jealousy mixed with sadness stabbed her chest. Why hadn't he talked more about such things? Why hadn't she asked? Maybe Belinda was making all this up.

"They fought constantly, sometimes threw things, sometimes hit each other. That convinced Nicholas no man and woman could live together happily for years and years. He told me so," she said.

Strange to discuss Nicholas's most private thoughts with Belinda, stranger still that she knew none of this, but curiosity kept her going. "Surely he's seen good marriages, where couples stay in love or at least enjoy being wed?"

"He says those people hide their misery and show the world false smiles."

"Doesn't he want an heir?"

Belinda picked up one of Amice's chemises and held it up to the light. "I'd have thought he'd have told you. Well, as he told *me,* he's not certain what, if anything, he will inherit. His mother holds any lands that might be his, and as a second son...."

No. Nicholas couldn't have spent so much time with her, said he loved her, made love to her, only to get access to her money, her lands. Amice wouldn't admit to Belinda that she and Nicholas barely discussed his family. Amice had looked forward to talking of such things, of goals and dreams. She'd delighted in images of the sharing they'd do. Politics and quarrels had gotten in the way.

Belinda was still talking. "...and working for the king, has probably not received his due. Well, I must go. Have a wonderful journey."

The second the door closed, Amice's tears began to fall. What had she been thinking, that Nicholas had been as miserable without her as she was without him? Belinda couldn't lie about spending time with him. It would be too easy to verify.

Belinda had encouraged her to write poems for York. But she had asked to get involved in the first place. Or had Belinda known Amice was behind the bush and read the letter aloud apurpose? Could Belinda be devious enough, clever enough to create a scheme to embroil Amice in the activity Nicholas would despise most? To draw them apart?

She rinsed the bad taste in her mouth with water from the pitcher by her bed and flexed her trembling hands.

Nicholas had never mentioned his hatred of marriage. How could he love her without wanting more? Perhaps love didn't mean the same thing to a man as it did to a woman.

Amice would be away from court for a few weeks. The queen had granted her request to visit her home because nothing had changed with Henry's condition and none was anticipated. She'd spend the majority of the time working up the courage to ask Nicholas many difficult questions upon her return.

Belinda waited until she saw her nemesis ride away. Now she'd be free to pursue Nicholas. As the French said, *Ou chat na rat regne.* Where there is no cat, the rat is king. Revenge would taste as delicious whether Amice was here to see it or not.

Amice's dismay had been priceless. Likely her doubts would grow as her time away from him increased.

Securing a seat next to Nicholas at the evening meal proved a simple matter. As servers made their way through the hall with heaped platters, she prepared to have the cupbearer keep filling Nicholas's cup with strong ale. That she'd never seen him so melancholy before bothered her, for it would make her task more difficult. But in her gown, cut lower than Henry would approve were he able, she had hopes of success. If only Nicholas would look at all she offered.

Why wouldn't he drink? If she imbibed, perhaps he'd join her.

"The ale seems particularly fresh."

"I prefer the cider." He turned to talk to the man on his other side.

Belinda wound up drinking a bit more than she'd planned, and as she was too excited to eat, her head spun. Time to make her move. She put her hand under the table, high on Nicholas's thigh. She tasted success when his hand rested atop hers. But he merely put her hand back in her own lap.

One advance rejected. No matter. She had many more up her sleeve.

The ale really was delicious. She waved for the cupbearer to fill her cup and top off Nicholas's still full one.

"The fairest daisy petals lack the power to keep all safe in this treacherous hour."

"What did you say?" Nicholas demanded.

She stilled. Now she had his full attention. But the flow of ale had to stop right now, or she'd end up in trouble. "It's from a poem I heard."

"And where did you hear that poem?" He leaned closer to hear her answer. His scent went to her head faster than the drink.

She couldn't think clearly. The first words that popped into her head were, "I wrote it."

Hmmm. He didn't look very happy about that. Nor was it true, was it? Why would she write such a poem? Why would she write at all?

"*You* wrote that poem? Do you know how many hours of work that and other seditious, slanderous tomes are causing me? I'm charged with finding all the copies that have been posted in a vain attempt to stop rumors from spreading."

Nicholas wouldn't want to be with her if he was angry at her.

Had she written the poem? Of course not. Who had? Ah, now she remembered. "I meant to say, Amice wrote it."

Let her be the one he was mad at.

He gripped her shoulders tightly. "Are you certain? Amice wrote those poems? How do you know?"

She giggled. Her head fell back because she could no longer hold it up. "'Prince of Nothing.' 'The Falcon Eats the Daisy.'"

Nicholas cringed upon hearing the title of one of the true poems, which referred to the Duke of York's badge, the falcon, and Margaret's symbol, the marguerite, or daisy. Was Belinda making this up, or had Amice's betrayal taken on a new dimension? He would get to the bottom of this.

Suddenly he realized that he'd been so focused on their conversation he hadn't thought how they must appear to the other diners. He must look as though he was about to strangle Belinda or kiss her. With her head lolling back, her full breasts were almost in his face. Neither they, nor she, held temptation for him.

He doubted any woman ever would again.

❧ ❧

Amice walked into her cousin's new brick castle at Tattershall, cheeks icy from her brisk walk. Lord Cromwell sat by the huge fireplace in the parlor. He looked older than she'd remembered. His light brown hair had thinned.

"Hello, Cuzralph!" Her childhood nickname for him used to make her smile.

"Amice. Please tell me what is bothering you. You've not smiled since you arrived."

"Am I that easy to read?"

He rose and took her hands. "I see sadness. Uncertainty, which I don't recall you having even as a girl. And something else I can't quite define, as though you've given up. Why?"

"Am I so different from other women, to want things I do not, cannot have?"

"Ah, there it is. What don't you have that you want?" He sat in one of the chairs by the hearth and indicated the other.

Amice felt tears gathering as she sank into the chair

embroidered with tiny yellow flowers. Could she tell Cromwell what she'd told no one else? Her cousin had done so much for her, even risking his standing with the queen to free her from the Tower.

She poured a cup of cider from a pitcher on a carved table. How could she explain? Her cousin fully supported Henry, like Nicholas.

Nicholas. Amice pushed his name and image out of her mind. If he'd known she was leaving court, he obviously didn't care, for he hadn't even said farewell. She hadn't gone to him, for nothing had changed.

Even if she agreed to never lift a finger for York again, what would she get in return? Nicholas's continued friendship, yes. Friendship alone wasn't enough to persuade her to change her mind. But if he could have, would have offered marriage...would that be sufficient? Was spending your life with the man you loved more important than your duty?

Apprehension clung to her like dust.

She wanted Nicholas to love her, but wouldn't settle for less than the security of marriage. She'd been a fool to think whatever time they could snatch would be enough. She yearned to wake up next to him every day, be able to walk proudly about court, Castle Rising, or anywhere with Nicholas at her side, as her husband. Not her secret lover.

Unfortunately, now that she knew what love was, she could never accept any other man as her husband. If what she now desired made her greedy, so be it. She didn't want to lower her eyes each time Nicholas was in the room for fear someone would read the affection in them. The religious and public confirmation of their feelings was important.

Her cousin sat quietly, waiting as she sorted through her thoughts. The patience he'd learned through long years of dealing with the king stood him well now.

"I am in love, Cuzralph, and don't know what to do."

"Ah. So that was why you refused Margaret."

"I didn't want this to happen," she said.

"Would Margaret approve of him? Would I? Who is he?"

"Yes and no, yes and no, Sir Nicholas Grey." Amice dropped her head into her hands.

"Let's take this one step at a time. In the right circumstances, Nicholas could be an excellent choice for you. The timing is wrong. Margaret and Henry naturally looked higher.

"For what would Nicholas bring to the crown? Nothing. He's already Henry's man. But wait." He leaned forward. "You've said nothing of *his* feelings for *you*."

Amice bit her lip. "At one time he loved me, so he said. But we quarreled over something serious…that I'd rather not discuss now. We haven't spoken since." *And I miss him so.*

Cromwell's eyebrows rose. "Is there anything I can do?"

"Not unless you can make him forgive me and love me again." She sighed, wishing she could will away the torment in her heart. "Just having someone to listen helps."

Unless she and Nicholas could resolve their differences, unless the queen changed her mind, there was nothing anyone could do.

❧ ☙

Harry finally had the cream, but thought he was going to lose his mind. And he hadn't even heard the mandrake root scream. He'd only seen Amice once. She'd been carrying a book, hurrying as if to spend as little time as possible in the freezing winds.

He'd observed the maids until he found a likely candidate, Bronwyn. Welsh, young, with sparkling eyes and sweet lips. Maybe he'd have other uses for her.

He wore Edwin's clothes when he approached her in the corridor near the hall. Wouldn't do for her to know he was a scullery boy. Scullery man.

Harry spoke to her several times before broaching the subject of the lotion. Each time, he gave her a little trinket. By the end of March, he felt she was malleable enough.

"Bronwyn. I was wondering if you could do me a favor."

She smiled back, the innocent, trusting smile of a virgin. "What do you need, milord?"

How he liked that she called him that. It sounded even better with her thick Welsh accent. "My cousin is visiting, and I'd like to surprise her with a gift. A special lotion with her favorite scent.

Since the gift is to be a surprise, I'd like you to leave it in her chamber. I cannot risk being seen." That was true enough. "I've written a note for you to leave."

"What does the note say?"

"Cousin, a gift to welcome you." The maid, of course, couldn't read. The note really said, "From one who will have you."

"I will do it. How kind you are."

"Please let me know when you'll bring it. I'd like to be nearby to share her surprise."

"Why don't we go now?"

After all this time, after exercising every ounce of patience, Amice would be his.

"Bronwyn, I almost forgot. The cream was quite costly and the scent is powerful, so she is only to use a very little. She's to put it on the sides of her head, here." He touched his temples. "Can you remember that?"

"Yes, milord."

But Amice wasn't in her room.

"We can try again on the morrow," Bronwyn said amiably, handing him back the blue jar.

The next morning, Bronwyn was found dead.

Upon hearing of her demise, Harry opened the jar, recoiling from the almost sickly sweet scent. How much had Bronwyn stolen? Obviously the girl hadn't been able to resist the lotion he'd made sound so wonderful and had used too much.

The setback proved that he'd have to apply the lotion. It would not do at all for Amice to end up like Bronwyn. Not at all.

CHAPTER 18

ension gripped Nicholas at the prospect of talking to
York face to face. Though protector, York remained
his liege's, and thus his, opponent. His nerves might
snap if they stretched any tighter.

His future, and England's, were at stake.

York nodded a greeting. He sat behind a large desk covered
with rolls of parchment and maps. As Nicholas sat in a high-
backed wooden chair, York indicated the cup of wine that had
already been poured. Nicholas pulled it closer, slightly wary, his
other hand resting on the lion's head carved into the chair's arm.
He'd have to stay on guard with this man.

For a moment, each sought to maintain his portion of the
battlefield; only the narrowest line down the center could belong
to both. If they handled their swords well.

Adjusting the embroidered collar of his robe, York seemed
weary. The creases beside his eyes were a bit deeper, the blue of
his eyes dimmer than the last time Nicholas had seen him. The
strain of responsibility was taking its toll.

"Your reputation for honesty precedes you," York began. "I
know you're devoted to Henry. Unfortunately, the essence of the
man is gone. For good, I fear. Despite what people say, I've
never wished Henry any harm."

Nicholas nodded, pleased York was so direct.

"We may never be able to call ourselves friends, but I hope
we can work toward a common end. I need men such as you. If
Henry's supporters refuse to follow me, there can be no peace."

Nicholas raised a brow. York, who'd more than once raised an army against his king, now wanted peace?

"I've come to realize I battle Margaret, not the people. They want food in their bellies and clothes for their backs. While Margaret wants the throne for her son. As I do for mine." He sipped his wine. "Most of Henry's councilmen want what is best for them," York continued, setting down his cup. "I don't want to butt heads with them, like a herd of goats."

Neither smiled at the apt comparison.

"You ask a great deal," Nicholas said. He needed time to think. He only made snap decisions on a real battlefield, where a split second of indecision could mean life or death. His mind flashed to William.

"Yes," York agreed. "I'm not asking you to change your allegiance. As I told Parliament, should Henry recover, he shall be king. I merely ask for what I'd hoped would be given freely. The council's complete support. Despite my belief that I should've been king, I'm loyal to Henry."

Was York telling the truth, or trying to manipulate him? He thought of Amice, of her faith in York, of the risks she'd taken for his cause. But was the potentially temporary protectorate truly enough for this man, who seemed to crave wealth and control as King Arthur craved the Holy Grail? Or would he accept what he had now then ask for more later, when each new demand would seem a small thing?

"For now, I'm with you. I'll do as you advise." Choosing was a relief. "But I'll watch and wait, like a hawk. Should you stray from your nest, I will stoop, and there will be no plea that can save you."

York nodded, then sat back in his chair, palms flat on the table. Nicholas knew the duke wouldn't reveal how much his concession meant. York would show no sign of weakness to a man who could yet again be an enemy.

❧ ❧

Amice relished everything about being home, from the scent of her soap to the familiar faces. She could almost slip into her old routine and put Nicholas out of her mind. He'd always inhabit part of her, but she'd summon strength to make his portion as small as possible.

Only pleasant thoughts would fill her stay at Castle Rising.

Amice spent so many hours with the tallies and accounts that Cyril sought her out to make sure she was well. She tended her garden, visited the villagers. She tried to write, but when no words came abandoned the pen for embroidery.

She'd been surprised to hear Harry had been released, but also relieved. He must've given up his mission to marry her, for he'd been on his own for months now with no contact. One less problem to worry about.

"Amice," Cromwell called as she walked toward to the stables.

"Cuzralph, I was going for a ride. Would you join me?"

"No, no, these old bones don't climb on a horse unless they have to. You've fit right back in here, have you?"

"Of course. This is my home," she answered, taking in deep breaths of fresh, familiar air.

"I meant you're trying to make life as it was before you went to court." Cromwell rested his hand on her shoulder. "I worry about you. You smile, but I know you're brooding about something. Or someone."

Amice's attempts to avoid serious thoughts failed at his kind words. The back of her throat stung and tears threatened. "Everything was simple before. I'm not certain I like all I've become. When the queen locked me in the Tower, I realized I'd been accepting my life, as women are taught we must, but I wondered why. I don't know how to get all I desire."

"By striving for things you can obtain, and learning to do without those you can't. Trust in God to provide. You'll find peace if you can teach yourself to appreciate what you have," Cromwell said.

"Father Heydon says it's wrong to want to better your lot. I already have much more than many." Amice took in the view of the bailey, the expanse of grass and oak and ash trees.

Would Cromwell, like Nicholas, view her actions as betrayal? "Those poems questioning who Prince Edward's true father is. I wrote some…mine were true, but favored the Yorkist cause. And I copied documents for the duke."

The relief at telling the complete truth felt as though she'd set down a basket of cabbages. The sun felt brighter and warmer on her face.

His mouth formed an *0.* "Why? Why would you do that?"

"York needed help. He believes this is one way to raise doubts about Margaret's ability to serve as regent. The worse Henry became, the more squabbling I heard...."

"I'm surprised that you would involve yourself so. You're right. I can't seek Margaret's aid knowing this. If you still care for Nicholas, you must go to him when we return. If he refuses you, will you be worse off than you are now?"

Amice imagined telling Nicholas the truth of her desires. She envisioned disdain and refusal in his eyes, how cold and harsh the blue of them would be. What if he laughed in her face? The humiliation of rejection couldn't be more painful than the misery she suffered.

"It would prove there's no hope for us. I'd have to forget him, and put Nicholas and life at court behind me. The ember of hope I cling to keeps the pain alive. If I could extinguish it, perhaps I'd recover from his loss. But I'll never forget."

She'd cut short her visit and return to court. Cromwell was right. She needed to resolve her situation with Nicholas.

One way or the other.

❧ ☙

Nicholas paced his narrow chamber like a caged leopard in the Royal Menagerie. Back and forth he strode, with a smooth turn to propel himself in the opposite direction. He tried to put words to his emotions, something he wasn't used to and didn't welcome doing. But it seemed the only way to make sense of the turmoil in his mind.

Never could he recall feeling at a complete loss. Bereft, dispossessed.

Martin entered, carrying a pitcher and two cups, which he set down on a small table. "Sir, you look as though a loved one had died. Is there bad news?"

There had been a death in a way, a death of love. Amice had become part of his life so naturally. Now it felt as though a part of him had been ripped away. She'd left court without even a fare thee well. And he missed her.

"No news of note."

"What troubles you?" Martin poured two cups of wine and carried one to Nicholas, then sat on a coffer next to the wall. He leaned back and crossed his feet at the ankles, settling in for a long chat.

Nicholas accepted the wine, but continued to pace. The movement somehow soothed his agitation. He wouldn't admit needing to voice his thoughts, yet was thankful Martin was willing to listen. "I can't seem to stop thinking about Amice, and that's driving me mad. I should be able to block her from my mind."

"Why?"

He ignored the unanswerable question. "I begin to understand why people want to live together and be bound by marriage," he confessed. "For the fortunate few, marriage might not be a prison sentence but an opportunity to unite. To form a team where before each worked alone. To have someone to stand with against troubles."

Martin raised his cup in a mock toast. "Sir Nicholas, how far you have come."

"But her perfidy shattered any trust between us."

"Ah, she has crushed your feelings as one tramples a violet in the forest. Step upon the tiny blossom, destroy its delicate petals under your boot and smash it into the dust without a care," Martin intoned.

"I'm serious and you make sport."

"I will be serious. Forgive me." He bowed.

"How could I continue to love a woman who believes as she does? Her way of thinking is opposite the path I've led." A sip of wine did nothing to improve his mood.

"I doubt a troubadour ever said true love was fostered by politics or religion. Imagine how difficult it must be for Amice to understand your devotion to Henry. He was your companion from your earliest memories, but she barely knows him. She's seen only the struggles in the kingdom. Now, he sits unaware as his kingdom struggles, as others writhe like snakes to gain control. While she supports the one man who wants for himself what Henry had. The only man in all of England who has the power to obtain that goal. Perhaps your feelings for her aren't strong enough to surmount these differences," Martin offered.

"Perhaps not," Nicholas agreed. "Then why does my chest ache when I think of her? Why do I think of her constantly?"

"To remind yourself what a fool you were to think what you shared was special?" He set down his cup and folded his arms.

Nicholas shot him a seething glare without interrupting his pacing.

"Beg pardon. I see this love can be a painful thing. I've never been pierced by Cupid's arrow. From the looks and sound of you, I hope I never am."

"It's worse than I thought possible. As though I've succumbed to some strange disease. Whenever I see a petite, dark-haired woman, my heart skips a beat and I hope it's her. I find myself enumerating reasons why any woman before me is lacking. Her hair isn't curly enough, her smile isn't as bright, her eyes aren't that interesting mixture of green and brown."

Martin gasped. "Oh, my, Cupid's arrow has struck you hard."

"Worse. Amice fills my dreams." At least he'd had fewer of Castillon.

"Do you believe dreams are whispers from God, as the Bible says?" Martin rose, matched Nicholas's steps and took his cup, refilling it before returning to his seat.

"No. I didn't remember my dreams until recently, nor did I give them much credence." Nicholas pulled a stool over and sat before Martin. "Amice is with me. We're about to kiss."

"Is this the good part?"

Nicholas couldn't bring himself to share the details, though he enjoyed recalling them. "She wants to tell me something important. But I wake up before she can."

"Hmm. Sir Nicholas, why didn't you ask her to stay?"

"Why would I? What are we to each other in the eyes of the court? Nothing."

"In the end it isn't the eyes of the court that matter, but your own."

"I wish I could agree," Nicholas said. "We couldn't even

appear to be friends because we feared our feelings would be exposed. How could I allow her reputation to be tarnished, to permit others to view her as less than she is? And she betrayed me by working for York, who has been and might again be an enemy."

"Because she didn't tell you immediately, or because she worked for a cause she believes in that you don't? Is there a way to reconcile the friend and the assumed traitor?" Martin asked.

"You are too dramatic and ask too many questions, my friend. I'd thought you'd prove useful or I wouldn't have told you."

All he knew was that he missed Amice more than he wanted to admit. He couldn't go on the way things were.

🐝❧

Harry's nerves danced with anticipation. He had his lotion, Amice was at hand. Within hours he'd have what he coveted.

All he had to do was get into Castle Rising. If he seemed thoroughly repentant, she might allow him to stay.

The reunion began exactly as he hoped. The guard brought him straight to Amice, who was embroidering some blue fabric. She was more beautiful than he remembered.

Amice barely concealed her surprise. She set the material on her chair as she stood, her lovely face and form mere feet away. "Why are you here, Harry?" Her tone was cool, her manner neither friendly nor hostile.

The guard hadn't relinquished his firm hold, nor had Amice asked him to do so. Annoying, but Harry couldn't let his temper get the best of him.

He swallowed burning envy. He owned little more than the clothes on his back while she owned everything in Castle Rising and more. "I heard you were home, and desperately wanted to apologize for my behavior last year. My days since have been filled with prayer."

A long pause. He could see her wrestle with indecision.

"Thank you for your apology." She sat back down. "Your journey, I trust, will continue with good favor."

Relief fled at being dismissed already. "I hoped, as your brother-by-law, to partake of your hospitality while in the area."

Now her generous nature warred with her knowledge of his past.

"I'll have a room made ready. But as I'll be leaving soon to return to court, I'm sure you'll want to continue your travels on the morrow." She nodded at the guard, who released Harry with obvious reluctance.

Victory! "My thanks. I'll treasure each moment of my stay."

They were almost alone in the hall. A lone servant was setting the table.

"In anticipation of your kindness, I brought you a gift. A delicate lotion. I was told if you apply small amounts to your head, so, it will soothe you."

Amice took the blue jar and looked at the intricate painted pattern. As she opened it, she sniffed the contents. "Lily of the valley. My favorite. This must have cost quite a lot. I thank you. I'll try some this evening."

He'd reach his objective. At last.

CHAPTER 19

mice was tired, but tossed and turned. Had she done the right thing, allowing Harry to remain under her roof? He'd apologized and seemed sincere, Cromwell was here, a man stood watch. She needn't worry.

Her thoughts turned from her unwelcome guest to Nicholas. The strain of not thinking about the man was as difficult as thinking of him. Perhaps Harry's gift would relax her. She opened the jar, scooping cool lotion onto her fingertips. A small amount, he'd said. Spreading half onto her other hand, she raised both hands and massaged the cream into her skin.

Her head began to tingle. So soothing. The sensation spread down her body to her fingers and toes. How quickly the cream worked.

Suddenly her legs felt weak. She wobbled to the bed and lay down, head spinning. She tried to plan what she'd do on the morrow, as she did each night. But she couldn't bring to mind a single task she had to perform. Nothing seemed to matter.

Drowsiness floated over her like a cozy blanket.

Harry waited with growing impatience until finally all was quiet. He poked his head out of the room she'd let him sleep in, standing motionless for several minutes, listening intently. Nothing and no one.

Tiptoeing to Amice's room, he wondered if she'd tried the

cream. What exactly would it do to her? Uncertainty added to his excitement. The apothecary had been vague about the effects, but had drummed home her warnings.

A board creaked, bringing him to an abrupt halt. After a long moment, he continued on.

He was in luck. No guard in sight. Her door was partially open. Amice lay on the bed, still fully dressed, her eyes half-closed.

"Amice?" he whispered.

There was no reply, no movement. He moved closer. "Amice?"

When she didn't answer, he touched her shoulder. No response. As he raised her into a sitting position, her head lolled onto her shoulder. Hmm. This wasn't what he'd had in mind. Had that wench apothecary known, and, wanting him to buy her costly wares, kept silent? Or had Amice applied too much? An inkling of fear niggled.

"Amice, it's Harry."

"Hullo, Harry," she answered sleepily, her head rolling back. That couldn't be drool oozing out of her beauteous mouth.

"Amice, I am your friend. I want you to write a letter. Will you do that for me?" He made his voice soothing, cajoling.

Her head bobbed. He dropped her onto the bed and spied a writing desk. He took out a piece of parchment and inked her pen, and carried both to her.

"Write, 'Cousin Cromwell, I've consented to marry Harry.' No, wait, that sounds silly. Write, 'Consented to wed with Harry. I know you won't approve but he is the husband I truly want.'"

She was writing too slowly. He tapped his foot and repeated himself. Her pen wove unsteadily across the page. He held her hand—so soft, inking the pen as needed. Though the letter might be a bit sloppy for the ever tidy Amice, it would suffice.

"Add, 'I am sure he'll bring me happiness and protect me from harm.' There. Now sign your name. That's very good," he said, as though talking to a small child. "I'll send this letter by messenger to Tattershall first thing."

And pray that Cromwell would convince the queen to approve.

❧❦

With Henry ill and York in control, the situation at court had calmed. For the moment. Nicholas requested and was granted a week away. At long last, some time to himself. Not enough for the pilgrimage he wanted, but enough for another important task.

He touched the leather bag that hung at his waist. The contents had convinced him to find Amice.

He'd gone to a market to purchase a birthday gift for his sister. But every ware displayed reminded him of Amice. She'd like this silk scarf, sigh longingly over this illuminated manuscript. After passing a jeweler's stall, he stopped suddenly. Backing up a few steps, he'd focused on the item that had caught his eye. There, on a piece of velvet, was a necklace comprised of eight amethysts set in links of finely wrought gold. Perfect for Amice.

Amice always wore the amethyst necklace with her mother's portrait to keep her close. Now he'd convince Amice to accept this one as a token of his love so she could keep him close. Somehow this was the answer to his problems, he felt sure.

"How much?" He could already see himself fastening it around Amice's neck. How she'd smile at him and place her delicate fingers on it.

"I'm sorry sir, but the piece has been sold. I'm awaiting final payment," the wiry goldsmith said, wringing his hands. "Perhaps you'll find another to your liking. This beautiful garnet necklace with inlaid pearls compares quite favorably. Or this, with emeralds.... "

"Perhaps if I pay double its cost, you'll see your way to making another for the original purchaser? I need this. Today." Nicholas untied a leather pouch of coins from his belt. He wouldn't bully the man into giving him the necklace, but he'd strike a hard bargain.

The goldsmith's eyes widened. "By all means sir, that will be satisfactory. Who knows when my customer will pay? I will make him another."

Nicholas had kept the necklace on his person ever since.

Why he couldn't wait a few more days until Amice returned to court, why he had to go to her, he didn't know. He was still angry, but his need to see her, to talk to her, overwhelmed his determination to stay away. She was with him always, his mind filled with visions of her laughing, smiling, her hair curling about his fingers. He couldn't wait to see her.

Nicholas realized he neared the place where he'd first met the muddy Amice fleeing from Harry. The memory brought a smile to his lips.

A woman stood in the road with her hands raised, blocking his way. She was tall and slender, with brilliant white hair and remarkable silver-grey eyes that slanted slightly up. "Milord, a moment if you please. My horse has gone lame, and I am on a journey of a most urgent nature." Her wrist turned gracefully as she pointed to her horse.

A woman traveling alone was an unusual sight in itself, but a woman garbed as she was, in flowing, bright-colored robes that sparkled in the sun, added to his curiosity.

"Who are you, and where do you go?" he asked.

She looked at him as if assessing his worth. "I have no choice but to trust you, for time is running out. I suspect evil is afoot and am trying to prevent it. I am Ninian, a London apothecary. A man asked me for a dangerous drug, which I deeply regret preparing and selling to him. I knew he lied about his purpose and sensed he was dangerous. I'm trying to set matters aright by preventing him from using it."

"What were you going to do, a woman alone?"

She shrugged. "Catch him in action and turn him in to the authorities? Persuade him not to use the mixture by buying it back? I only know I had to try. I couldn't accuse him without proof of his intent. It may already be too late."

"Where was the man headed?" Nicholas asked. He could take her where she needed to go and then be on his way. Amice would be at Castle Rising for several more days.

"I heard him tell a peddler. To a place called Castle Rising."

Nicholas's blood froze. "What did the man look like? What was the drug? When did he leave London?"

Ninian appeared taken aback by his stream of questions. "He was tall and very thin, with long, curving fingernails. The drug was a lotion of mandrake root and other components to induce sleep and calm," she explained. "Why do you ask?"

"We must go immediately. You can tell me the rest on the way." Nicholas held out his hand. When she took it, he pulled her up behind him.

Amice, back in Harry's clutches. He had to get to her. He should've known she needed him. Nicholas urged Merlin on, though carrying two he couldn't run as fast.

"What exactly is it you fear?" Nicholas asked as they raced down the road.

Ninian spoke into his ear. "The danger is that if too much is used, the victim will die. Usually I don't concern myself with the use of my products. But this one is dangerous, and I had a bad feeling about the man. He said he needed it to calm his wayward wife, but I believe he lied."

"I think I know the man and who he intends the lotion for," Nicholas answered, fighting churning panic. "He wants to force a woman to marry him." His woman.

"Then I was right to pursue him. Perhaps if she has used too much and is still alive I can help you save her."

Faster, Merlin, faster. The landscape blurred green as they flew.

Nicholas feared the dread in his heart would overwhelm him. How had Harry escaped his locked cell, traveled to London and back? Amice must not have known, of she'd have said something.

He'd have the tale as he wrung Harry's scrawny neck.

❧ ☙

Amice's head pounded. As she pushed herself into a sitting position, Harry appeared at her door, a letter in his hand and panic on his face.

"What are you doing in my room? Why am I still wearing this gown?"

"I saw your cousin Cromwell breaking his fast. I wanted to know if you'd join us. Did you like the lotion I gave you? Try some more." He swept up the jar and smeared some on her temples before she could protest.

"This is a drug. You're trying to poison me!"

She tried to wipe the cream away, but much had blended into her skin. She opened her mouth to scream, but Harry slapped his palm over her mouth.

Amice wriggled, tried to bite his hand. But he was so thin there wasn't enough flesh for her teeth to latch onto. Her tongue wet the fingers smashed against her lips. She retched at his salty, unclean taste. She kicked against his bony weight pressing her down, his hip biting into her thigh.

Keeping his fingers over her mouth, Harry climbed upon her. He lifted her skirts with his free hand. "Finally. I've waited years to have you beneath me. Where you belong."

Fear sizzled and spots danced before her eyes as he yanked up her skirts. *Oh, no. Please, no.* Her teeth finally found purchase on his thumb. She bit him, hard.

He yelped and leaned back, then slapped her. Pain exploded. Her head snapped to the side.

"Stop blathering. No one can help you now."

Amice's energy was fading fast. As the drug took hold, her limbs failed her. *Oh, Nicholas, if only I'd been brave enough to tell you that I still love you....* She couldn't will her body to move.

Harry paused, poised above her. This wasn't good. Amice was sound asleep. He shook her until her head tossed on the pillow, then swiped her hair away from her face.

"Amice. Don't you dare play games with me. I will have you."

No response. He wanted her aware of what he was about to do. He wanted to please her and himself.

"Did I apply too much cream? I was careful, wasn't I? If you die, this will be no fun at all."

Still no response.

New plan. He'd saddle a horse and carry her away. As he put his hand on the door, it opened, pushing him backward.

Nicholas entered, his jaw set with more anger than Harry had ever seen, followed closely by that witch of an apothecary. How had she found him? How had Nicholas gotten involved?

He could only think of survival now.

Nicholas grabbed him by the throat and shoved him into the wall as the apothecary hurried to Amice.

Ninian opened one of Amice's eyes. "She's in a deep sleep,

not yet the sleep of death. Thank the gods." She grabbed a blue jar from the coffer. "But very little of the lotion remains."

"I am going to kill you. Now," Nicholas ground out, holding Harry against the wall and squeezing his neck with both hands.

"Wait!" Ninian cried. "I need to know how many times the cream was used."

Nicholas relaxed his grip a fraction of an inch. "Answer her."

Harry feebly gestured to his throat. Nicholas opened his fingers another infinitesimal amount.

"Two," Harry croaked.

Ninian gasped. "Only two? Almost all of the cream is gone. There was enough for eight applications."

Nicholas smashed Harry's head against the stones, rendering him unconscious. He fell in a crumpled heap, a trickle of blood oozing down his neck. Nicholas hurried to Amice's side.

"What can we do now?" he asked, gently pushing Amice's curls from her eyes.

"Wait. And pray. Time will tell. She's used more than I anticipated, so there's nothing I can do. I know of no antidote. It must wear off on its own," she said.

Cromwell hurried in. "Nicholas? What are you doing here? I saw you rush into the keep. And who is this?" He pointed at Ninian. "What happened to Amice?"

Without taking his gaze off Amice, Nicholas said, "Harry drugged her. Obviously he continued his earlier campaign."

"What campaign is that?"

Nicholas glanced briefly at Cromwell. Her cousin truly didn't know, shock evidenced by his fish-like gasping for air.

"Shortly after Edwin's death, Harry asked Amice to marry him. Of course she said no. He held her prisoner. We met as she fled her captor to seek aid."

Cromwell looked old and sad. "I have failed her. As her nearest male relative, I should've prevented this. I was too concerned with the king and my two daughters to pay attention to Amice's problems." He joined Nicholas at the side of the bed.

Nicholas sympathized with Cromwell. *If she dies, I'll live in anguish the rest of my days. Amice, I too have failed you. In defending my beliefs, I left you open to attack. I was too proud to accept the value of your gift, the greatest gift of all. Yourself.*

Thank goodness for his dream, for the necklace, for the unbidden urge prompting him to go to Castle Rising. But it still might be too late.

"My lord, I am Ninian. I sold Harry the drug, though I suspected his hostile intentions. How can I express my grief at what I've done?"

Cromwell took her hand. "I see the suffering and sincerity in your eyes. Thank you for trying to save her."

The three waited and prayed as their vigil continued through the night with no change in Amice's condition.

CHAPTER 20

arry moaned, conscious only of the pain consuming his body. Forcing his eyes open, he peered into the dark room. Several shapes surrounded the bed. None moved.

Slowly he straightened from his crumpled position on the cold floor. Shooting cramps attacked his legs, so agonizing he had to bite his hand to stifle a scream, but they eased as he stretched. His head had never hurt so badly, even after a long night of drink.

"If I were him, I'd have locked me up right away," he whispered to the door. A tiny chuckle escaped him as he squinted at the outline of the knight's strong body, rendered ineffective by the throes of sleep.

Harry crept away. Not a servant stirred. The agony of his injuries slowed his escape, but he made his way to the castle entrance. *No need for a horse, the bouncing would do me in for sure.* Carefully, so as not to jar his head, he continued on.

He was free. Free to find another way to have Amice.

Nicholas was by nature a light sleeper, but yesterday's events had exhausted him. Even so, he awoke before the windows let in any sign of day. Cromwell, Ninian and Amice were motionless. And Harry was…gone.

He let out a yell as he ran into the hall and out to the bailey.

No sign of him. If he hadn't been so concerned for, so focused on Amice, he'd have had Harry imprisoned.

"Harry has escaped after trying to kill Lady Amice," he told the first servant he saw. "We must stop him."

Servants raced to do his bidding.

Nicholas hurried to the stables for Merlin. He rode out bareback, hair flying in the wind.

Cromwell and Ninian jerked awake as Nicholas cried out. They looked at each other.

"We must help him find Harry," Cromwell said, pushing slowly to his feet.

"Of course." Ninian opened Amice's eyes, checking for any reaction. She listened to her shallow breath. "I'd hoped for good news as the drug wore off. Unfortunately, Amice's condition hasn't changed. At least she's not worse."

"I'll send someone to sit with her and report every hour." They hurried out of her room. "Harry won't get away with his crimes."

The pair searched the castle with the help of some still-drowsy servants. But for a smear of blood on the stone floor outside of Amice's room, there was no trace of Harry.

Ninian prayed Nicholas would find him.

A nightmare gripped Amice.

Harry was on her, his body forcing her onto the hard wooden floor. Rushes tangled in her hair. She couldn't move or scream. She simply lay there, frozen. He leered and laughed, his mouthful of yellow teeth descending toward her. His foul lips met hers. She tried to shove him away, but couldn't.

He tossed up her skirts and reached between her legs. No!

Suddenly Nicholas appeared. Her limbs and heart were free. She tried to reach for him, but he was gone.

Her eyes opened. She was alone. Had Nicholas really been there, or was it only a dream? Of course it was a dream. He wouldn't come for her—wouldn't leave Henry and court to be with her. He no longer loved her. Maybe he never had. Words of the moment, not words of forever.

Amice's head throbbed. "Nicholas," she whispered.

Her eyes closed once more.

❧ ☙

Hours later, the disappointed, tired and hungry searchers sat on benches in the hall. Harry hadn't been found, though the dogs had hunted him down as they would a fox. Nicholas's bones ached, he was so weary. Ninian rested her head on her arms, and Cromwell breathed heavily. No one spoke. They'd run out of ideas. The servants went quietly about their tasks, preparing and serving food and drink.

All turned toward a movement at the door, where a rumpled Amice stood, propping herself against the carved stone, blinking awkwardly at the crowd.

Nicholas rushed to her.

Her eyes gleamed with obvious hope, then disbelief and confusion. She shook her head, as if not certain she was seeing correctly. "Nicholas?"

"I'm here," he said as she swayed. He caught her before she hit the ground, and carried her back to her room, followed by a concerned Cromwell, Ninian and Ginelle. Worry ate at him, yet she felt so good in his arms. He'd missed her so.

Gently he laid her on the bed, arranging pillows for her comfort.

Amice stirred. She sat up.

"Rest now. All is well," Nicholas said, stroking her hair.

"Harry?" she asked. "He tried to…he wanted…."

"He's gone. You have nothing more to fear."

Cromwell raised a brow, but said nothing. He started toward the bed, but Ninian gently tugged on his sleeve and pointed toward the door.

Ninian pulled harder, whispering, "They need to be alone."

Nicholas and Amice stared at one another as if one looked away for but a second the other would disappear.

Amice pushed herself higher on the pillows. Her smile

dissipated the chill in his heart. "You *are* here. You came for me."

"Did Harry…hurt you?"

Her cheeks reddened. "No. But he would have. He was atop me, about to…but the drug must have taken effect. He didn't harm me."

Nicholas counted ceiling beams to calm his nerves. The thought of Harry anywhere near Amice was bad enough, but picturing him ready to pounce on her, to defile her, was beyond bearing. He forced the thoughts from his mind even as they sickened his stomach.

"I should have been here."

"What, you're my guardian, to follow everywhere I go? You couldn't have known what Harry planned. You have responsibilities," Amice said.

"I want you to have this." He placed a tooled leather pouch on her lap.

"You came so far to bring me something? Why?" She took it, opening the flap. The eight large, deep purple amethysts set in engraved squares of gold sparkled in the candlelight. "It's the most beautiful necklace I've ever seen."

Words stuck in his throat. He couldn't bring himself to discuss his feelings, to tell her he not only cared, he loved her. He loved her enough to combat any obstacles. Together they'd find a way. Being with her was all that mattered. If she would have him.

But to tell her would make him feel, well, naked. Vulnerable, like a knight without his sword. He needed the protection of his weapons.

Did the gift please her? He couldn't bring himself to look. Yes, of course he could. If she didn't want the necklace, so be it.

"This is extraordinary." She glanced at him, then returned her attention to the necklace. She tilted it to catch the light. "The workmanship, the gems…. I can't accept such a generous gift."

Nicholas wanted only to hold her in his arms, to feel her against him, but sensed she wasn't ready. He fought awkwardness threatening to keep him from speaking, turning him into a young lad wooing his first girl. Why was this so difficult?

"I bought it to show how much you mean to me."

She raised a brow. Their gazes met again, blue and green joining, communicating what neither could say aloud. But something had to be said. If neither was willing to bare his or her heart, he'd leave as he had come. She'd have the stunning necklace, nothing more.

"I don't believe the same things you do. I can't change who I am." The necklace glittered in her hands.

"Neither can I change. I'm sorry we don't agree, but hope we'll not argue or try to persuade the other to join our cause. Our differences may seem insurmountable to some. I hoped I could put you from my mind. But I missed you. So much."

He sat on the edge of the high bed, taking the other end of the necklace. "You were even in my dreams. When I saw this as I passed a jeweler's shop, I had to have it. Though I'd convinced myself I no longer wanted to be with you. Loved you, yes. Wanted to build a life with you, no."

"And now?" She seemed to squeeze out the words. Was that hope in her eyes?

"Much has happened in the short time you've been away. I admit I can see why you believe in York. He's powerful, strong and shrewd. But he and Margaret seem to get along one day, but then are at each other's throats the next. As to Henry...he was weak in government. Now his spirit has fled his body. There is no king left in him." He settled into a more comfortable position, still holding his end of the necklace.

"I'd just returned from yet another futile, depressing visit to see if Henry's condition had changed. Each time I leave the senseless king, I feel a year older. Even Margaret has given up hope of his recovery. The endless hours of prayer, the myriad bizarre treatments Henry has endured, all for naught. So much time has been wasted when York could've been working for the betterment of England. We could have moved forward, instead of waiting.

"Two weeks ago, a page handed me a note with York's seal. I can't quite describe how I felt, just seeing his seal in my hand. York had requested to meet me. This would be our first talk alone. Yes, York is protector of the realm, a long climb back from being Henry's enemy. But I couldn't shake twinges of doubt about his long-term loyalty.

"He said he wanted some of Henry's men to openly support him, to promote peace and reduce discord among the factions. A show of unity, he believes, will ease the people's concerns. I'm to be one of his advisors. So how can I continue to be angry at you for aiding the very man I now assist? Certainly not because you recognized his value and the need for him to be in charge sooner than I."

"I believed I was right," she said, "yet I was torn between being open with you and worrying about how you'd deal with the knowledge. Would you be angry or feel compelled to bring me before the council? Would you hate me, and no longer want to be friends? I couldn't bear that."

Amice took his hand. Its warmth revived him. "When we were together, I let my feelings for you take precedence. Nothing mattered but being with you. But we couldn't wed, just share a few stolen moments now and again. How could I tarnish those wonderful times with words that could pull us apart?"

What was she holding back? He sensed a mental tug of war.

"With you I've found a depth of feelings I didn't believe possible. There's an indescribable pull that grows each time I see you. Even in anger, my thoughts are always with you."

Nicholas bowed his head, shading his eyes from view. *How can I be worthy of such a love? If our desires were to again conflict with my service to Henry....*

The time had come to take a stand. Did he want Amice in his life or not? She'd be in his mind in any case, if not in person.

He fastened the necklace around her neck, as if to bind her to him always. His throat felt thick, clogged. Could he ask it, the question he never thought would pass his lips? There was no other way to be with her. But could love survive what lay ahead?

Sensing her anxiety at his prolonged silence, he touched her cheek, stroking her chin with his thumb. "Amice, I love you. More than I thought possible. Even as the words pass my lips, they sound strange. But true. I need to be with you. Will you wed with me?"

Instead of the uneasiness and dread he'd expected after asking her to spend the rest of her life with him, he was filled with peace. Utter peace.

Fat tears splashed his fingers, but her eyes were bright with joy. "Yes, Nicholas. Yes, I will."

He'd done the right thing. Brimming with happiness, he wrapped his arms around her. And wished he never had to let her go.

She kissed him. Nicholas held her closer, tighter, never wanting to let her go, reveling in the desire sweeping through him. How could he have thought of a life without her? His would've been empty. Even in her rumpled state, she'd never looked more beautiful. With reluctance, he pulled away, having saved one last item.

A small smile reached his eyes at her forlorn expression over having their kiss interrupted. "We'll make plenty of time for that, later, I promise. Have you considered how our marriage will come to pass?"

Instantly he regretted his question, for her face fell and a frown creased her smooth brow. But he could fix that. Holding her hands, he continued, "I've obtained permission for us to wed from York himself."

Now a look of wonderment lit her eyes. How he enjoyed watching her.

"When he asked for my support, I made his consent to our marriage the price. Naturally, it's to his benefit as well…he needs as many York and Lancaster couples as he can find to help keep the peace. And your cousin Cromwell approves also."

Amice flung herself upon him again, knocking him onto his back on the bed.

"Wait, wait!" he cried, laughing. "There's one other issue." He returned to a sitting position, keeping her on his lap. "When I asked York for you, he mentioned how helpful your copying documents had been. But when I brought up those troublesome poems you wrote, he told me you hadn't written any. I pressed for the poet's name, and he said he thought the author was Belinda. What have you to say? If you did write those poems, I might add, I should still be angry. They were humorous, yes, but some were also scandalous and even cruel, and I was one of those charged with finding them and taking them down."

It was Amice's turn to laugh. "I did write some poems, but made sure mine were all true. Belinda delivered them to York. I told her I wished to remain anonymous. Obviously she wanted to claim the credit for herself."

"I suspected as much. We can tell York the truth when we return to court. I want us to be married as soon as possible. We've been apart long enough. I can't wait until the day you're mine."

"And I can't wait until the day I can wake up in your arms, in our bed, as husband and wife."

He tipped his head and kissed her, long and slow.

After a hot bath, Amice joined Nicholas in the hall. He'd gathered everyone, from the steward to the stable boy, promising an important announcement. With all eyes upon him, he drew her to his side.

Amice couldn't stop smiling. The happiness that coursed through her wouldn't allow anything to breach its boundaries. He loved her. He had asked her to marry him. For Nicholas, she knew, that was the hardest task of all.

Nicholas poured a cup of wine and raised it. "Let us drink to your lady, who has consented to become my wife."

Cheers resounded in the high-ceilinged hall as the residents of Castle Rising jumped to their feet as one.

Harry skulked in a clump of trees near Castle Rising, nursing his bruises. If Nicholas had another chance at him, some body part would be broken, or worse.

He told a tree, "Nicholas will never let Amice marry me. I think he wants Amice for himself. That will never do."

Harry lacked the strength to fight Nicholas. He needed another way to deal with him. A way that didn't cost a great sum or require much time. He'd waited long enough to have Amice where she belonged. Beneath him. So close he'd been, close enough to touch her.

In addition to his physical pains, Harry felt the pain of rejection, of not being good enough. Why didn't Amice want what he wanted?

"No, no, no. None of those thoughts."

Obviously, Nicholas couldn't be allowed to interfere again. He would have to die.

CHAPTER 21

The hardest part was waiting.

For two days, Harry tried to be patient, hiding outside the castle, living off almoner's scraps, waiting for them to leave the protection of the stone walls. It galled him to eat Amice's leftovers.

Still recovering from his injuries and with fingernails bitten to the quick, securing the rope to the trees spanning the road had been painful.

In the bleak light of dawn on what promised to be a cloudy day, Harry sucked in his breath as a rider approached. It was time.

Wait. He heard more than one horse. What had he done? Too late now; the riders drew near. A smile warmed him. Nicholas led the pack. So what if a few of his men also took a tumble? They were all guilty, for they supported his enemy.

Oh, no. Amice followed close behind. If her horse tripped over the rope and she fell, she could break her neck.

All would be for naught.

"Should I untie the rope? Stop them, revealing my trap? What if I say it was someone else's trap and I couldn't untie the rope?"

The trees didn't answer.

How would he explain his presence? Such a short time to make an important decision. His heart pounded as the horses drew closer.

"Do something, do something!" called the wind.

He whipped out his small eating knife and sawed at the rope. If he partially severed it, maybe only the first horse, Nicholas's, would trip. He couldn't risk Amice's life or expose himself. But if he cut too much, Nicholas might ride by unharmed.

A chance he had to take.

The dull knife refused to shred the stout rope. He sawed harder, frantic, out of time. Nicholas turned to the others. Had he been facing forward, secure in his seat, he might've seen the rope. His horse tripped as Harry had planned, snapping it at its weak point. Nicholas flew over the horse's head, landing in a heap in the middle of the road. The others rode too fast to stop. They pulled at their reins to avoid trampling him beneath thundering hooves.

"Yes! Yes!" Harry jumped for joy, savoring their expressions of horror. Nicholas's horse whinnied and scrambled to his feet. Other horses stepped gingerly past Nicholas, motionless in the dirt. Amice screamed as one narrowly missed his outstretched arm, which rested at an unusual angle.

Mere seconds later, with the horses settled a safe distance from Nicholas, the riders jumped off and ran to the prone body. Amice reached him first, ignoring his injured arm and reaching for his head. Her fingers lightly rushed over Nicholas's scalp.

"Martin, you and the others get a litter. Tell someone to alert Maia and Ninian of his injuries," she cried.

Harry fairly danced behind his tree. After he ensured Nicholas wouldn't awaken ever again, Amice would be his.

Martin hesitated. "My lady, if I may, one of us should remain with you."

"Your lord needs help. Now. I'll be fine. Go!"

"Leave, leave," Harry hissed. His mouth watered.

"I know what Nicholas would say if he awoke to find that we left you on the road alone." Martin indicated the pieces of rope. "Someone set a trap. I can't leave you unprotected."

Amice gasped. She looked around as if trying to catch sight of an enemy. Her pretty mouth tightened. "I see. Do what you think best."

Harry itched to make his presence known, but forced himself to wait, even as Amice's gaze took in the tree he hid behind.

Martin signaled for two knights to stay. He mounted and led the others away.

Amice hovered over Nicholas. The tears gathering in her eyes burned Harry's gut like sour milk.

He couldn't take two knights with only a dull eating knife. But perhaps he could distract them long enough to get Amice on a horse.... Taking a deep breath, he picked up a heavy rock.

This could very well be his final chance.

Harry threw with all his might. The rock landed with a loud thud on larger rock. One of the men, sword drawn, hurried toward the sound. Harry picked up a small boulder. As the man passed Harry's tree, Harry hit him on the back of the head. The knight dropped to the ground with a thump.

Amice and the remaining knight looked worried. He shook his head, clearly not wanting to leave her alone. He drew his sword and looked from side to side.

When he turned his back, Harry hurried from his hiding place and smashed the knight's head with a rock. The man fell at his feet.

Two knights in two minutes. Harry smiled at his prowess as he grabbed Amice from behind and hauled her onto the nearest horse. At first she must've been too stunned to scream, but as Harry clambered up behind her she found her voice. Though he doubted anyone would hear, she screamed so loud Harry wondered if he'd ever hear out of his right ear again.

"Let me go! Help! To me!" she shouted.

Harry reached around Amice to grab the reins, but she writhed and twisted. The horse ran as though his life depended on it.

"Fool!" Harry yelled. "Do you think to jump?"

She took the reins and tried to haul the horse in. Amice's hair flew behind her, getting in his eyes. The mass of curls itched, but he couldn't release her or the reins.

His every dream hinged on the next few moments.

※☙ ☙※

From the depths of unconsciousness, Nicholas heard a faint scream that grew louder and faded. His pain-dulled senses recognized Amice's voice. Compelling himself to awaken, to move, he opened his eyes to see her on a horse galloping into the distance.

Where was she going in such a hurry, away from Castle Rising and without him? Why was she screaming? Throbbing agony in his left arm, which must've broken when he fell, prevented him from thinking clearly.

Someone rode with her. Harry. Holding her.

Ignoring the pain as best he could, he stood and mounted Merlin, who'd been placidly munching grass. As Nicholas cradled his injured arm to his chest against the bouncing gait, he and Merlin sped toward Amice and Harry. His heart raced faster than his horse.

Slowly they gained on Amice. If anything happened to her.... She meant everything to him. He could not, would not, lose her.

"Amice!" he yelled.

Hooves pounded ever closer toward Amice, drums of doom sounding for Harry. His horse breathed heavily and slowed. "Go, go, go, you sluggard!"

❧ ☙

He twisted. A furious Nicholas approached, left arm pressed against his chest. Damn the man, how had he mounted and caught up so fast?

Harry kicked and kicked as he led his horse toward the right side of the road.

With an injured arm, Nicholas couldn't pull either of them down. He drew alongside and edged sideways to cut them off. Despite Harry's desperate kicks, his horse trotted to a halt.

There was no place to hide.

Amice slid down as Nicholas pulled a sword from a saddlebag, pointing it at Harry.

Who had no weapon, nothing with which to defend himself.

"Let's make this a fair fight." Nicholas tossed him the sword.

Before Harry could grab it, Nicholas had drawn a second sword.

Amice cried, "Nicholas, no!"

"It's the only way, Amice. I can't kill him without giving him the chance to defend himself." He dismounted with care.

Harry and Nicholas assumed the age-old positions of adversaries. Sweat dripped down Harry's face as they circled. Nicholas appeared calm, as though he awaited a meal instead of a fight to the death.

"Wait," Amice ordered, pulling the cloth sash from her gown. She wrapped it around Nicholas's neck, then secured his arm against his chest.

Harry chafed at the delay, but feared he'd hurt Amice if he attacked.

She gazed at Nicholas with obvious love.

That was all Harry needed to see. He lunged at his rival, pushing Amice aside. She stumbled back, out of harm's way.

Harry knew he was no match for the king's man, but fought with the recklessness of one who had nothing to lose. Nicholas swatted Harry's strikes like a horse swishing its tail at flies.

How could Nicholas exert minimal effort, while he, Harry, was almost too weary to stand? With no thought to technique, he swung and swung.

Floodwaters of panic rushed through Harry's veins. He was running out of energy, and thus out of time. Any second he expected to feel Nicholas's blade slice through him.

To watch his lifeblood spill into the dirt.

❧ ☙

Still parrying Harry's swings with ease when Martin and the others rode into view, Nicholas said, "Take him. And give strict, specific orders to keep him secure. We'll turn him over to the King's Bench and let them hand down a sentence. He's not worth killing."

With that, Nicholas moved in, coming alive as he pounced on Harry. A single stroke sent Harry's sword flying. Defenseless, Harry had no choice but to submit to Martin. Harry hung his head.

Martin tied Harry's hands behind his back.

Nicholas said, "You ride on, we'll follow."

Despite the throbbing agony in his arm, he wanted a moment alone with Amice, to reassure himself she was all right.

His heart still raced too fast. He could've lost her.

As the others rode back to Castle Rising, Amice rushed to Nicholas's uninjured side to receive a one-armed hug. Their lips met with the passion of reprieve and the aftermath of danger. Despite his pain, despite standing in the middle of the road, he felt the sizzle of desire.

Nothing would keep her from him now.

"Amice," he breathed.

Fat raindrops began to fall as they resumed their kiss, mouths melding. Rainwater slithered down their faces.

Sinking to their knees in the road, oblivious to the dirt, Nicholas pushed a damp strand of hair off Amice's face. "Now," he said.

He needed to reaffirm his life and love. Only she could do that for him.

"Here? Are you sure?"

"More than anything."

The rain became a downpour. Not bothering to remove their drenched clothing, Nicholas reached under Amice's skirts. He couldn't undo his own garments with one hand, but Amice willingly applied herself to the task.

Nicholas knew this was love. He'd suffered a painful injury, they were soaked, in the middle of a public road, but their need for each other overrode their bizarre circumstances and actually heightened his desire. "I want to be inside you."

She straddled him and guided him into her. Deeper, still deeper he plunged, then moaned with his release. Amice joined him seconds later with sweet gasps.

"How I love you," he said.

"And I you." She kissed him once more.

They mounted and rode toward Castle Rising. Toward home.

The first time he'd seen her, she was wet as she was now. Had some part of him known even then that she was the woman for him, the love of his life? He watched her with a small smile of satisfaction on her face.

To love and be loved was far better than anything he'd

experienced. He couldn't define what made Amice different, what made her inspire such deep feelings in him, and he no longer wanted to try.

All he needed to know was that he believed in their love.

❦ ❧

The announcement of their wedding kept the gossips' bellies full for days. Everyone clambered to attend, each woman trying to anticipate and outdo the bride's finery.

Nicholas was honored that both York and Margaret would be present. He realized the gesture was also political, to prove the factions were getting along.

When Amice entered the crowded chapel, Nicholas's heart stopped. She looked incredibly beautiful and radiant in a blue brocade gown. The amethyst necklace he'd given her sparkled around her neck along with her mother's. But the gems couldn't compete with the sparkle in her eyes.

When she stepped into his arms at the end of the ceremony, when his lips met hers for the first time as his wife, his heart overflowed with love.

During the feast, Nicholas ignored ribald jokes and suggestions shouted by guests succumbing to drink. He told his wife how beautiful she and her gown were.

"Remember the day we argued when I was dying wool? I'd wanted to match the color of your eyes, but the finest cloth I could buy or weave couldn't replicate the shade. I happened upon this fabric at a market. The way it catches the light was exactly what I'd been hoping for.

"I planned to wear this gown for my wedding to another. Where only I would know it was a symbol of my love for you," Amice said. "But now I can proclaim it to all."

She leaned forward and kissed him.

"Yes," he agreed. "We can proclaim our love to all."

Belinda strolled up to their table. "I came to offer my good wishes to the happy couple." Her tone was bitter, not friendly.

Nicholas decided Belinda should be found out. She didn't deserve the praise and recognition she'd garnered for Amice's work. Though the poems were scandalous and against Henry, though Nicholas couldn't approve of them, York deserved the truth. For one thing, it would strengthen his and York's reluctant alliance. For another, the protector needed to know who his true supporters were.

"My beauteous bride, I must speak briefly to York. I shall return shortly." He bestowed a loving kiss on her, lest Belinda had any lingering hopes that he wasn't a happy groom..

A few moments later, York stood and offered a toast to the newlywed couple. He turned to Belinda, seated nearby. "Lady Belinda, mayhap you could honor us with a verse in tribute to our friends?"

Belinda blushed and bit her lip. "Your Grace, I'd be happy to prepare a ballad, to be sung later. Composing cleverly takes thought."

"Surely you can come up with a verse that captures the spirit of this moment. Can you not think of one? Any little rhyme will do," York replied.

All the guests waited and watched.

"What, no humorous and witty words for us?" York pressed.

The silence lengthened. He turned to Amice. "Perchance you could come up with something?"

Amice stood, ready to acknowledge her contributions. Typical of the protector to take charge of the situation and make the outcome clear to all. She glowed with pride that Nicholas had discussed her poems with York.

Creating verse on the spot, and one in honor of one's self was a bit awkward, but she'd give her best effort.

"When two once far apart in love unite
The heart shall sing its joy throughout the night.
Entwined as one the couple greets the day
For decades full of happiness they pray."

Amice couldn't help but enjoy the looks on the nobles' faces as they realized what was happening. She felt a twinge of guilt at Belinda's suffering, but decided she'd earned it.

A round of applause began slowly, then gathered in volume. Belinda rose and swiftly walked out of the hall.

Relief soared through Amice. It was over.

She couldn't wait to begin her life with Nicholas as husband and wife. To sleep in his arms every night. The security and contentment of snuggling against him would be the perfect completion to a productive day. She hadn't comprehended the depth love could add to every moment.

They'd spend as much time as possible at Castle Rising, but would return to court as his duties demanded. She vowed that unlike many couples, they'd live together. She wouldn't spend months alone, even at her beloved Castle Rising, while Nicholas served at court. And when he was ready to go on his pilgrimage, she'd go with him.

Amice wanted to shout from the battlements so all would know of her happiness.

Nicholas crossed the crowded hall, astounded by his sense of fulfillment. How much time he'd wasted believing marriage was akin to being taken prisoner by the enemy. His desire for Amice grew each day. He still reacted like an infatuated youth. Whenever they were separated, he longed to be in her company again.

He reached his bride, who sat with her hands folded and her eyes closed.

"What are you doing?" he asked softly, not wanting to startle her.

She opened her eyes and smiled. "Being grateful. For you. And because dreams I barely dared to dream came true."

EPILOGUE

December 1454

wo days after Christmas, Amice and Nicholas continued the twelve-day celebration with the court, still clouded by Henry's continuing illness. But this year, the clouds were thinner due to York's successful protectorate. And because of the thriving heir to the throne, Prince Edward, now over a year old, who represented England's future.

Amice knew Nicholas, too, wished the festivities would end so they could return to Castle Rising. Yet they enjoyed the musicians entertaining the court with merry tunes. Sharing a bench, they held hands, happy to be able to openly acknowledge their love.

A page ran into the room.

All recognized the youth as one of the pages who constantly attended King Henry. The musicians abruptly ended their song on a discordant note as the page tried to speak. His haste to deliver his message was so great only squeaky whines emanated from his mouth.

Bishop William Waynflete patted him on the shoulder. "Out with it boy, what is it?"

Puffing out his chest, he announced, "The king is recovered!"

The well-dressed crowd stared at him as if his clothes had fallen off. Amice wasn't sure she'd heard the boy aright.

"Do you jest?" Bishop Waynflete demanded.

"No, my lord, I swear 'tis true! The king spoke, I heard him," the boy said.

"Then what are we standing here for? Take us to the king."

The page and Waynflete led the hasty procession to the king's chambers. Everyone wanted to witness this auspicious moment.

Amice overheard speculation that began even before the last courtiers left the hall.

"What will happen now? York won't be able to remain protector if the king is well…."

"You can be certain he'll not step down willingly."

"If York has to resign, we'll all be in the same place we were before Henry took ill, with Margaret and the council disagreeing. What are we to do?"

The page had spoken true. Henry gazed about, appearing a bit dazed, but clearly lucid.

"Why do all of you stare so?" he asked of the awed group in a voice weak and thin.

No one knew what to say. How to tell your king he'd been senseless for seventeen months? That events had progressed without him? That he had a son? Gossip and theories would flow later, but for the moment all absorbed the impact of Henry's recovery.

Bishop Waynflete looked behind him to see if anyone was willing to step forward and inform the king of his illness. But everyone, even the council members, looked at the pointed toes of their shoes rather than take on the awesome responsibility of passing on such news.

Waynflete squared his shoulders. "Your Grace, I lack the words to tell you what has transpired. You have been gravely ill…for a long time."

Henry sat up straighter. "Have I? How long?"

"Nigh on eighteen months, Your Grace," Waynflete offered.

Had Henry been healthy, he might have jumped to his feet in surprise. As it was, he would have fallen to the ground had two attentive pages not caught him and eased him back into the cushioned chair.

"That's impossible," Henry began. "But the expressions on

your faces convince me what Waynflete says is true. What day is it?"

Waynflete licked his dry lips. "This is St. John's Day, in the year of our Lord 1454."

"Eighteen months.... Margaret?"

"You have a fine son, Your Grace," the queen said with a proud smile.

Henry leaned his head against the back of the chair. "Thank the Lord, the Merciful Almighty. I'll make offerings in honor of my son and my recovery to Canterbury and Westminster. And at the shrine of St. Edward's. See it done, Waynflete."

He bowed. "Aye, Your Grace. I shall return to pray with you soon, if you will."

A servant rushed into the chamber, Prince Edward in her arms. As Margaret displayed their son to her husband, tears filled their eyes. Even the most jaded of courtiers was moved by the sight of the newly recovered king viewing his son for the first time.

Amice knew Margaret couldn't believe the miracle before her eyes. Henry was well at last and had publicly acknowledged his son. Now they'd endeavor to regain power. There was no need for York to remain protector.

Margaret breathed a sigh of obvious relief, perhaps thinking her troubles were ending. She feared they'd begin anew.

Amice realized her joy at the king's recovery was tinged with selfish dismay. In all likelihood, she and Nicholas would need to spend more time at court than they'd planned, for Henry would want to keep his friends close.

As the rest of the court rejoiced in Henry's return to awareness, she took Nicholas's hand.

"Whatever our future brings," she said, "we'll welcome it together. But when it comes to the king, we're still at his command."

AUTHOR'S NOTE

Dear Reader,

Thank you for reading *At His Command – Historical Romance Version*. I hope you enjoyed the book as much as I enjoyed writing it. I couldn't have done it without the support of writer and non-writer friends and Romance Writers of America®.

I'd appreciate feedback on what you liked and even what you didn't. You can contact me at RuthJK@ruthkaufman.com and learn more about me and my writing at www.ruthkaufman.com. I'm on Facebook at Ruth Kaufman Author & Actress and Twitter: @RuthKaufman.

If you're so inclined and have the time, I'd appreciate a review of *At His Command*.

Thank you again for reading *At His Command* and spending time with Amice and Nicholas in 15th century England.

What really happened to Henry VI in late summer 1453? Much scholarly debate surrounds the illness that suddenly affected the king and its impact on the civil wars sparked by a feud between the houses of York and Lancaster, later known as The Wars of the Roses.

Was his condition a mental illness such as catatonic schizophrenia or a depressive stupor? Insanity? Did it stem from shock upon learning of the defeat at Castillon? Some sources maintain it was madness inherited it from his grandfather, King Charles VI of France. Henry was in such a state he didn't even acknowledge his own long-awaited son, Prince Edward.

Whatever the ailment, Henry was incapacitated and couldn't reign. No remedy essayed by his team of physicians worked. Queen Margaret and the council kept the king's illness from the public for months. In 1454, Richard, Duke of York was named Protector of the Realm instead of the queen…until Henry regained his senses more than a year and a half after onset, just as suddenly as he lost them.

ABOUT THE AUTHOR

Ruth Kaufman is a Chicago on-camera and voiceover talent, and freelance writer, editor and speaker with a J.D. and a Master's in Radio/TV.

Writing accolades include Romance Writers of America® 2011 Golden Heart® winner and runner up in *RT Book Reviews'* national American Title II contest. Her true, short story, "The Scrinch" is in the St. Martin's Press anthology *The Spirit of Christmas*, foreword by Debbie Macomber.

She's appeared in indie features, short films, web series and national and local TV commercials, and has voiced hundreds of explainer videos, e-learning courses, commercials and assorted characters.

Learn more about her at www.ruthkaufman.com and www.ruthtalks.com. Follow her on Twitter: @ruthkaufman or Facebook: Ruth Kaufman Author & Actress.